"I just like the fire in your eyes when you think I'm going to tell Jake about your little crush."

I had the strong urge to bite him...though as sick and twisted as he seemed to be, I was starting to think he would like it. "Cut it out." My hands balled into fists and I tried to calm down by chanting to myself that I was a pacifist.

"Can't." He grinned, and his white teeth blinded me. Did he eat toothpaste? Was there any part of him that wasn't model status perfect? "I like you too much."

"Don't say that." I shook my head at him. "That you like me. You don't even know me."

"I know enough that I'd like to get to know you."

My heart skipped a beat. Stupid heart. "I'm not interested. I know you're not used to a girl saying no, but it's officially happening." I had no interest in a guy who reminded me so much of cheating Eric. They even had the same sexy grin: the one that promised hot nights and broken hearts. "Forget about what happened earlier today and please, leave me alone."

I was proud of my success in getting through the speech without stuttering or letting my gaze lower to his lips. The way he moved his face closer and closer to mine did a good job of distracting me. His lips were mere inches away, curling up at the ends.

"But not leaving you alone will be so much fun."

Praise for M. K. Hale

"If you're looking for a beautifully written love story full of great characters, comedy, angst, and love, I suggest you read *Hating Him*. Now. Stop. Don't pass go. Get this book immediately. Brandon and Mandy captured my heart from the beginning, and I know they will captivate you, too."

~*Rose Croft, author of HIGH SCHOOL LOVER*

"Meredith Hale has a great grasp of new adult romance, especially romantic comedy... Brandon and Mandy together really make the story! I keep laughing and then fanning myself every time they're together!"

~*Linda Kage, author of A PERFECT TEN*

"Love, love, LOVED this! I was so addicted to it, I read it all in a few hours."

~*Jennifer Lewis, author of the MARRIAGE OF CONVENIENCE SERIES*

"There is absolutely nothing to hate about M.K. Hale's new novel, Hating Him. A perfect blend of humor and a crazy amount of sexual tension. Once you start, you won't be able to stop reading this enemies to lovers/fake relationship romance!"

~*Marie Cole, author of the JUST FRIENDS series*

"Funny, intriguing...truly unique, unpredictable, and exciting. Once I started reading, I couldn't put it down."

~*Katie Santee, author of YOU WERE MINE FOR A TIME*

Hating Him
by

M. K. Hale

This is a work of fiction. Names, characters, places, and incidents are either the product of the author's imagination or are used fictitiously, and any resemblance to actual persons living or dead, business establishments, events, or locales, is entirely coincidental.

Hating Him

Cover Art by *Diana Carlile*

The Wild Rose Press, Inc.
PO Box 708
Adams Basin, NY 14410-0708
Visit us at www.thewildrosepress.com

Publishing History
First Champagne Rose Edition, 2018
Print ISBN 978-1-5092-2194-3
Digital ISBN 978-1-5092-2195-0

Published in the United States of America

Dedication

To my parents: I love you more than the world itself for you are my world.

Chapter One
Head Over Heels

Mandy

"What do you mean they broke up?" I asked my best friend, Ashley, as she held a pair of unattractive, shrimp-pink heels in one hand.

She'd obsessed over this particular shoe store for over a week. When I first walked in, the desire to run right out the door plagued me, but she yanked me back inside. As a college junior, majoring in art with an extreme couponer of a single mother, whenever I stepped into a store with price tags carrying three digits to the left of the decimal point, I tended to stay away.

The chic black and white walls matched the expensive marble looking floor. I hesitated to step on it and dirty up the pretty shine with my discount store boots. The enormous gold chandelier hanging from the ceiling screamed: 'you don't have the paycheck worthy of breathing the same floral scented air as me, much less buy shoes here.' Even the workers appeared too wealthy and too important to talk to. Their uniforms looked like they had been designed by Vera freaking Wang. For the first time in my life, I felt uncomfortable in my jeans and camisole.

"She didn't show up to Thanksgiving dinner," Ashley said, cuddling the shoes in one palm like a newborn baby. "I asked Jake if something was wrong.

He said he broke up with her two weeks ago."

She checked the price of the horrid looking shoes one more time and put them back. Thank goodness. I did not want to tell her something as strange as shrimp colored shoes made her ankles look fat. Whenever we shopped together, I came up with ridiculous excuses as to why she should keep her credit card in her purse. Friendship and all that.

"Anyway, now's your chance." Her squeal of enthusiasm reminded me of how lucky I was to have a friend like her. "He's single and ready to mingle. Think about it, we could become actual sisters if you married my brother." Most girls hated when their best friend liked their brother. Ashley embraced it and swore to help me in any way she could.

I had loved Jake Kane since I was fourteen years old, but timing never worked for us. Plus, I had no clue if he would ever see me in the same way. To him, I was his little sister's best friend, the girl with frizzy blonde hair and who once ate all his Halloween candy at the mere age of eleven. Now as a twenty-year-old, I was ready to go after him.

"But what if I ask him out, and he doesn't feel the same way? Then it'll be awkward and then—"

"Mandy. Calm. Down." Ash squeezed my hand. "Jake has always liked you; he just has yet to realize it." It sounded like what people in the movies told the girl with the unrequited crush to comfort her.

My stomach twisted with nerves. "I don't know…"

My mother and I spent every Christmas at their house. If this didn't work out, I feared it ruining my relationship with Ashley, her brother, and their family.

"Oh, come on," Ash said. "You've pined after him

for six years. Now you can finally take him. Why are you not jumping up and down?"

She'd tried to get me my 'groove' back ever since I walked in on Eric, my boyfriend of two years, and caught him having sex with some other girl. A year had passed since our break up, and I still struggled to get my confidence back to where it had been.

Using her super sleuth skills, achieved from an addiction to mystery and crime shows, she found out Eric had cheated on me with a girl he had known for two months. I still didn't know what hurt more: him cheating with someone he barely knew or him cheating with someone for whom he had real feelings.

Since that time, I'd shied away from boys. A week after I walked out on Eric, I found myself crying at Ashley's house.

"Mandy?" Jake took me in his arms, letting me sob for close to an hour on his expensive, brand name shirt. "It'll be okay."

"Am I really not good enough to keep one guy's interest?" Even my father had left me as a kid.

"Cheating is always about the cheater's issues, never the person cheated on." He stroked my hair and did not wince at my puffy and red face. Ugly crying was my specialty, right after saying the wrong thing in awkward situations. "You'll find someone. Trust me."

I trusted Jake. Trusted that he was the someone I needed. A nice guy, who would never cheat on me, never hurt me. A guy I knew and understood. I wanted love. Real, sweet, comfortable, and uncomplicated love. I had always seen Jake as a knight in shining armor. He cared for me; he just would have to see me as more than a friend.

"Did you hear me?" Ashley demanded. "My brother is finally free. You should be jumping up and down. Jump, damn it."

I defended myself. "First, we don't know if Jake will ever see me as more than his little sister's best friend since elementary school. Second, I twisted my ankle going down the steps this morning. I couldn't jump up and down even if I wanted to."

She waved a finger at me like it was my fault that my legs did things of their own volition. "You're always hurting yourself."

I spotted a cute pair of sandals and checked the price… *Oh look, groceries for a month.* I moved on from the shoes to trail after her as she searched for her next target. "Not on purpose."

"I still don't understand how someone as klutzy as you took our high school cheerleaders and girls' basketball team to the state championships."

The frown deepened on my face as I continued looking at the over-priced shoes. "I've always been good at sports, you know that."

"You also trip on air like the ground is your eternal banana peel."

She walked down a different aisle of shoes. The parallel stacks of multicolored heels reminded me of a grand library with its endless selection of novels. The difference here being that libraries were free, and this shop contained merchandise bearing price tags that put most people, like me, into cardiac arrest.

Ashley stopped. I tried not to run her down. "I know a way to make my brother fall for you."

"I should trip on him?"

"No." She picked up a shoebox. "You wear these."

She lifted the lid to reveal the sexiest black satin heels I had ever seen. They were so hot, she touched them and acted like they burned her, making a '*sss*' sizzle sound.

I still did not understand where her reasoning or confidence came from. It was not like he had a foot fetish or something... Oh God, did he have a foot fetish?

"Why would a pair of shoes make your brother fall for me?"

"Trust me, he'll fall head over heels for you." She elbowed me. "Get it. Heels."

"I got the pun."

Ash had a bad habit of explaining her jokes. She also had a bad habit of telling jokes that weren't amusing even after she explained them. "You didn't laugh."

"It wasn't funny."

"Whatever." She flipped her hair and went back to the subject at hand. "As I was saying, my brother will fall for you because you'll be wearing these shoes."

I waited for her to convey the rest of her plan. The look of mischief in her eyes scared me to the core, but I still wanted to know the details of her plan. "And?"

Her wicked grin sent a chill down my spine. "And only these shoes."

Ten minutes later, Ashley bought the sexy satin heels for me.

I tried to take her credit card away from her, but she had lightning reflexes and strong fingers from carrying shopping bags and texting so much. "Ash, this is never going to work."

Ashley did not even blink when the cashier announced the price of the shoes. The Kane family was the wealthiest bunch in our small town. Sometimes the issue of money strained our close friendship, mainly because I had none and Ashley always wanted to buy me things. I did not think of myself as proud, but her spending money on me in amounts I would never be able to reciprocate, made me uncomfortable.

"Fine, buy them." I gave up because I'd sooner win the lottery than convince her not to buy me the expensive heels. "I'll just return them later."

The cashier fashioned her dark red lips into a perfect sneer. "No returns." Apparently, she found our boisterous conversation and my attempt at stealing Ashley's credit card to delay the sale annoying.

"You hear that?" I looked at Ashley. "Don't buy them. It's not worth it. You know your crazy plans always blow up in my face." I did not want to think about all the other shenanigans she had gotten me into.

She waved away my concerns and signed the receipt. "It won't this time; my plan is un-blowable."

I wanted to put my head in my hands and groan. She had just bought a hundred-dollar shoes in order for me to seduce her brother. It was crazy. "Un-blowable isn't a word."

"Why don't you check Webster's Dictionary and get back to me?"

"You always say that because you know I won't look it up, but I'm telling you right now, it's not a word."

Ash picked up the bag carrying the shoebox and handed it to me. "Okay, Ms. English Major."

I took the bag from her and continued to frown. My face, either frowning or smiling, always conveyed the status of our relationship. Either way, it would give me

6

wrinkles in thirty years. "I'm an art major."

She winked at me again as we walked out of the expensive shop. "Point made."

"I don't know about this…"

She bought the nonreturnable expensive shoes for me, but that did not mean I would go along with her scheme. Her confidence dwarfed mine in comparison. Her plan for seducing Jake did not sound like me at all. I would have more luck lighting him on fire than sending him a heated gaze.

"You will seduce my brother in these shoes," Ash said loud enough that two guys crossing the street turned around and grinned. My face heated as I pushed her toward her car.

The smell of orange chicken and pizza filled the air as we passed by the Chinese buffet that served American food in addition to Chinese. Apparently, people had wanted to pair sushi with mashed potatoes for a while. Our town, Launasville, was weird. A gust of cold wind pushed through my thin jacket and I gasped at the chill. Fall was fading into winter. I hated that it was November and my breath was already visible. Yet, knowing the temperamental weather for this part of Pennsylvania, it could be hot enough for short-shorts in another week.

"I bet once he sees you on his bed, he'll jump on top of you and—"

"Shh." I clapped a hand over her mouth, and she licked my palm. It was worth it, however, because a mother and three young kids walked by us. Her glare told me her kids weren't ready to learn about the birds and the bees quite yet. "You can't be so loud. And anyway, isn't this weird for you? I mean he's your brother. Me *seducing* him…" It was weird even for *me* to think about it.

"I'm not twelve. I know how babies are made, and I want you to be the mother of my nieces and nephews."

"You really are weird, Ash."

"And you really are my best friend. Now come on, my brother is one of the most popular guys at Arden University. You need to snatch him up before another sorority girl does."

We climbed into her bright red car. She had a random 'baby on board' sticker on her trunk because she said it made crazy drivers leave her alone.

I played with my fingers to distract myself from the knots tightening in my stomach as she turned the key in the ignition. "Yeah…" Once the car started, the volume on the radio set out to deafen all inside a five yard radius.

"Listen to me." Ash grabbed my chin and pulled my gaze up to meet hers. She had the same striking, dark blue eyes as Jake. "You've loved him for forever, and you've never done anything about it. You have never really done anything just for yourself in general."

"That's not—"

"It sure as hell is true. You've lived your life for a dad who was never home and a mom who made all your decisions for you. Plus, you committed two whole years to a guy who didn't deserve you and sucked away all your confidence. Aren't you ready to finally do something for yourself? Something that will make *you* happy?"

I smiled. "Yes."

****

"Let me get this straight, you convinced Mandy to seduce Jake?"

I groaned and hid my head in my hands. "Rachel..."

After shopping, Ashley and I met up with a group of friends for dinner in order to celebrate the end of Thanksgiving break. We were all heading back to Arden University tomorrow, where Ashley and I lived together in the dorms.

The restaurant we picked was our traditional hang out because Ashley had proclaimed her undying love for one of the hot waiters while Rachel declared her devotion to the chef's famous peanut butter chocolate pie. The faux magenta leather booths were roomy enough for the four of us and the never-ending cheesy jazz playing in the background always made us laugh.

Ashley, Rachel, Elizabeth, and I, inseparable friends since high school. We all went to college together and met for weekly dinners when we were available. I was lucky to still have the same friends from high school. Most people from our small town went to Arden, the closest big public university, a little over an hour away.

"What? I'm just pretty amazed." With a sigh, Rachel Sann leaned against the padded back cushion of the booth. "I mean, you've been in love with Jake for forever. All last year, you followed him around campus like a shadow."

"Don't call her a shadow." Ashley tapped me on the head with a salad fork. "She's more like a cute little puppy."

"Wouldn't be the first time someone called me a dog." I took another bite of key lime pie.

Elizabeth Lee waved her hand, as if to shoo me out of their conversation. Like their discussion of my love life was none of my business. "Shut up and eat your dessert, gorgeous."

"You're going to have her show up in his room wearing nothing but a trench coat?" Rachel questioned Ashley. "What do you expect to happen exactly?"

"All my brother needs is to see Mandy as an actual girl, not a—"

"A man? Thanks, Ash," I mumbled through my bite of the sweet and tart pie.

"You know what I mean." With another pat, she turned back to the other two. "The goal is that when he sees her—and I mean sees *all* of her—he'll realize how amazingly beautiful and awesome she is and fall in love with her."

Elizabeth voiced my worst fear. "And if it doesn't work?"

Rachel shrugged as if me giving up on a six yearlong crush was as simple as choosing a dinner entrée. "I'll set her up with one of my guy friends."

Elizabeth huffed. "All of your guy friends are douches."

"Zach isn't that bad—"

"Zachary Brandt is the personification of the word 'eeww.'"

Ashley brought them back to the original subject. "Guys, she wants Jake, so we're going to help her get him."

"I just can't imagine Mandy seducing a boy." Rachel's lips fought off a smile. "Don't get me wrong, you're hot and everything. But I keep picturing you taking three full awkward minutes to unbutton a coat and then saying 'fancy, seeing you here…in your dorm room…where you live.'"

They laughed but her words stuck in my head. Me seducing a guy was hard to imagine.

****

When I got home from the shopping day with Ashley, then the night out with the girls, I opened the shoebox one more time. The heels, higher than anything I had worn before, shined like satin sin. I slipped off my boring sandals to try them on.

Trying not to wobble as I walked to the mirror, I took slow, small steps. The shoes fit like they had been carved for my feet. I twirled and stabilized myself on the edge of my dresser when I almost fell headfirst onto the floor. On a normal day, I wore sneakers or flip-flops, not six inches of commercially manufactured death. When I looked at my feet in the mirror, they didn't look like mine. The black stilettos made me feel sexy, on top of the world. Literally on top of the world. I felt really tall.

My phone dinged, so I grabbed it. Ash texted me.

—*Try on those heels yet?*—

—*I think I'm in love.*—

—*With my brother? Already knew that.*—

I bit back a smile at her response and messaged back.

—*No, with these shoes. I might run off to Vegas with them. Notice I said run off 'with' and not 'in.'*—

—*They hurt?*—

—*Fit perfect but I can barely walk.*—

I imagined Ash laughing at me after I sent it.

—*You won't need to walk in them for the plan to work.*—

11

Waiting for Jake in his dorm room while wearing *nothing* but the heels was a daunting idea. It sounded like something I'd do in high school, back when I still had my wild streak, but now... Ever since Eric broke my heart, my self-assurance had dwindled to uncertain levels. Like oceanic abyss levels.

Even thinking about seducing Jake was hard. Now, I knew I wasn't ugly. Heck, I used to be a cheerleader and an athlete, so I was fit in all the right places. However, my last set of crunches had been a year ago, and I liked pie. A lot. Tomorrow was the first day back to school after Thanksgiving break, so I still had some turkey and mashed potatoes fat on me.

Jake Kane dated the most attractive girls around. What if I wasn't good enough? Eric hadn't thought I was good enough—

Stop. I would not be the sad, shy girl who had lost herself in heartbreak. I would not be the girl who let life happen instead of taking charge and living it.

However, I was not the kind of girl to show up at a boy's place dressed in nothing but heels and a trench coat. I wasn't a prude. I just was not—

My phone dinged again and I checked it.

—I have a chilly feeling that you're backing out of the plan.—

I smiled. It was spooky how well she knew me.

—I don't know if I can do the whole trench coat 'come and get it big boy' thing...—

—Ewww. Firstly, never call my brother 'big boy.' I love you and I want to help you two get together, but that made me nauseous. If he brushes you off (which I'm sure won't happen), then we will team up and either kill him, or give him amnesia and try again.—

—. . .—

—*Don't '...' me, Mandy Cross. You're doing this. Tomorrow. And you are going to steal my brother's heart.*—

—*And never give it back?*—

—*That's my girl.*—

I smiled. And nodded. I would do this.

I *could* do this.

I needed to move on. I wanted something special. Something real. I wanted Jake. Tomorrow I would seduce a boy and steal a heart.

Chapter Two
Blonde In A Trench Coat

Brandon

Thank fucking God Thanksgiving break was over.

I missed Arden University; I missed partying; I missed girls. Thanksgiving dinner had been a silent hellhole of cranberry sauce and tofu. Of course, my mother chose the worst week of the year to turn vegan. Tofu turkey was not meant for growing college football players; I needed meat. Real meat. Not some soy thing I had no idea how to physically describe.

For the entire break, my dad blathered on and on about my football season, and how I 'better be better than the best.' How the hell can someone be better than the best he can be? It's the best he can be. All I wanted was to get to my dorm room and take a goddamn nap.

"Brandon!"

A bunch of guys passed me in the hallway, weird grins on their faces as I took my room key out of my pocket. One was my neighbor who I'd talked to before. He spent too much time studying chemistry and not enough time studying anatomy. He'd never had a girlfriend. He opened up to me at a party once and asked me for advice on girls. I told him I didn't do anything special and therefore had no tips to share.

"Dude, ready for the football game this Friday?"

"Bro, how was your break?"

The other two guys standing next to my neighbor were complete strangers to me and yet they greeted me like the God I was. People always did that. It was understandable, everything interesting at the university revolved around me. As clichéd as it sounded, everyone at Arden either wanted me or wanted to be me: I was Brandon fucking Gage.

I nodded. "Break was fine; I'm just exhausted. Have you seen Jake yet?" My opportunity for a much needed nap would go up in flames if my roommate tried to talk to me about his time with the folks.

"I don't think he gets here 'til eight tonight," a random guy in the hallway informed me. I struggled to remember his name but gave up because in the end it didn't matter. Everyone already knew mine.

"Okay." I turned to my door. "See you guys later."

One of the guys winked, which made me suspicious. "Have fun, man."

I hesitated and shot him a confused look. "What do you mean?"

"I don't want to ruin the surprise," he said and went back to talking to his friend.

I unlocked my door, then turned the knob. Once I peered inside, I saw the surprise and boy, did I like it.

Napping was far from my mind.

A girl in high heels sat on my bed.

A really sexy girl dressed in almost nothing but really sexy heels.

Her slender body and curves screamed 'woman.' Long blonde hair flowed down her shoulders, blocking my view of the cups of her bra. However, her hair did nothing to cover her cleavage. *Hell yeah.*

I closed the door quietly. She looked at her phone

and nibbled on her adorable bottom lip. The blue halo of light coming from her cell allowed me to see her in the dark room.

"Hey."

She jumped as if something burned her. She looked up from her phone and squinted in the dark. "Hey," she replied and put her phone away.

With the absence of the light, I made sure not to bump into any furniture and risk ruining the mood. I sat next to her and the added weight on the mattress tilted her even closer to me. *Mm, gotta love gravity*. The lace of her bra scratched my arm as I worked to eliminate any distance between us.

"U-um, I'm sure you're wondering what I'm doing here—"

'*Not really,*' I thought. After hitting the green button on my speakers, light music played, helping to set the mood.

"Wow…" she said. "Very prepared of you."

I dipped my head and captured her lips. A husky sigh came from her when my fingers tangled themselves in her long hair. I didn't need to hear the back-story of why she was here. I needed to forget about my horrible Thanksgiving.

Damn, I was always thankful for an almost naked girl in my bed.

A strange, new heat filled me as she kissed me back with just as much intensity. Her lips were as plump and puffy as pillows, as if she'd been biting them all day. Her fingers traced my chest, and I savored the moan she released when she began to explore the ridges of muscles. Each one of those breathy sighs sent electricity from my lips, straight down to my groin.

I'd never been so turned on and all we did was kiss. Tingles spread through my body as she moaned against my mouth again. When her tongue joined mine, I no longer cared how new the feeling was. I wanted her and she wanted me. That was as complex as it needed to be.

"Don't you want to—" She broke off mid-sentence as I lifted her by the waist, and she straddled me like she needed no further instruction. "Talk about this before we…"

Once our hips met, she gasped as my arousal pressed against her inner thighs. She seemed to forget where she was going with her question. The knowledge that she was as into this as much as me turned me on even more.

Who was this girl? How had we never hooked up before? We both moaned when I kissed down her neck. My right hand trailed up her rib cage.

She said something again but her muffled speech hindered my ability to understand anything but, "ake."

"Mmm, I think I know exactly where you're aching, beautiful…" I nibbled her ear and licked away whatever sting I may have caused. "Trust me, once I'm done with you, you'll be—"

"Jake?"

The edge in her voice made my entire body freeze. Jake? She was here for *Jake*?

She leaned over and clicked on the desk lamp next to my bed. I flinched at the sudden brightness. We both blinked a couple times. Then her eyes went wide.

She screamed.

"Damn, girl." I clutched at my ears, half fearing the high pitch sound coming from her throat would make them bleed. "I love the screamers, but I've barely even touched you."

"Who the hell are you?" she shrieked and grabbed a trench coat from the floor.

No, please don't cover up. "Who the hell are *you*?" I shot back at her.

Did her reaction mean she wasn't here for me? Why wouldn't she be here for me? She would rather have *Jake*? That made no sense. Everyone knew I was better than Jake. He came second to everything involving me: girls, grades, football...

"I don't have to answer to you."

Her electric blue eyes collided full force with mine and the fire in them had me wondering how much passion might be hiding there beneath all that blue flame. And that body. It got harder and harder not look at everything she had to offer. Every time my gaze dipped below chin level, her frown went from a glare to pure disgust.

"What are you doing here?"

"This is my room." How was this my fault? "What are *you* doing here?"

Her eyes grew wide at my statement. "I-I thought this was Jake's room."

I nodded, still not sure what to make of the situation. "Jake is my roommate."

"Roommate." She closed her eyes and whispered, "A roommate."

I started to think she was crazy, until she yelled a very unlady-like word, then blurted, "I'm sorry. I didn't even think that he might..." She buttoned up the trench coat, hiding her amazing body from my eyes. I hated that coat. I would burn it someday. "Sorry."

"Don't be sorry. If anything, you got a better deal."

Looking confused, she stood, wobbling on those slim black heels. "Excuse me?"

"Jake is okay, I guess. But girls who come to this room come for me for a reason." I walked closer. "And I do mean *come*."

Her expression changed from what first looked like confusion then to repulsion and then rage. She flew through emotions like I flew through football practices. "You think I came here to sleep with you?"

Dang, this girl was loud. I would love to see how loud she was when I got her in bed and pushed every inch of my body against hers—

Jesus, stop. I calmed myself. "You said you were expecting Jake, so I figure you came here to sleep with him."

Never in the history of my life had I ever been jealous of another guy, but right now all I wanted to be was Jake for this girl. Hell, I would be anything, do anything for this girl. The way she bit that sexy bottom lip turned me on. God, even her breathing turned me on. What was wrong with me?

"I—I wasn't going to sleep with him," she stuttered, and busied herself with looking anywhere but at me. Damn, her flustered expression was the cutest thing I had ever seen. "I—I just wanted his attention."

"You got mine."

I yanked off my t-shirt, threw it on the floor, and inched closer to her. My abs were phenomenal, but she looked at me like she wanted to spread Nutella all over my skin, then devour me whole. *Oh baby, yes please.* I moved another few inches toward her and she appeared even more flustered. She took a step back.

She glanced from my bare chest to my eyes, then down again. "I don't want yours."

I took a step back. "Excuse me?"

"Sorry to tell you, but not everyone wants you."

She attempted to step around me, but she tripped and fell into me instead. I caught her with ease. Stunning turquoise-blue eyes dropped from my gaze to my lips. Her breathing became heavier and her pupils dilated. She wanted me; I knew it, and God did I want her. She licked her lips and her eyes met mine again.

I kissed her.

Heat erupted inside me when I captured her bottom lip with mine and, damn, did she kiss me back. A moan escaped both of us at the same time. Her nails clawed at my back while my grip on her waist tightened. My left hand snuck into the soft gold of her hair to pull her even closer.

Her phone dinged. The sound had the same effect as a bucket of ice water pouring over her. She jumped and pulled back and…slapped me.

"What—" I started, but she cut me off.

"Who do you think you are? You start making out with me in the dark, letting me think you were Jake, and now that I know you're not, you still think for some ungodly reason that I'll just switch to you? God, you're just like Eric."

"Who's Eric?" The way she sneered the name made me think he was not a person I wanted to be compared to.

"Are people that replaceable to you?" Jesus, the emotion in her eyes could set an iceberg on fire. Hell, she set me on fire from just a kiss. "Do you typically find random girls in your bed?"

"Do you really want me to answer that?"

Her eyes widened. "Why did you even kiss me?"

I rubbed my sore cheek. "Because I haven't kissed a girl in a week."

Her eyes widened. "You are such a jerk!"

She pushed me back. I tried to ignore the sparks of heat coursing through me as she touched my bare chest. She started to run out of the dorm room when she again tripped on nothing. She caught herself on my dresser and attempted to stabilize.

"Why are you wearing such high heels if you don't know how to walk in them?"

She turned around with an insulted expression on her face. Why was she so mad? I swear, it was like everything I said—

"Why are you such a pompous, supercilious ass?" She ran out of the room and slammed the door behind her. Pompous? *Supercilious?* Was she a walking SAT booklet?

I stared at the door for a second until I walked over and collapsed onto my bed. The sheets still smelled like her. Like...strawberries.

I fucking loved strawberries.

****

Light knocking on the wall woke me up from a fantastic dream of the hot, blonde girl in a trench coat. My roommate, Jake Kane looked as tired as I felt. He must have gotten a haircut over Thanksgiving break because his normal long hairstyle was now similar to my shorter one. I wanted to tell him no matter what he changed, he would never come close to looking like me, but I was still bitter about the blonde preferring Jake over me.

His bag dropped with a thunk on his bed. "How was your break?"

"It sucked." I leaned back and crossed my arms behind my head. "How was yours?"

"Family drama."

"I feel that." I checked the clock and hoped I had not missed dinner. I had been starving since my mother force-fed me that terrifying tofu turkey for three days straight. "I thought you were supposed to be back at eight tonight. It's only five."

"I got back early; no traffic. Do you want to grab dinner at seven?"

"Sure thing."

Even though Jake often competed with me, he was still my roommate and my teammate, which meant civility was a must. My thoughts then drifted to the blonde who had been here earlier. "Are you dating someone new already?"

"No. I plan to play the field for a while." He looked kind of curious as to why I asked about his love life. Which was understandable considering I never had before. "Why?"

"No reason." I wanted to change the subject, but my thoughts centered around the fiery blonde. If Jake didn't keep her, I sure as hell would.

Wait, what? I did not keep girls. I didn't have time for a girlfriend, not with football and school. I had time to have fun with them, nothing more. My reputation on campus was well known: use them and lose them.

Maybe I could convince the blonde to be another one of *them.* I wanted her; from her reactions to me— before the scream and the slap—she'd felt the same. With her breathy sighs and moans, that girl begged to be seduced. I was eager to be the man for the job.

After catching up with Jake, I attempted to fall back to sleep but every time I closed my eyes, I saw the blonde in the trench coat.

Chapter Three
Disgust To Lust

Mandy

"What do you mean he wasn't there?" Ashley whined as we ate dinner at the University dining hall, nicknamed the Diner. "You were supposed to wait."

The gray carpet on the floor brought out the glossy red and black of the tables now filled with students. An unknown aroma filled the air and did nothing to ease the queasiness in my stomach. I glanced to the entrance to see if Jake would be eating here tonight. Embarrassment still plagued me from what had happened earlier. What if his horrible roommate told Jake I'd been waiting for him? He did not know my name, but he could easily describe me, considering how much he got to see.

"I did. I waited until his roommate barged in and tried to seduce *me*."

Though he had not needed to try hard. That guy was a s'more: hot, sweet, irresistible, and delicious. Heck, I still wanted another taste... *Stop*.

"Oh no." Ashley put her hands against her cheeks. "I forgot Jake has a roommate. He was in a single last year. I'm so sorry, my plans really do always blow up."

I hung my head and attempted to suppress the memory even though every detail branded itself into my brain. "You think? Oh my God, it was humiliating."

"Wait. Isn't his roommate—Oh. My. God," she shouted, loud enough to make heads turned. "*Brandon Gage* saw you naked."

"Not so loud, Ash. I don't want people to think—"

"Oh my God. Brandon Gage tried to seduce you!"

More heads turned. I was two seconds away from duct taping Ashley's mouth and pulling her out of the Diner. "Would you stop? And why do you keep saying his full name like that? He's not a god." Though I had to admit, he was close to it, his ego and everything. "Anyway, I was lucky I hadn't gotten fully naked by the time he came in."

"You still had the trench coat on?"

"I went in with a bra and panties underneath it."

"I told you not to do that. I knew it would make you end up chickening out. I said totally naked under the trench coat. Totally. Naked."

"I understand, but today my reservations worked out for the best because at least—what did you say his name was? Braidon?"

"*Brandon*. How could you not know his name? He's the most attractive, popular guy at Arden. He plays football with my brother."

"He does?" At games, I paid attention to Jake and nothing else. Well, Jake and the delicious pretzels they sold there.

"He's the star athlete!" Her eyes bugged out. "His father is like super rich. Every girl in school has tried to date him since the beginning of time."

"Anyway, I'm glad he didn't get to see...*all* of me." Even though there had been a moment when I wanted to see all of him. My throat dried up like the Sahara Desert after he took his shirt off. The muscles on that boy put a male model to shame.

"He's *Brandon Gage*. I would *pay* for him to get to see all of me."

I pushed food around my plate with my fork. My stomach performed constant flips whenever I thought of Braidon, making it harder to eat. "Sorry to burst your bubble, but he is the biggest jerk I have ever met, Eric included."

Even if he didn't know I expected someone else, he was a jerk for not caring enough to ask. How many strangers had tried to seduce him in his room before today? Considering his sensual talents and apparent popularity, maybe a lot.

"Damn," Ashley said. "I'd already started planning our wedding out in my head, too. How big of a jerk? Forgets to write his vows or sleeps with the maid of honor?"

"Try sleeps with all the bridesmaids and is late to the ceremony so the bride is waiting for *him* at the altar. And excuse me, if you got married, I would be your maid of honor and I would never sleep with him. I wouldn't even want to talk to him. Anyway, you can't marry him because you can't be married to someone I've kissed."

One. Two. Three seconds passed before my words registered.

"What?" She came up out of her chair with a shriek. "You *kissed* Brandon Gage."

Every person in the Diner watched us like the dining hall had become a dinner theater and we were the live performance. Great. Now everyone knew the intimate details of who had kissed whom and where. "Would you stop that?"

"I'm sorry." She put a hand over her chest and took a couple of deep breaths. "I just—I think I'm having a heart attack."

"Then you finally know how it felt when he walked in on me half naked. It was dark and it took a couple of minutes of…making out to even realize it was Braidon instead of Jake."

"*Brandon*. His name is Brandon."

"You girls talking about me?" a male voice asked from behind me.

No. Oh no.

She looked up at him and radiated excitement. "Hi, Brandon Gage."

"Hi. Ashley, right? Jake's sister." His smile was audible. God, I think I hated him. Hated and lusted. *Whoa, where had that thought come from?*

"That's right and this is my friend, M—"

I cut her off before turning to him. "Hi." I did not want him knowing my name.

Once our gazes met, a flush of heat filled my cheeks and hit me in all the wrong places. God, why were there butterflies in my stomach? I was a junior in college, not a freshman in high school, and I did not even like Brandon whatever-his-last-name-was.

"Blondie. I missed you when you ran out earlier. You're the first girl to leave my room without a smile on her face."

Ashley choked back giggles, but I didn't break eye contact with him. God, he was a melt worthy, cavity-inducing, sweet bundle of hotness. His light brown hair resembled autumn leaves, with its tint of red. It made him seem older, mysterious…sexy. *Stop. You hate him.* But damn, were his eyes brown? I wanted to jump into those chocolate waves and drown in the decadence.

"I'm sure every girl is happy to get away from you. It was nice catching up." I attempted not to sound nervous. It didn't work. "Bye, bye." I shooed him and turned back to Ashley, who was yet again looking at me like I was crazy.

"Brandon, what are you doing over here?"

Oh. My. God. Jake.

Jake, Ashley's brother, the boy I had failed to seduce mere hours ago, was behind me. I met Ashley's gaze only to see her jumping up and down in her seat like the dramatic person she was. I could almost hear her in my head, '*Look, both your men are here.*'

"Oh, hey, Ash." Jake smiled. "Man." I flinched at the nickname he had given me. I understood that 'Man' was short for Mandy, but calling me 'Man' felt like friend zone 101.

"Hi." I strived to think of something else to say but nothing came out. As always. God, he was beautiful too. Why were college boys so attractive? Dark hair. Blue eyes. *Be the father of my children, please.*

"Your name is Man?" Brandon raised an eyebrow; one lip curled up. "Do your parents hate you?"

So. Rude. "It's Mandy, not that it's any of your business." This was the first time I had seen Jake in weeks. I needed to talk to him. I needed to attempt flirting.

"What if I want to make it my business?"

I gaped at him, my mouth opening and closing like a fish fighting for air…or would it be water? Why could he not just leave me alone?

Ashley took the reins of the conversation after witnessing me freeze up. "Why don't you sit with us?"

He looked from me, to his sister, and then to the table across the diner, which his friends occupied. "I don't know…"

"Oh, come on." Brandon nudged him. "It'll be fun. Scoot over, Blondie."

Brandon swept in and pushed me to the side, fitting himself on the seat next to me. His warm leg pressed against mine and a liquid heat settled in my lower stomach like a knot. No words described how being so close to him made me feel. My fingers twitched from annoyance of his personality, while my lips still tingled from his kiss hours earlier.

"I guess it'll be okay for tonight." With reluctance, Jake sat next to Ashley. My heartbeat accelerated. There was an awkward silence until Jake took the liberty of filling it. "What have you been up to, Man?"

Great. This was my chance to impress him with my confidence and flirting. *Do not mess up. Do not mess up.* "Uh, I—"

Brandon the Jerk interrupted me. "You came over earlier today to see Jake, right? What was it again that you needed to tell him?" His eyes danced with laughter. My fist was seconds away from colliding with his jaw.

Ashley coughed; Jake slapped her on the back. "I'm fine."

"What did you need to talk to me about?" Jake asked. "You never come over to see me. I didn't even know you knew which room I was in."

"I-I—uh—" I struggled for any possible answer but my mind went blank, yet another reason why the Arden University improv troupe rejected me.

"I told her what room you were in." Ashley jumped in to save me. "I was busy so I told Mandy to go ask

29

you if you wanted to eat dinner with us tonight." Thank God for her quick thinking and ability to lie. It always seemed to come in handy…sadly.

Jake looked at his sister in confusion. "You could have texted me."

"Silly me. I didn't think of that." She twirled a strand of hair. "You know how crazy I get sometimes."

"I know." He turned to me. "Remember when she tackled Batman at my thirteenth birthday party and said she wouldn't let go until he proposed?"

I laughed at the bizarre memory. "She wanted him to be her boyfriend because you said he would never like her."

"He was my favorite super hero." Jake wagged a finger at his sister. "Always wanting the person who is off limits, that's my sister for you."

"I'll bet Ashley isn't the only one who wants someone who is off limits." Brandon looked pointedly at me. "Am I right, Mandy?"

"What?" My voice came out louder than I had meant it to. Damn nervousness. "I don't know what you are talking about."

His eyebrows rose to the top of his head. "Sure, you do. You know with—"

I slapped my hand over his mouth before he said another word. Trying to ignore the way his soft, warm lips pressed against my fingers, I attempted to look threatening. "Can I talk to you for a moment?" I sent daggers at him with my eyes, but his spirit dodged each one as he grinned. "*Alone*."

Brandon fanned himself. "Why, of course you can." He motioned to Ashley and Jake. "If you both will excuse Blondie and me, she needs to proclaim her undying love."

I led him to a vacant area of the diner, then pounced. "Who the hell do you think you are?"

"My name is Brandon Gage, born May twenty second, Arden University student, sex god, and football player. You are?"

I scowled at him. "I think I hate you."

"Hello, 'I think I hate you—'"

"No need to be a smart-ass."

"There's never a need to—"

"You just are one?" I offered to finish his sentence for him.

He laughed. "You're quiet when you're nervous, but, damn, you are so feisty when you're angry." He brushed a strand of hair off my face, and I pulled back from him slower than I meant to. "It's adorable."

"I'm a catch. Now why are you trying to destroy my life?"

His good looks made appearing angry and confident impossible. My fingers twitched as I remembered how good it felt to run them over his sculpted chest. Even now he was close enough for me to touch—

Control yourself.

"I'm not trying to destroy your life. I just like the fire in your eyes when you think I'm going to tell Jake about your little crush."

I had the strong urge to bite him...though as sick and twisted as he seemed, he might like it. "Cut it out." My hands balled into fists as I chanted to myself that I was a pacifist.

"Can't." He grinned and his white teeth blinded me. Did he eat toothpaste? Was there any part of him that wasn't model status perfect? "I like you too much."

"Don't say that." I shook my head at him. "That you like me. You don't even know me."

"I know enough that I'd like to get to know you."

My heart skipped a beat. "I'm not interested. I know you're not used to a girl saying no, but it's officially happening." I had no interest in a guy who reminded me so much of cheating Eric. They even had the same sexy grin: the one that promised hot nights and broken hearts. "Forget about what happened earlier today and please, leave me alone."

I prided myself on the success of getting through the whole speech without stuttering or letting my gaze lower to his lips. The way he moved his face closer and closer to mine did a good job of distracting me. His lips hovered mere inches from mine, curling up at the ends.

"But not leaving you alone will be so much fun."

****

"He was totally flirting with you."

Ashley found it impossible to stop talking about our dinner with Brandon. She thought he made bedroom eyes at me the whole time. I thought of it more as him trying to dig my grave, push me in, and bury me alive.

"Less flirting, more threatening," I corrected her. Brandon said statements hinting at my feelings about Jake *in front* of Jake the whole time. He also found an excuse to use a sexual innuendo every five minutes, making me blush so much I went a little lightheaded. My hatred of him grew every minute at dinner. Now, it settled at an all time high.

Ashley, Elizabeth, Rachel, and I all hung out in my dorm room. Elizabeth and Rachel had been filled in on the most embarrassing moment of my life. They laughed for a full five minutes after hearing about how I managed to seduce the wrong guy on accident.

"He knows that you like Jake, big deal." Ashley acted as if her news had not just blown my mind. "It's not like you do a good job hiding it."

"What?" Did everyone know? "Do you think Jake knows?"

"Jake is oblivious, just like every other boy. The only reason Brandon saw it was because he was watching you like a starving man watches hot gravy being poured over turkey and mashed potatoes."

I rolled my eyes at Ashley. "You're always so descriptive in your analogies."

"I try. It was a food analogy because I'm hungry. I couldn't eat at dinner because every time Brandon tried to hint about your feelings for Jake or what happened with the trench coat, I started choking." She shrugged. "Look, I know you love my brother and everything, but Brandon has never looked at or paid attention to a girl as long as he did to you at dinner."

"What do you mean he has never looked at a girl that long?"

"He's just not the type to date or...care. Don't get me wrong, he sleeps around a lot, but that's it. He doesn't have girlfriends. I've heard he doesn't even sleep with the same girl more than once. If Brandon Gage is showing interest in you, more interest than he has ever shown to a female before if I might add, then maybe you should..."

My eyes widened with disbelief as I stared at her. "But I love Jake."

"You've always loved Jake. You've never really

had much fun." The pity in her eyes made me feel even worse.

I defended myself, "I've had fun."

Rachel wiggled her eyebrows. "But not *Brandon Gage* fun." I blushed again as they all explained to me how intense his reputation was. The stories they told did nothing to help my thoughts for him stay pure.

"I'm not interested in the Brandon Gage type of fun. He's just as much of a jerk as Eric." I said, "I've done the whole one night stand thing and that's not what I want. I want a relationship. I want Jake."

"Why do you want Jake?" Elizabeth questioned.

"What do you mean?"

"Why do you love Jake? What about him makes you want him?"

"I…" I had never needed to make a list and explain it before. I had just always liked him.

I liked him when I was a kid and I rode my new bright purple bike into Mr. Kennil's mailbox, and Jake helped me up, then lied to protect me. I liked him when he baked brownies for Ashley and I after we cried while watching *Titanic* for the first time. I liked how he was the only guy in my life I trusted. My dad had left me; boys had bullied me until I discovered make-up and exercise; and my long term, serious boyfriend cheated on me. To me, Jake was a rock.

"I've always liked him. He makes me feel safe; he was my first kiss… He's always been there for me."

"Look, we're not saying to give up on him," Ashley met Rachel's hesitant gaze, and continued in a cautious tone, "Maybe you should go after Brandon—"

"No. I love Jake. He's the one who will help heal me from Eric. I've waited for him for forever. I thought you understood."

"I do. It's just… I want you to be happy and even though I know you think Jake is great and all, the way you looked at Brandon… The fire in your eyes… I have never seen that in you before."

"The 'fire in my eyes' was me trying to mentally burn him. I hate him, guys."

"Come on. All that heat?" Ashley teased, "You know what they say: disgust turns to lust."

"Who in the history of the world ever said that?"

She grinned at me. "Me, just now."

"Anyway, I'm sure I will never even see Brandon again." I was torn from feeling disappointment and relief at that realization. I might never again see his sensual smile, his caramel coffee brown eyes, his amazing chest… Wow, my thoughts needed some self-control.

Just like Eric, Brandon Gage was the same kind of self-centered jerk who broke girls' hearts after he got all he wanted from them. I knew guys like him and I read about guys like him. He would never change, and there was no need to assure myself of that fact. He paid attention to me because I refused to give him what he wanted.

Resisting Brandon would just be another step in getting Jake to fall in love with me. It would not be that hard…not if I didn't have to see him, be around him, or talk to him. Arden University held thousands of students. What were the chances that I would ever even see him again?

Chapter Four
Pushing Buttons

Brandon

Un. Fucking. Believable.

I had a class with Mandy. How in the hell had I never noticed her before? I mean, sure it was a lecture hall full of one hundred and fifty students, but still. Once I realized that the blonde hair was not a figment of my imagination and that she was really there, I made sure to sit as close to her as I was able. AKA, two rows behind her and a couple of seats to the left.

Goddamn it, I had to talk to her. I wanted the attention of those fiery blue eyes on me, so I did the first thing that came to mind. "Hey, Blondie," I shouted over two rows of people and bit back laughter when her entire body stiffened. And, man, what a great body. "Blondie!"

She didn't turn to look at me. Not even to glare. Every other person in the huge lecture hall stared at me like I was a lunatic. I didn't care. Her gaze wasn't on me, so I did what I knew would crack her.

"Blonde girl with the long legs and the big pair of—" She turned around faster than my mother spent my father's paychecks. The fire in her eyes blazed so hot, for a moment, it stunned me. "Earrings," I finished my statement. "How's it going?"

"An obnoxious asshole is stalking me, so not that

great," she yelled back. The people in the rows between us chuckled. I couldn't blame them; she was adorable when she got angry. There was almost steam coming out of her ears.

"Who is he? I bet I can handle him." She rolled her eyes at my response and turned back around. I wasn't having any of that. "How do you think Jake will respond when I tell him you love—"

She cut me off before I had time to finish. "Do you have a death wish?"

"Only if you're the one doing the killing," I said. "Slowly."

"Don't be so sure I won't. I'd love to straddle—"

Mandy stopped. My grin opened ten times wider at her look of absolute mortification. An image of her straddling me branded itself into my brain. Inappropriate thoughts of other ways to make her blush flooded me. Of course, I felt less inclined to vocalize any of those due to the listening ears of everyone in the lecture hall.

Her blush went scarlet as she spoke to fix her mistake. "Strangle. I meant strangle you. I'd love to straddle you—strangle you!" She put her head in her hands as if that would hide her words from me.

I could not speak through my smile. Hell yeah, she thought about me the same way I thought about her. Knowing that made my heart beat faster and my pants become uncomfortable. My plan was working. All I needed to do was get Jake out of her head.

Then the professor entered the lecture hall and Mandy turned to face the front of the room. For the rest of class, it was hard to focus on anything Mr. Ken said because I couldn't stop imagining my hand tangling in that gorgeous blonde hair.

God, she was hot. Those striking blue eyes that resembled the hottest kind of flame, and those fit long legs that I just wanted to wrap around me like my letter man jacket. Ugh, when did this class end? I needed to talk to her again.

Something strange was happening because talking to girls was my least favorite activity to do with them.

"Mr. Gage?" the professor's voice stole me from my thoughts.

I tore my gaze away from Mandy. "Yes?" Every person in class stared at me including the teacher. Mandy also craned her neck to see me.

"You appeared in deep thought on the subject, do you wish to add anything?"

Mandy snorted and I took that as a challenge. I was no stranger to people thinking of me as nothing but a dumb jock. The slide show revealed that he was in the middle of talking about Socrates, a subject I knew well. The few things I watched on TV were sports and documentaries.

I straightened in my chair, not glancing at Mandy, but knowing full well that her eyes were on me. "Something we have yet to discuss about Socrates is his 'art of measurement' philosophy."

The professor smiled and nodded for me to continue. A couple female sighs sounded as I went on. None came from the girl I most wanted to hear speak.

"He believed that people commit morally bad or wrong acts only when they think the benefits will outweigh the consequences. The 'art of measurement' is meant to analyze the disconnect between benefits and consequences."

"And what do you think about that philosophy?"

"I think it's crap." My classmates laughed but I did not stop there. "It's all about weakness of will, which he disagreed with. People may weigh their options, but in the end, it doesn't come down to choice, it comes down to weakness. People do wrong things all the time fully knowing they are wrong. A strong man does the right thing because of willpower and commitment, not because thinking about the consequences of doing the wrong thing swayed him away from it."

A hand shot up in the air. I held my breath as I awaited Mandy's response. "To say that means that every person with weak willpower would choose to do bad instead of good," she said.

"We all have weaknesses." I stared at her. The atmosphere of the classroom transformed until I forgot we weren't alone. "But promises are the proof of will, not of weighing benefits against consequences. The 'art of measurement' is about people doing something only for themselves. Willpower and commitment are strengthened by those whom we want to do better for."

"And you think someone has the power to focus on another's needs before his or her own?"

I did not miss the sadness in her eyes. I wanted to abolish it. Who had hurt her in the past to make her think she wasn't worth putting first? She deserved happiness and nothing less. "I think when you care about someone, you should find thinking of yourself first as a challenge."

When the professor dismissed the class, I pushed through the people sitting next to me to catch up with Mandy. Somehow, she moved like a ghost, weaving through the crowd to escape. After knocking over some people in the process, I spotted her before she exited the building. I took a deep breath and ran a hand through my hair to make sure that I appeared calm and not like I had just sprinted to find her before she left. I bumped into her to get her attention.

"Sorry," she muttered, head down, eyes glued to her binder as if she were contemplating a subject as complicated as human existence. She did not even look up to see who had bumped into her. Why did she apologize when it wasn't her fault? The girls I knew would push the person back and then proceed with insults capable of making a nun's ears bleed.

"Sorry, darling, that was my fault." Her head bounced up like an eight-year-old on a trampoline after hearing me. "Oh," I acted surprised to see her. "Look who it is. Good points in class today, are you a philosophy major?"

"Are you stalking me?" Her expression surprised me. Did my speech about willpower somehow make her less repulsed? Thank goodness for Socrates. "Should I be scared? Do you have a shady past?"

"I'm not stalking you," I said even though I was not sure if it was the complete truth. "You just…make me curious."

"You make me curious about murder but I don't think that's a good subject to explore, so I would love it if you would stay away from me."

Mandy walked away and once my eyes met her quite lovely behind; I hesitated to watch for a bit longer before jogging after her. "I don't know, I think straddling would be a great thing for us to explore. It would be a great way to go, that's for sure."

"I meant strangle and you know it."

"Did you know you look downright edible in those jeans?"

"God, you really just…push my buttons!"

Could she get any cuter? "Baby, I don't want to *push* your buttons." I pulled her closer to me in order to stop her from walking away again. Her pupils dilated from, hopefully, what was arousal and not demonic rage. "I want to *undo* them."

She let out a sputtering breath.

"And anyway, I think the reason you didn't say the word strangle was because you were secretly thinking about us doing another S word together."

"Or maybe I was busy thinking about Jake," she shot back and pushed me away.

Direct hit. Could she have been thinking about Jake?

No way. She was just denying it. I had seen her eyes drift to my lips. I had heard her moan against me when we kissed once the lights had been turned on and she knew I wasn't Jake. I had been the one to put that blush on her cheeks. Not Jake.

Mandy started speed walking away from me again, but I kept up with her. That aggravated her even more. "What do I have to do to get you to leave me alone?"

"I don't know. I've never met a girl like you before."

She raised her eyebrows and put her hands on her hips. *Aw, she's trying to look sassy.* "A girl like what?"

"Feisty, adorable, funny…" A smile stretched across my lips at the memory of how flustered she got. "You fascinate me… Plus, you're hot."

Mandy walked up close enough to kiss me, and tilted her head, her eyes locked onto mine. "You know why I think you won't stop following me around?"

"Why?" I wanted to lean in and show her skills that would have her eyes rolling into the back of her head. I had it on good authority that I was very talented.

"Because I'm the first girl who has told you no and I think we both know that once I tell you yes, you'll leave me heartbroken and alone just like you do every other girl."

I was silent for a moment because I did not expect her to verbalize my exact plan. It took a minute before I tried again to lighten the mood. "Why don't you tell me yes and we'll find out?"

She looked disappointed. "You are a pig."

"Oink, oink." I tried to joke but it didn't work. I wanted to tell her that all the rumors about me were falsified and dramatic. I wanted to tell her that I was a good guy. But I couldn't. It wouldn't have been true.

She went to turn away from me again, so I reached out to catch her arm.

"Brandon?"

As Jake called my name, an enchanted look washed over Mandy's face. I should kill him. How did he get this kind of reaction out of her when all I got was a frown? Jake was not especially handsome or personable. He was not even that great of a guy. I still remembered the girls I'd sent home crying because he was already in the room with someone else.

"Jake," Mandy said in a voice a full octave higher than normal. She flinched at the severity of her pitch, but he didn't seem to notice. He'd not noticed Mandy at all in fact, until my hand was on her arm.

"What's going on here?" His eyes narrowed on where my hand touched her. When neither one of us offered a response, he asked again, "Mandy?"

"Um, uh—"

I had known her for a mere two days and I already knew that she never worked well under pressure, so I offered some help. "We, um, I was killing a mosquito...that landed on her arm."

I gave her upper arm a soft slap as if it would reinforce the legitimacy of the story. *A mosquito? Really?* Maybe some of Mandy's inability of winging it was contagious. Like stammering smallpox.

She nodded a little too quickly. "That happened."

Jake's gaze switched from me, to her, and back to me before moving on. "Okay, well um, I just wanted to say, I'll be late coming home tonight because Elliot's frat is having a party."

"Okay."

I would have said anything in that moment to get Jake to leave us alone, so Mandy would stop looking at him like he was some sort of God. I was the God at Arden University. She should have been looking at *me* that way.

"I, um..." Jake tilted his head like he was confused, then made a gesture to include both of us. "I didn't know you two hung out."

"Oh, us? We don't—"

"We don't want to put a label on it yet." I slipped an arm around her and bumped my hip into hers in a playful go-with-it way. "She's difficult to tie down."

Though I had no plans to be a part of any label, even if it was with Mandy, I wanted Jake to stop looking at her like he had just realized the meaning of life. She would be mine.

He looked at me with disbelief. "I didn't know *you*

would be able to be tied down."

Why wouldn't he take the hint and walk away already? "She's that amazing, I guess. I just hope she lets me scoop her up before any other guy does."

"Yeah." Jake's eyes left mine to examine Mandy from head to toe. She let out a little yelp when my grip tightened around her waist. I cleared my throat and he looked up. "Yeah…" he repeated. "It was nice seeing you again, Mandy. Maybe we should hang out sometime, too."

She all but swooned.

I should kill him.

Who the hell flirts with a girl after a guy says that he wants her? Jerk-face Jake apparently. Asshole.

Mandy smiled so wide, bystanders might have thought she'd won the lottery. "Th-that would be great."

"Cool, I'll text you." He nodded at me before jogging away. "See you."

"Is it me or did he seem kind of jealous that we were hanging out together?" I asked her when he was out of earshot.

Mandy appeared just as confused as me. "What? I don't know." The hopeful twinkle in her neon blue eyes made my heart jump, and then ache because that gorgeous gleam was for him, not me. "Do you really think he was jealous?"

"Of course, he's jealous."

She blushed, then looked away. Maybe she was not as impervious to my charms as she claimed. I needed to convince her I wasn't the pig she thought I was.

I wanted to show Mandy I was worth a try.

****

"Let me get this straight, you're not coming to the party tonight?" My closest friend, Michael, gaped at me. I snickered at his and Lucas' shocked expressions. We were in the locker room after our three-hour football practice. I threw on a clean shirt while they questioned why I wasn't going out with them tonight.

"I just don't want to go."

"Since when?" Lucas asked in his heavy southern accent.

"Since I have better things to do with my time than drink cheap beer and make out with strangers."

Michael gawked at me even harder than Lucas had. "Since when?"

"Oh my God..." Lucas gasped as he closed his locker with a bang. "You met a sweet little peach."

"Peach?" Comparing Mandy to a piece of fruit was almost laughable. She was much more tart than something so sweet.

"Lucas." Michael frowned at him. "You seriously have to learn to be less southern. Call a girl a girl. I'm tired of you getting all the cheerleaders because you use words like sugar and darling. It's not fair."

Lucas smiled until his dimples appeared. "Sorry, Mikey."

"He calls you Mikey?" I teased Michael. We'd been hanging out with Lucas since the first day of the semester, so he still surprised us.

Michael put the attention back on me. "What's this about finding a peach?"

"I don't know what you guys are talking about."

"Oh, come on, I know the look you've been having." Lucas wouldn't let it go, probably because I teased him about how he wanted 'something real.' I had no interest in girlfriends, but that was all Lucas imagined for himself. "You found somebody."

"Not in the way you're suggesting. I just met someone who…intrigues me."

"Intrigues you?" Michael made fun of my word choice. "For real, who are you?"

"It's not that weird."

"She must be super hot," Michael commented.

Lucas made a face. He was the gentleman of our little group.

"Oh, she is."

"What's her name?" Lucas inquired.

I did not want to tell them. I wanted to keep Mandy a secret. She was too fascinating to give up. Plus, I already had enough competition with Jake in the way. "Blondie."

"Hm, a nickname. You must either like this girl or you weren't listening when she told you her name."

"I know her name. Besides, she didn't even want to tell me her name at first."

"Wait, wait, wait. This girl wouldn't tell you her name?" Michael and Lucas chuckled at my frown. "Is she blind?"

"Doesn't even need reading glasses." I slammed my locker door closed after I finished getting dressed. "She just hates me for no reason."

Lucas' jaw lowered. "Goodness, the girl hates you?"

"A female being hates you? How is that even possible?" Michael said with heavy sarcasm, "It's not like you constantly act like you're a self-centered God."

"You sound just like Blondie."

"Then I like her already."

****

I was kissing Mandy. A bit more than kissing...
One of my hands tangled itself in her hair, while the
other trailed up her inner thigh. Her body trembled
against mine as my fingers moved closer and closer to
where she wanted me most. She released a breathless
moan against my neck when I rubbed her—

The most annoying sound in the world interrupted
me from the best dream in the world. God Dammit.
Fucking alarm clocks. I rubbed my eyes as I tried to
calm down my breathing. Cold shower this morning
then. Again. Man, I was Brandon Gage. Cold showers
were supposed to be for guys who couldn't get any.

Talking to Mandy yesterday decided it for me, the
next girl I'd have would be her. I could wait until then.
Once Jake had left us alone to talk, I walked her to her
next class without getting her mad at me again. Making
her laugh was like the equivalent to winning a gold
trophy.

My new plan was clear. I knew how to get her into
my arms instead of Jake's. She wanted his attention,
and what better way than to convince her to fake date
me to make him jealous? It would give me an excuse to
kiss and touch her and persuade her that I was the
superior choice. I just needed to make it so that she
believed she had come up with the idea on her own.

When I walked into the Diner for breakfast, I did
not miss the way every girl checked me out as usual
while I stacked my plate with five scrambled eggs and
three pancakes; a man has got to eat. Their stares
pierced into my back like needles when I turned to find
a table. Then I saw her again.

Mandy.

Three days in a row, it had to be a sign.
I would make her mine.

Chapter Five
A Strong Supporter of OJ

Mandy

I could not get Brandon Gage out of my mind. Face or body. I daydreamed about those abs every waking moment. Last night, I woke up sweating, no matter that it was far from summer time, after a realistic dream. Even my subconscious recognized that Brandon knew how to kiss me until my knees went weak. Dream Brandon was sweet and tender... I liked him much better than real life Brandon. That arrogant, self-centered, son of a—

"Blondie." He appeared out of nowhere. Like a fungus. Hot fungus.

Gross. What am I thinking?

He wore a snug black shirt and blue jeans that made me want to take a bite out of him... I told myself that my thoughts were due to my late start to breakfast and hungry, growling stomach. My tray at the Diner consisted of two empty cartons of orange juice, a plate of half eaten chocolate chip waffles, and what appeared to be an over ripe plum. I always had at least three cartons of orange juice to start the day with breakfast; it was my favorite.

His disheveled hair brought to mind all the ways I wanted to tangle my fingers in it. How could his eyes be so cheery so early in the morning? It was hard not to stare at him as he stood there, looking like a model in front of me. My mouth went dry.

I cleared my throat and raised my drink. The straw missed my mouth and instead went up my nose, causing yet *another* embarrassing moment for him to witness from me.

He chuckled. "I think straws are supposed to go in your mouth." I glared, sipping from my orange juice. "I see you're a strong supporter of OJ." I choked at the velvet in his voice. My eyes watered as the liquid burned going down my throat. "I meant the juice, not the man."

"I got what you meant." I cleared my throat again and looked him over. "Is this going to be a regular occurrence now?" Keeping my guard up around him was hard enough, and seeing him everywhere I went did nothing to help me. Lust had never suffocated me like this before. Not even when Ashley had convinced me to watch a popular movie featuring attractive male actors playing emotional strippers.

He took the seat across from me as if I invited him to do so. "What?"

"Annoying me every day."

I picked the purple plum up, off my red tray and took a bite out of it. The juices from it dripped onto my thumb and I licked it before it made my hand sticky. I looked back up, as Brandon's eyes went from my thumb to my lips. Feeling self-conscious, I licked my dry lips and jumped at the abrupt husky noise Brandon released from the back of his throat.

I waved my hand in front of his dazed face in order to get his attention. Whatever he was thinking about affected him. "Brandon?"

He jumped right back into the conversation as if he hadn't just been staring at me like I was a giant plum that he wanted to take a juicy bite out of. "I'm annoying you?" He slid back in the chair and relaxed. It seemed he expected to stay for a full conversation. He stretched his legs under the table until his knees knocked against mine and caused a rush of heat to sink below my stomach. "Why would you say that?"

"I would say that because you annoy me," I shot back and wondered when he would get the hint to leave.

He mock gasped and clutched at his heart. "And here I thought you lived for our conversations."

I tried to suppress my smile at his goofy humor. I shouldn't find him amusing at all. I shouldn't want to be around him. I attempted to distract myself by looking around the dining hall.

A group of who I assumed to be his friends watched us. The girls appeared angry and the boys perplexed. I understood their confusion. Brandon Gage sat with girls who were tens. Heck, not even tens. The girls that Brandon surrounded himself with were always thirteen on the classic zero to ten scale. Even I was bewildered as to why he chose to cling to me like fleas.

"Why are you over here talking to me when all your friends are over there?"

He motioned between us. "We're not friends?"

"I barely know you." I threw my hands up in the air in vexation. "Before I discovered that we share a class together, I never even saw you."

"But I've *seen* you."

The innuendo made me want to crawl into a corner and die. The way we first met would forever haunt me.

Leave it to me, to seduce the wrong guy by accident.

As if sensing I was uncomfortable, he changed the subject. "Are plums good?"

"You've never had a plum?"

He speared at a section of his scrambled eggs and ate a fork full. "Correct."

"How have you never had a plum?"

"Sorry, I don't go to the plum convention every weekend."

He took another bite of eggs. His plate was the largest serving of scrambled eggs I had ever seen one person take. How did he stay so fit? *Football, duh.* And 'fit' he was. I didn't think I was a muscle kind of girl and yet, I had a real problem taking my eyes off of them. I swear, sometimes he flexed for no reason other than that he saw I enjoyed it.

"There's no such thing as a plum convention."

He stared at me for a moment before breaking into a smile. "Do you get sarcasm?"

"I get it when it's funny."

He laughed at that. I didn't want to make him laugh; I wanted to make him leave. "Come to my game tomorrow night."

"Your game?" I never went to games. Plus, it would be my last day off before I had to start back working at the Arden University Health clinic for students and faculty.

"You know, football. Weirdly shaped brown ball, tights, helmets…"

"I know what football is."

My irritation seemed to fuel him. "Great. You'll come then?"

My heart pounded harder than it should have at the

word 'come' on his lips. His chocolate brown eyes held a spark of excitement that reminded me of the way a kid looked at a cookie jar, like it was full of possibilities.

The sincerity in his expression made me pause before I spoke. "I...don't think so."

He grinned. "Too busy trying to get Jake to notice you?"

I wanted to smack the smile off his smug face. "No. I..." I tried to come up with an excuse that wouldn't make me sound lame, but I wasn't the best at coming up with things on the spot. "I have a hot date."

A dark emotion flashed across Brandon's face, but disappeared before I could place it. "With who?"

"You wouldn't know him."

"I know everyone on campus, darling."

Not the imaginary boy I created in my head. "Correction, everyone knows you. I doubt you know one fourth of all of their names."

"Why would I need to know their names if they already know mine?" He took another bite of eggs as if he had no clue that his statement was so self-centered and egotistical. "Anyway, who is your date?"

I tried not to give it away, but I was a pretty bad actress. "His initials are HW."

He looked somewhat disappointed in me. "Is your hot date homework?"

"My notes can get intense sometimes."

He shook his head at me and then leaned in across the table, one of his hands moving over mine. "Why don't you take one night off, away from school work, and come to my game? Please." His deep brown eyes dissipated my resistance. "I promise you'll have fun."

"I don't know…"

"Exactly, you don't know what fun is, but don't worry. I can teach you. When you look back at your college years ten years from now, you're not going to remember your homework assignments. You're going to remember your experiences. Come *experience* with me." The huskiness in his voice sent a chill down my spine and I found myself responding before I thought it through.

"Okay." What? Damn it.

"Great, I'll see you there." He picked up his lunch tray. "Oh, and if you ever want a real date that will raise your temperature, I'm a text away."

I wasn't the only one in the Diner who turned to watch him go. He looked just as good walking away as he did from any other angle. Brandon Gage, always at the peak of sexiness, had a smile that resembled something sinister because it never faded. I did not know why I agreed to go watch his game, but I was pretty sure no girl ever resisted him for long.

For some reason, it felt like I had just made a deal with the devil.

****

Jake texted me the next day while I was in my art class, and I stared at the message for two full minutes before realizing it was real.

—*Want to hang out some time? I miss how close we were in high school.*—

I typed '*definitely*,' erased it, wrote '*I'd love to*,' deleted it, and then sent a '*yes!*' without the exclamation point after some deep thought about how to show interest but not desperation.

"I don't think I've ever seen you on your phone

during art class. Whoever it is must be pretty special."

I jumped in my chair at my art professor Mr. Stratten's comment from behind me. The sudden movement shook my easel and paintbrushes. "Sorry, sir." I tucked my phone back in my purse and picked up my paintbrush. "It won't happen again."

"Don't apologize." He looked over my half finished streaks of whites, grays, and blacks which were meant to show the hints of a storm cloud brewing inside a woman's iris. "You sure like working in black and white."

The fact that he frowned made me want to cry. "It's kind of my style."

In my opinion—one shared by many students—Mr. Stratten was the best art teacher at Arden University. He had all the professional connections an art major needed to find a job with a stable income after graduation. He was also in charge of the exclusive art New York internship that was offered to one Arden student every year. I needed that internship. My mother allowed me to major in art as long as I promised that if I failed after one year out in the field, I would go to medical school.

The New York internship was a golden ticket that guaranteed a future for myself in what I wanted to do. I would have no chance without Mr. Stratten's recommendation. In fact, my goal was to get him to love me... So far, it was not working out the way I planned.

When I applied for the art program for Arden, my portfolio made it clear that I exclusively painted in black and white. The admission counselor loved that. She said that my colorless style was something unique.

Mr. Stratten disagreed.

Since the beginning of the semester, he criticized every one of my paintings. It made me feel insecure and stressed me out more than a passion in life should. Art once put me at ease. It filled me with…energizing sparks. Once an image popped into my head, my fingers twitched until I took up a pencil or paintbrush to create it. Yet, Mr. Stratten remained unimpressed.

"I know you…*prefer* black and white, but art is about expression." The white noise music he played in the background emphasized his spiritual tone. "Trying new things. Becoming comfortable in the uncomfortable."

Worrying over how much to say, I bit my lip. "I haven't used color since middle school." Color was too bright. My designs were too dramatic with it.

"Hmm." Mr. Stratten made a noise then moved on to another student.

A sinking feeling made itself at home in my chest as my confidence wavered even more. How was I going to get Mr. Stratten to like me? Using other colored paints would not be enough. He wanted a soul and a story behind every painting, which I only managed in black and white. Art had always been my refuge, but now it became more and more like another thing to feel torn about.

I had enough to feel torn about.

****

The tightest top and push up bra known to man prevented me from sucking air into my lungs. No wonder corsets went out of fashion. "Ash, I need to breathe."

"You can breathe when you're dead," she

mumbled as she stroked my eyelashes up with mascara, helping me get ready to go to the football game.

After screaming for ten very loud, very long minutes when she learned Brandon had invited me, she proceeded in digging through my closet and throwing every piece of clothing she didn't like on the floor. When she picked out a top two-sizes-too-small and a pair of skintight leggings, she grabbed her make-up supplies and pushed me down onto my desk chair.

"I believe no one breathes when they're dead."

"All right, then you can breathe when you're married. To Brandon."

She finished my eyelashes and proceeded in lip-glossing my chapped lips. I had been licking and biting them all day due to nerves about seeing Brandon again. I turned into a roller coaster of emotions whenever he was around. One second, I wanted to suffocate him with a pillow and, the next, I wanted to suffocate him with my lips.

"I can put on make-up myself, you know."

"That's funny. Last time you tried to put on make-up, your eye shadow and blush made you look like a clown." For my first date in high school, I had not listened to Ashley and done my own make-up. I didn't look atrocious… I just looked really, really bad.

"A cute clown," I mumbled, trying to maintain some of my dignity.

"That's right," she said in her high pitch, baby-talk voice and even went so far as to pinch my cheeks. "And you were the cutest darn clown the world has ever seen, but, honey, the whole point is to not look like a clown. And darling, tonight…" She smiled when she moved back to examine her handiwork. "You look hot."

I pulled at the tight top strangling my cleavage. "My chest hurts."

Ashley patted me on the head and pulled my shirt down even farther until my bra peeked out. "Life hurts."

I pulled the top up to cover more of my chest, and fooled with my leggings as I attempted to somehow make them less second skin-like. "I'm serious, I think it's too tight."

She clucked her tongue in disapproval. "Your sense of adventure is too tight."

"That doesn't make sense."

"Shh, don't let your mouth ruin this for me. You never let me dress you up." She hugged me and kissed my contoured cheek. "You know this is why I always wanted a sister. Jake would never let me curl his hair or paint his nails."

"I'm glad I could save him the horror."

"Are you excited to see Brandon play? I bet at half time he'll be all sweaty. Probably pull off his helmet and shake his hair out in a way that's super sexy. Maybe splash some water on himself to cool down—"

"Sometimes I question your sanity."

She shrugged. "My brother says the same thing."

"Maybe that's why we're meant to be together."

She petted the top of my head. "Don't lie. You didn't get all dressed up for Jake."

I hid my face behind strands of my hair. "Whatever."

"Oh, is that a natural blush I see? Mandy has a crush!" She sang, dancing around the room. "Mandy has a crush!" At times, she was so immature.

"I do not. The main reason I'm going to this game

is because Jake will be playing. I find Brandon infuriating, horrible and…completely unattractive." I huffed and my breath got caught in my throat because I was a terrible liar.

"She says, lying to her best friend."

"I'm not lying."

"Then I guess we shall see." Her wicked grin would have scared me if my mother hadn't been the one to teach her it in the first place. "You look so good. When Brandon sees you, he might end the game early, grab you, and take you away, so he can claim you in every way that a man can claim a woman—"

My cheeks burned with embarrassment. "Ash!" Ever since she had found my stash of romance novels, she had been addicted.

She handed me her mirror and my eyes widened. "Ready to go to the game, princess?"

My blonde hair appeared brighter as it framed my contoured cheeks. The make-up made it look like I had an actual sharp jawbone structure. My lips looked as edible as a piece of bubble gum. In contrast with the eye shadow, the blue in my eyes shined like the bright, hot flames used in buffet lines. She was right…

I looked hot.

I tried to suppress the excitement eating away at me. "Ready."

Chapter Six
The Player's Play

Mandy

Hard as it might be to believe, I went to a football game in an act of free will. For the other games, Ashley either dragged me or I attended because Jake played. For some reason, it was important to Brandon that I went to his game and that excited me more than it should have. Adrenaline pumped through me as a stadium filled with half-drunk, over-competitive college kids roared and cheered for their favorite players.

When Jake ran out on the field, I screamed and shouted. He danced a bit and bowed like he was on a stage instead of fake grass. My hands were still clapping when Brandon's name was announced over the P. A. system.

I almost lost all ability to hear as every girl in the stadium screamed at the top of their lungs for him. Someone even flashed him. He did not appear to notice though. If he noticed, he remained indifferent. From my spot in the bleachers, I saw him scan the massive crowd. His gaze stopped on me. I had grown so accustomed to seeing his grin that I knew it from a mile away. My skin heated and the edges of my lips curled into a smile. The same one that I always fought back whenever he was around.

God, this boy had gotten under my skin after a

mere couple of days.

When he waved, at me, all the girls sitting close to me jumped up and down like he had picked them out of the crowd. I bit back my smile and saluted him like I was a soldier in the massive army for his affection. Even though he was too far away to *see* me, a wave of electricity washed over me as we stared at each other. My top suddenly felt too tight.

The game moved in slow motion. I didn't understand football, but I sure as hell watched it like an episode of my favorite TV show. I tried to keep my eyes on Jake but Brandon kept tearing my gaze away. He was the fastest on the team and if I blinked, he would be somewhere else the next second. I now knew why his abs were so incredible.

At half time, everyone got up to either go to the bathroom or buy food from a concession stand, so I got up too. Mob mentality and all. As the giant groups of people pushed by me, I wished Ashley had joined me. Moving through the crowd to get to the lemonade stand was like attempting to speed walk behind a herd of zombies.

"Excuse me," I said it a million times, but no one paid attention. My throat burned from all my screaming; I needed to get a drink before half time ended.

I nudged and weaved myself through the crowd, the way I had seen others get around, almost making it to the stand before strong, warm arms wrapped around my waist. For a split second, I expected it to be Brandon and was equipped with a smart ass comment. When I turned, I was instead filled with a sense of dread and fear. A drunken college guy more than a couple feet taller than me, had his hands on my hips as if they had the right and permission to be there.

I put my hands over his and strained to pull them off of the waistband of my leggings, but he refused to budge. "Um, excuse me."

I looked around for someone to help me with him and found that a group of boys, who looked stronger and older than me, had surrounded me. They were all good-looking and resembled athletes, but I knew they weren't on the football team. Soccer, maybe? Hockey? Their eyes were bloodshot and their balance seemed less than ideal. The vinegar, harsh smell of alcohol wafted from them and assaulted my nostrils.

The one still holding me by my waist said, "What's a sexy girl like you doing here all alone?" I wanted to ask if he could try to sound less like a cliché villain, but the feeling of his cold breath against my neck shut down any attempt at humor. He took my shudder of discomfort as an act of arousal. *Not really, buddy.*

"I-I'm not alone," I said loud enough for all the boys to hear. There was no way they would try anything. We were on the side of a busy walkway that had intersections with the bathroom as well as the exits and entrances for the stadium.

"I think you're lying," one said.

"I'm not lying," I lied.

I attempted to make eye contact with other bystanders to get their help, but the boys formed a dome around me, inching closer and closer with each second that passed.

"Oh, really?" The one with an iron grip on my waist asked me, "Then who are you here with?"

I turned my head to look at him and regretted it. He

licked his lips as his eyes drifted toward my mouth. "My friend."

He pulled me until my back pressed against his stomach. The situation grossed me out more and more as it continued. "Then where is she now?"

"*He*'s in line getting two cheeseburgers because he has to eat every couple hours since his boxing career burns so many calories." I hoped they believed me because that may have been the first lie in my life where I did not stutter or give myself away.

A couple of them looked around and made a gap wide enough for me to see that the line close by for hotdogs and burgers had decreased. The few people still standing in it were four girls and a gray haired male professor. Great.

One of the boys forming the circle around me grinned and walked up until he was toe to toe with me. "Looks like your imaginary friend left."

I contemplated punching him, but their sheer numbers alone made starting a fight impossible. "What a rude thing to say." I tried to keep the charade alive, but they were all getting way too close for comfort. "Don't imply that my friend is imaginary. Maybe he went to the bathroom." The one behind me lowered one of his hands to fool with the waistband of my leggings while the other moved up my rib cage. "Hell no," I proclaimed. This guy was getting a black eye.

He nipped at my ear. "Who's going to stop me?"

My blood boiled with rage. "I can protect myself."

"Sorry, sweetie, but I don't think you can protect yourself from all of us."

"But I can," a familiar voice said. I almost fainted with relief. In that moment, I didn't care about the cliché-ness of the situation. My knight rescued me.

Brandon Gage looked ready to commit murder. His jaw appeared tenser than my mother on tax day. His eyes narrowed on the boy holding me. As if his gaze burned, the boy tore his hands off of me and backed away with them up in a surrender position.

"Gage, man. We didn't know she was yours."

I pushed him. "I'm not his, jack ass."

Gage advanced. "It doesn't matter if she's mine, which she is." His hands clenched into fists. "It matters that you would try to take advantage of a girl who's all alone."

I'd heard enough about my lack of friends tonight. "All right. I just want to make one thing clear because there has been a lot of discussion over it. I do in fact have friends. Many. And they are not imaginary, if I might add."

"Mandy, what are you talking about?" Brandon looked at me like I was crazy, so I let him take over. He turned back to the group and shot them an expression that had the power to scare a war criminal. "If I ever see you guys again, it'll be a different ending."

"You won't touch us man, you'd get kicked off the team," one commented. The rest looked at him with wide eyes like he'd wished for a slow, painful death.

Brandon responded by putting an arm around my waist. "I can do whatever I want."

I maneuvered out of it. "Eh, no, you can't." I speed walked away from them, but a hand grabbed my wrist before I made it to the entrance of the stadium. "I'm going to go find my seat now."

Brandon frowned and released me when I stared down at his hand on my skin. The sparks that hit me everywhere we touched never helped me focus on the task at hand. "Wait."

"What? Were you expecting me to cling to you with gratitude? Shower you with compliments?" It was easy to do so when he looked that good in a jersey. The pads on his shoulders made the bulges of his muscles appear more pronounced. His hair was darker and damp with sweat. A true athlete. A true man. *No, Mandy, focus.* "I am thankful, but I'm not some damsel in distress you can go around saving. I'm—"

"I know, I know. Feminism. I was just going to say that I have a better seat for you."

I used a warning voice as my cheeks filled with a blush. "If you're going to say your lap…"

"I wasn't, but it's good to know that you've been thinking about such an interesting position. Anyway, I came up here to offer you the seat that's always saved for my dad. I don't feel comfortable leaving you alone again, but I have a game to play. It's a great seat with the best view of the game. Plus, I'll be able to keep a close eye on you."

I pursed my lips in deliberation and nodded in agreement. I did not feel comfortable going back into the chaos of the crowd by myself.

"Thank you." He grabbed my hand and proceeded to pull me along. "Follow me."

I didn't stop him this time when his warm fingers interlocked with mine. He took me through a special doorway and led me to the front row of the stadium.

"How are you even allowed to be out here right now?" I questioned him. "I thought players had to stay down on the field."

"They do. I wasn't exaggerating when I said I can

do whatever I want."

I rolled my eyes. They widened when he gestured to an open seat in a row just above where the players sat on the bench and discussed plays with the coaches. I was close enough to talk to one of the other football players, if I wanted to.

I may not have been a football fan, but I knew great seats when I saw them. "I'm sitting here?"

A knot of liquid heat lowered in my stomach as he grinned at me. "Yup."

The announcer came back on the P. A. system and said something I didn't understand. I assumed it had something to do with the second half of the game starting soon.

I pointed to the field. "You need to go."

He smiled and shocked me when he pulled me in for a quick hug. He didn't seem like the type of guy who hugged. I liked it. "Be safe."

"I have a black belt," I told him, not informing him that it was just a black belt I had bought from a local department store when it was on sale.

"Enjoy the game, Blondie."

He disappeared. A minute later, he ran onto the field and over to the coaches. They appeared angry with him for leaving but didn't care enough to take him out of the game.

Every time the game had a second of rest, Brandon's eyes were on me. Every referee whistle, every time out... All of his attention had me wondering what he wanted from me.

Did he really like me? Or just like that I said no to him?

Did I like him? Could I trust him not to be another

Eric even though they were so similar? Was I really thinking about who I 'liked' as if I was back in high school? My thoughts transported me away from the game and it took me a minute to notice Jake walking over to my seat.

"Hey," he shouted up at me. Whenever he was around, a blush enveloped my face. He was someone I always liked. Why did I let Brandon…distract me? Jake was the one I wanted. Brandon was…he was self-centered and bad for me.

"Hi," I shouted back.

"How are you liking the game?"

This was one of the few conversations that he had been the one to start with me. I could not blow this. I would not blow this. Please, God, let me not blow this. "It's good. Um, I like the uh, tackles and…funnels." Those were football terms, right? Before he had left my mother and me, my father taught me how to throw the perfect spiral but never any of the official terms.

"Funnels?"

"Are they not called funnels?"

"I think you mean fumbles. That or the funnel cakes they sell at the stands."

"I do love funnel cakes," I commented. He laughed and the melodic sound of it coming out of his perfect mouth shocked me. I had made him laugh few times in my life. This was progress. "But, um, to be honest. I don't like or know a lot about football."

He tilted his head at me. "Then why are you here?"

"Brandon asked me to come."

"Really?" Jake scanned behind him before turning back to me. "Does Natalia know?"

My eyebrows furrowed as I racked my brain to

67

place the name. "Who?"

"You know… The cheerleader." Still not ringing any bells. I shook my head. "Brandon's…well, she's his—"

My eyes locked on the cheerleader whom Jake pointed to. "They're together?"

She had long, flawless brown hair and what appeared to be the smallest waist I had ever seen. Did she do two hundred crunches each night? She dropped down into a split faster than I could say 'ow' and waved her pompoms. Could Brandon already have someone like her when he paid so much attention to me? Maybe he was just another Eric… Then again, Brandon said he didn't even *do* girlfriends.

"I mean…Brandon doesn't do the whole 'together' thing, but if you ask her then yeah, they're together."

I wanted to run and hide when the butterflies in my stomach transformed into nauseous knots. "Oh."

"Sorry. I think you should stay away from Brandon. I don't want you to get hurt, Man. After all, you're my sister's best friend."

I would have given anything for him to say that he cared about me getting hurt because I was *his* friend. "I'm not hurt." My heart beat hard in my chest, as if cracking under the pressure.

Time seemed to slow when the coaches called time out and Brandon jogged off the field toward me. His pace slowed down when he noticed Jake talking to me. The cheerleader whom I assumed was Natalia ran over to him. She jumped on him and wrapped her legs around his waist. Her fingers tangled themselves in his light brown hair as they kissed.

"You okay, Man?" Jake asked.

I ripped my watering eyes away from the pair to look down at him. "I just… I feel sick." I jumped out of my seat and ran up the stairs to leave the stadium. I made it to my dorm before the first teardrop fell.

****

"Boys suck. They should just all be gay because they all suck."

Ashley made noises of commiseration as she rubbed my back. "You should write poetry."

Rachel agreed. "You have such a way with words."

I choked on a sob and a laugh. "You guys are ridiculous," I said around Elizabeth's hand, which patted the tears off of my cheek with a tissue. Needless to say, my make-up was ruined.

I let my body sink against Ashley as she wrapped her arms around me. "You were complaining about boys, remember? Boys. Not us."

"He just kissed her? Right there in front of you?" Rachel asked. "Even after he saved you from those jerks who, by the way, I will find and personally exact your revenge."

"Yup."

"I bet without all the make-up and the cheer leading uniform, she's super ugly." Rachel cracked her knuckles. "What's her name? Natalie?"

"Natalia," I mumbled. "She looks like a damn model."

"I bet she has a drinking problem and messed up teeth."

Elizabeth gave her a disappointed expression. "Don't be mean."

"She's trying to steal Mandy's man."

"Brandon is not my man." I took a deep breath.

"It's stupid for me to even be crying. I'm not sad about Brandon. I barely know him and he's been clear that he wants one thing from me, so I shouldn't feel shocked that he kissed some girl. It's just that…it feels like another example of how I can't keep a guy's interest."

"Do not feel that way."

Ashley walked over to our refrigerator and took out a soda for me. "This whole thing seems weird. I mean he has been practically stalking you, and then he invites you to his game and kisses a cheerleader right in front of you?"

"I can't believe I wasted my last free night on him before I have to start working at the health clinic again." I groaned and fell back on my bed. "I could have been watching TV."

"Or doing homework," Elizabeth suggested.

"Get your priorities straight." Rachel messed up Elizabeth's short, red hair. "TV comes first."

"What are you going to do if you see him again?"

"I don't know…" I closed my eyes for a second. "Either run and hide or punch him in the jugular."

"Seems like the appropriate reaction."

****

I had to wake up early the next morning because of my internship for the physical therapy department of Arden University's Health Clinic. I did not want to become a doctor, or nurse, or therapist. But the job gave me the money I needed to live on campus. I had been hired because of my experience with therapy in the past, my high testing in biology and science, as well as my—or rather my mother's—interest in me going to medical school after I graduated. My mother was a nurse and I had to have PT every year because of my superior ability to always hurt myself when I was a cheerleader or played basketball.

My boss at the clinic, Mrs. Sweet, decided to make my day even worse. "Since most assistants are busy with other clients at the moment, we'll have you observe and guide someone today instead of doing paper work."

"Okay. Did the physical therapist outline a list of needed stretches and exercises?"

She nodded. "We need you to make sure he does them."

This was the first real responsibility she had given me. "That's fine with me, what's his injury?"

"That's another reason why we wanted you to take care of him," Sweet said. "Since you've had an incomplete ACL tear before, we thought it would be easy for you to handle and relate with him. The injury is not too bad. It should only require about a month of physical therapy."

I was not in the mood to deal with anyone. Last night, I had cried myself blind, then passed out later than my normal bedtime. I'd looked forward to the usual mundane work of filing papers. "All right. When is he coming in?"

"He should be here any minute. Oh, wait." She glanced over my shoulder when the door chimed, signaling someone had entered. "There he is now."

I turned. And cursed.

Fate hated me. I would have accused the jerk of faking an injury so he could stalk me, if he had not limped through the doorway.

When our eyes met, his mouth stretched into a wide grin.

Chapter Seven
The Modesty of a Model

Brandon

I couldn't believe my luck. Mandy would help me recover. I had been about to pay whoever it was to sign off saying I was fine to play, but, with her, I wanted to go through all the sessions. My lips hurt from the wide stretch of my smile.

Fuck, she had looked so good at the game. Practically edible. Those skintight pants made my head dizzy from lack of blood flow. That low cut top should have been illegal in most states. A small part of me wanted to hope that she had dressed up for me, and another part of me had wanted to cover her up so none of those douche bags who harassed her could see her beauty.

I had never known such a fascinating woman. She had been outnumbered and yet the fire in her eyes made me think that she was prepared to fight each one of them. She had been happy with me when I led her to those great seats, so why had she left? Did Jake say something to her? I'd been so distracted worrying about her that I didn't pay attention on the field and got hurt. The aching feeling in my knee added to the unstable feeling in my leg. ACL tears sucked.

Her blue eyes turned icy. My goal for the day:

warm them up. "Blondie."

"Gage," she growled it and not in a sexy way. Correction, in a sexy way but from her expression, I assumed she didn't mean it to be seductive. What did I do to piss her off this time? She seemed perpetually angry with me.

She motioned to my bent leg. "How did it happen?"

"The game." I wasn't about to tell her that my confusion as to why she'd left the game distracted me. "Which reminds me, why did you—"

She picked up a clipboard, avoiding eye contact. "I'm assuming you have already gone through PRICE."

The cold, professional treatment. Fine, I would find a different way to make her blood boil. "Price?" I played dumb which made her cheeks redden. "I've paid it if that's what you mean."

"No. Protection, Rest, Ice, Compression, Elevation. It's meant to help reduce the pain and inflammation of the injury."

"I've used an ice pack."

"All right." She spoke without looking up from the clipboard. "Do you have your personalized treatment plan signed by your physical therapist?"

I handed it to her.

She bit her lip as she scanned it. "Hmm." She nodded as if she understood the messy, hand written suggested activities designed to help strengthen my leg. "Okay, so today we are going to be using various joint and tissue mobilization techniques. They will help the range of motion."

I raised an eyebrow, waiting for her to clarify. "And by joint and tissue mobilization techniques, you mean…"

The way her lips moved when she pronounced the multi-syllabic medical terms turned me on. Her bottom lip puffed up like she'd been nibbling on it all morning. Plus, her tongue made frequent appearances when she spoke. I loved that tongue.

"Heel raises and single leg stances are a good way to start." She turned away and led me to a private room. "After that, we'll move on to hamstring curls and squats."

"Mmm, I might need you to demonstrate some squatting for me," I muttered, half hoping she'd not heard me.

She ignored my comment and opened the door to a private therapy room. "This is where we will be doing our sessions—those times when you're not on one of the exercise machines."

The beige walls resembled the same color as the khaki slacks my fraternity brothers wore around campus. A blue medical bed, a chair, and a computer on a wheely stand occupied the room. Mandy motioned for me to sit on the bed as she sat in the chair and logged onto the computer. My knee ached a bit when I bent it and sank down onto the plastic covered bed. She typed information into a database.

"You sure you wouldn't be more comfortable next to me?" I wiggled my eyebrows at her and patted the navy blue bed. "We could even lay down if you want."

"First, we are going to stretch."

I leaned my back against the wall. "I love stretching." I tried to not let the pain in my leg show on my face when I moved farther back on the bed. "Are you flexible? I would love to stretch you out."

Inappropriate ass was my default setting when I tried to distract myself. The truth was, my emotions were on the highest level of freak out. ACL tears ruined careers. My career had not even started yet. My dream had not yet been achieved. It was like seeing my life flash before my eyes and being stuck continuing to live it without doing what I loved most. Thankfully, my injury was a minor incomplete tear. It would heal within a month or so of intense physical therapy, but that still meant a month off the field. A *month*. Fuck. And it hurt. My knee throbbed whenever I climbed a flight of stairs or bent it at a certain angle.

"Are you going to be this obnoxious and inappropriate the whole time?"

I let my jaw drop like such an accusation shocked me. "I'm being inappropriate?"

"Every second of every minute I've known you so far."

I tried to feel bad about embarrassing her, but her red face was the most adorable thing I had ever seen. "That's a little harsh. I am injured after all. Are you going to hurt a man's self-esteem while he has an injured ACL?"

"You are not a man; you are a boy."

"Damn, girl, that's cold." I grinned. "I kind of like it though. You'll keep me humble."

"I don't want to keep you humble. I want to help your ACL heal, so I won't ever have to see you again."

"Why do they call it ACL?" I continued to waste time. "It sounds like a disease. Like athlete's foot."

"Neither of those are diseases." She pushed back a strand of her golden hair and her beautiful face hypnotized me. "ACL is an acronym for the anterior cruciate ligament. It connects the thigh bone to the shin bone and provides stability to the knee. It is called an incomplete tear because it's only partially torn. You jumped or moved or pivoted wrong but were lucky enough to escape a full tear."

"Still, ACL... It just sounds unattractive."

She rolled her eyes. "God forbid you're associated with something that's unattractive."

"Exactly." She got me. "Are you always so straight forward and witty?"

She pushed my shoulders back. "Lay back on the bed, please."

"Mmm, there's my straight forward girl." I leaned back until I laid flat on the padded, plastic-covered bed. It crinkled under my weight. "You like being on top?"

"I hate you." She closed her eyes and pinched the top of her nose. "So much."

I winked and it had the same result of pouring gasoline on an open flame. "Let's use that fire in your eyes for something else."

She glared at me and raised her voice to show her seriousness. "What would your girlfriend say if she heard the way you act around other girls?"

This time my jaw dropped from real shock. "I'm sorry... What?"

"Your girlfriend," she repeated, but it still failed to clarify things. "Natalia."

It took me another minute to think through what was happening. "I'm sorry... What?" I said again, in hopes for more clues about how she had come upon such ludicrous information.

"Don't try to play dumb." She huffed. "I saw you two."

"Saw us two, what? I hate Natalia. She's a bi—"

"Jake said you were dating."

My hands clenched into fists. "*Jake*...told you that Natalia was my girlfriend?" It was officially planned. Jake would be murdered tonight, six o'clock, sharp.

"I mean..." She bit her lip again. "I guess he just implied it."

"Blondie, stop biting your lip. You do it all the time and I swear to God, one day I'll have to lick it better." I did not regret the way her cheeks turned scarlet and a breathy gasp escaped her beautiful mouth at my comment.

"You're not with Natalia?"

"I'm not with anyone. I mean Natalia and I used to have sex a lot—"

She put her hands over her ears. "I don't need to hear about your sex life."

"You're right. It's better to experience it."

"You two kissed at the game. I saw you."

"Oh." I had forgotten. If Mandy had not been to games before, she would not know. "She kisses me every game; ask anyone. She always tries and I always push her away."

Her expression revealed nothing to me. "Oh."

"You were jealous?" I loved this. If she had seen Natalia kiss me and that was why she had left, then Mandy liked me. "Mmm, interesting. You wanted to be the girl I kissed?"

She leaned over me and rolled up my pants leg. "Shut up. We should focus on your leg."

"I know a different body part that wants your attention."

****

"Let's go to the movies," I said after we finished with some of the exercises.

She had first surveyed my leg and had me elevate it twenty times, and then she insisted that I do some weird knee bending positions. At one point, I accused her of simply wanting to watch me model for her. She told me that she'd never seen such an ugly model, but I had the right amount of modesty for the job. I liked Mandy…

"When are you free?"

She smiled. "It's America, I'm always free." I loved when she smiled at her own jokes. She was so cute… Fuck, what was I thinking? Cute? I did not refer to girls as cute. I did not care enough to refer to girls as anything.

"Great. I'll pick you up at eight o'clock."

"That was a joke, Brandon. I'm not going to the movies with you."

She motioned for me to sit straight and she pushed my pants leg up again. My body jumped at her warm hands against the bare skin of my calf. She rubbed her thumb into my sore muscles and I held in my groan. Fuck, why was her touch so arousing? She just massaged the injury. It should be more painful than pleasurable.

"It was a funny joke, and so was you saying you're not going to the movies with me."

"I'm not."

I nudged her with my foot. "You are."

"I'm not."

"Oh, you so are."

She laughed, continuing to massage and examine my injury. My reaction to the work of her magical fingers became noticeable as a bulge formed behind my jeans. I hoped she would not see what such a simple action caused.

"What are you? Six?"

"Eight," I shot back even though she would not get my joke of the innuendo referencing inches. She finished with the massage and took a step back. Apparently, it was already the end of my session, which meant I would have to leave her. "Why won't you go to the movies with me? I don't have a girlfriend."

Her slight hesitation gave me hope. "I still hate you." She opened the door of our private room to lead me out.

Every part of me screamed 'stall.' "What? Why?"

She crossed her arms over her chest. "Because you're a self-centered jerk who has no respect for women."

I tried not to look down at her amazing cleavage. I really, really tried. "Not true. I respect the way they make sandwiches and bake kick-ass pies." Her face scrunched up, fighting off a smile. "You know I'm kidding. And anyway, why not give me a chance?"

Her next words were like bullets to the chest. "Because I love Jake."

"Why?"

"Because he's who I should be with."

"Should?"

"Look, you're funny and…cute," she told me. "But you're just one of those guys who only cares about himself."

A noise escaped me. "Wow." No one had ever spoken to me that way. "You know, Blondie, next time you try to fit someone into a box like that, you should stop to consider which one you'd occupy."

****

—I'm sorry.—

I texted Mandy in hopes to get back on her good side. It bothered me that she thought of me as the jerk-stereotype. At the same time, I had not given her a reason not to think that way. Flirting was fun but maybe if I opened up more she would think of me differently. I had not been real with someone in a long time. It was easier to stay casual if I remained playful and…not me. '*Show a shallow surface, and no one will want to drill into you for oil,*' my mother told me when I was in middle school. Living by those words became easier and easier, the more people close to me managed to use or hurt me each year.

Mandy responded.

—Who is this?—

—You know who it is.—

—How in the world did you get my number?—

—A detective never reveals his secrets.—

—I thought it was 'a magician never reveals his secrets.'—

I loved how fast she texted me back.

—Either way my secrets will not be revealed, so don't think you can get them out of me. Unless, of course, you want to offer up a trade. Secrets for kisses? I suppose I could agree to that.—

—I bet you could.—

Time to plant the seed of my plan.

—It was weird for Jake to say I was dating Natalia. Think he was jealous?—

—Do you think he was?—

—Maybe that would be a good way for you to get his attention. Making him jealous.—

I knew how I would get Mandy. I'd use Jake to get her to use me, so that I could convince her to like me instead. It sounded like some complex plot of a chick flick that I would never watch, but in that moment I didn't care. Mandy would be mine.

She wouldn't even remember the name Jake once I finished with her.

****

Michael stole the beer from out of my hand and took a slug. I threw my hands up to express my displeasure. "Dude."

"You need to heal." He shrugged and drank from my beer again. "Beer isn't good for healing."

"How is your leg feeling?" Lucas asked as he leaned back in the dark green chair of their apartment.

I had taken to spending more and more time in Lucas and Michael's living room because I didn't want to bump into Jake, in or out of our dorm room. I did homework, hung out, and sometimes even cooked meals in their apartment. Every time I saw Jake, I saw the guy that Mandy *thought* she loved and who didn't acknowledge her existence unless I was around her. I could no longer stand him.

I sank further down into the sofa cushions. "I'm fine." We all sat across from the TV that played reruns of college football.

"Coach doesn't think you're fine." Michael pointed out. "He said you'd be out for the rest of the season."

"It's a minor injury."

"A minor injury that affects your ability to run," Lucas said.

"Like I said, I'm fine." I hated this. This injury was huge for me. I would miss games, games that scouts might watch and decide who was ready to go pro. My phone log indicated that my dad had already called twice. He probably wanted to scold or accuse me of getting hurt on purpose just to disappoint him. I needed to be back to playing as soon as possible. I *lived* for football. "I have to be in physical therapy four days a week."

Michael finished what used to be my beer and grabbed a new one. "That sucks."

"Yeah…" But then there was the fact that I got to be around Mandy for a guaranteed four days a week. "Not completely. You wouldn't believe who the physical therapy assistant is."

With a grin, Lucas tossed me a bottle of water. "The sweet peach?"

"Damn it, Lucas." Michael groaned. "I told you to stop saying weird country things like 'peach.'"

"Blondie is the one helping me recover."

"Congratulations," Michael said and snickered. "You have to pay her to be around you."

"Maybe the universe is trying to tell you something," Lucas offered. "I mean, you two keep getting pushed together."

"Brandon doesn't believe in the universe. He just wants to sleep with her." Michael turned to me. "Right?"

I ended the conversation by turning up the volume on the game. "I guess."

I did want to sleep with her. I did…but I also wanted to talk to her and tease her and joke with her and laugh with her and kiss her until both of us needed to break away to breathe. But damn, who would need oxygen if he had a girl like Mandy?

Chapter Eight
Use Me Anyway You Want

Mandy

"No. Way." Ashley exploded. "Wait, wait, wait. Let me get this straight. He's your patient?" Others in the library jumped at the sound of her squeals.

"That's all you got from my whole story?" I wanted to talk about Jake being jealous, not that Brandon would annoy me for the next month—or longer—until he healed.

She kept on grinning. "Oh my God, he's your patient."

"Patient, no. It's more like 'client.'"

"Can you imagine how sexy that is for him? I bet he has had the nurse-patient fantasy a million times. All the guys do. Before we broke up, Matt used to make me check his heart rate after sex."

"Ash." I covered my ears. "I *so* did not need to know that."

"Sorry." She laughed when I glared at her. Ashley and Brandon were a lot alike; they both took pleasure from my pain. "I'm just saying, he must love that you're going to be his nurse for the next few weeks."

"I'm not a nurse and I don't care what Brandon Gage will love. I told you this because I wanted to know if you thought Jake might be jealous."

"Here's the thing," she said. "I preferred you and

Brandon together, but then I hated him cause he kissed that one chick, but now I like him again, cause she's crazy and he clearly has eyes for you. Jake being jealous doesn't—"

I bounced in my chair. "You think he was jealous?"

"Calm down. Here's what I think, I think you should try to make Jake jealous. Like you know, maybe with someone who has made him jealous before... Hmm, and who was that again?" Ashley tapped her chin in fake, over dramatic thought. "Brandon."

How could I use a guy like that? "I'm not going to use Brandon to make Jake jealous."

"Why not?" she whined.

"Because... That's not who I am."

She placed her hand over mine. "You've wanted Jake for forever. You and Brandon hanging out has somehow triggered Jake's interest for the first time. Don't you want to do anything and everything you can to keep his interest? This could be your last chance."

****

Brandon grinned at me when he walked into the clinic. "Good morning, Blondie."

"We'll be in the same room as yesterday," I told him and led him to the private therapy room. I was on the edge about asking him for help. I attempted not to let my nervousness show. "We're going to start with foot stretches."

"Why don't you wear a uniform?" he inquired from behind me. "You'd look sexy in scrubs."

Nerves twisted my stomach when he sat down on the dark blue bed as I closed the door. Being alone with him in such a small room was awkward. "Scrubs are for hospitals and I'm not a nurse, now stretch your foot."

"I love it when you get all physical therapist on me."

His smile made me shiver. Must. Be. Professional. "Shut up and stretch your foot."

"You're cute when you're angry. Your face gets red and it makes me think about other ways I could get you to blush—"

"Do you even want to get better?"

"If I get better, I won't see you every day."

"And what a shame that would be."

He tilted his head and looked up at me with his chocolate brown, puppy dog eyes. Was he so spoiled because no one could say no to those eyes? "I think you would miss me."

"I'm sure you and your messed up leg will become what I look forward to every day." I rolled my eyes and put my hand over his foot. "Now, stretch out your toes by pointing them at the ceiling and then at the wall."

"Why do you do this?"

"It's meant to warm up your muscles—"

He cut me off. "I mean, why are you a physical therapy assistant? Do you want to go into the medical field?"

He seemed legitimately curious so I told the truth. "I'm an art major, but my mom only agreed to help me pay for college if I had a back-up career plan. She doesn't make much money but it helps. I wouldn't be able to afford Arden if it wasn't for her. I'm already in debt— Why am I telling you this? Sorry, that's personal. I don't want to bore you."

"I was the one who asked and you could never bore me." He titled his head and leaned in until his face was mere inches from mine. "I find you fascinating." I rolled my eyes and pushed him back down onto the medical bed. He stretched his foot like I had asked him to do. "It's true."

"Good, now I want you to raise your knee up and down twenty times." He flinched every time he moved it. I remembered how painful a damaged ACL felt. I nodded when he finished. "Good, now we're going to do a balance exercise."

He stood and copied my motions as I bent one knee and balanced on one leg, switching after twenty seconds to the other one. "This is very yoga-like," he said, wobbling a bit before stabilizing and holding the pose.

"It's a classic stance. A lot of your stretches come from yoga, so you may want to look into attending some classes on campus."

He laughed. "No way."

"Too girly for you?"

"I was at the gym a month ago and made the mistake of walking into one of the yoga rooms. Literally, three girls straight up jumped on me."

This was the guy I would ask to fake date me? "There is no way that's true."

"I was shirtless, so I get that the whole animal magnetism thing could have come into play, but I draw the line when strangers jump on me."

"Half the things you say sound like lies."

He shrugged. "I would only go back if someone went with me to fend off my admirers." His brown eyes lit up with the same mischievous amusement and excitement as a child's. He was going to have the most adorable children one day. Oh my God. Where had *that* thought come from? "What if you went and—"

Pain flashed across his expression and he leaned too far to the right with one leg up. Before he gained back his balance, he reached out to support himself on something at the same time I stepped forward to help him. His hand slipped from my shoulder to my chest, grazing the side of my breast.

Our eyes locked. My heart pounded so hard, my eardrum thrummed along to it.

"I know you won't believe me, but I swear I was not meaning to touch your..." He blushed. *He* blushed. The player, the 'king of campus' blushed. And it was adorable. "I didn't—I wouldn't... I'm sorry."

I continued to stare at him. Words not forming.

He shook his head a bit as if to shake off the awkward moment. In an attempt to lighten the mood he joked, "Did I mean to? No. Do I regret it? No."

A snort mixed with a laugh slipped out. "You ass—" I cut off when the door to our room creaked open.

Mrs. Sweet peered in. "Mandy."

I threw on my instant polite smile. "Hello, Mrs. Sweet." I had never gotten used to the fact that 'Sweet' was her real last name. I sent a prayer that she had not heard me call the top Arden football player a donkey's backside or seen him accidentally touch my breast.

"I've told you before to call me Jess." She grinned at Brandon. "How is our super football star doing?"

He gave her the same smile that the cheerleaders competed for. "I'm doing great, Jess."

"Is Mandy doing a good job with you?"

She appeared friendly but the twitch of her eye betrayed her. If Brandon Gage was not tended to in the expected manner, his father would complain, then pull the funding which I recently learned existed.

Brandon Gage was not only a popular player, but he had a rich father who gave major amounts of money to any part of the University involving his son. After Brandon was injured, Mrs. Sweet told me funding for the physically therapy section of the Clinic bumped up by seventy thousand dollars so new equipment designed for his son's recovery could be bought.

I held my breath, waiting for his response. If he told her anything negative, I would be fired. After all, he was the golden boy who ran the school. It was hard to believe that I had not even known about him before letting him see me half naked on accident.

"She's phenomenal." He smiled at her and she blushed like any other girl he made direct eye contact with. "I'm going to start calling her Sunshine because she's so bright and cheerful."

"That's great. I didn't know if Mandy would be the right one to help you, but she's dealt with ACL injuries before. Since the other therapy assistants' schedules were booked, she was all we could do for you."

"I'm glad. She's the best; my knee is already feeling better. I'm thinking I'll be able to get back to playing soon."

Mrs. Sweet's frown mirrored mine. "I don't think that's a good idea. You still have a ways to go." His eyes lost their sparkle at her words. "Good luck to you both." Mrs. Sweet closed the door after waving.

Brandon turned to me. "You've dealt with ACLs before? I didn't know you were cheating on me."

"Don't say I'm cheating on you."

"Who was he?" Brandon prodded in a joking voice,

but a slight coldness appeared in his eyes. "Was he better looking than me?"

"Nobody is better looking than you," I mumbled under my breath without thinking. My face heated into a blush. Brandon just grinned at me like he always did. "Shut up." I was tempted to stick my tongue out at him but he would like it too much.

He laughed, the joy returning to his brown eyes. "I didn't say anything."

"You're always saying something," I commented and he laughed again.

"Can you read my mind?" He put both hands over his head as if he could block his thoughts from being seen. "Let's test it. What am I thinking right now?"

"Are you ever serious?"

He poked my nose. "Are you ever not?"

I wanted to answer but I stayed silent. My responses fueled him.

"Who was the other guy you helped with a hurt ACL?" He brought it up again and I knew he would not let it go until he received details.

"Why do you need to know?"

"I need to know if I have any competition."

I huffed and looked at his knee to see if any bruises covered the injury. "You don't have any competition."

"Good to know."

"That's not what I meant." I needed to learn to keep my mouth shut when I was around him. I wanted to change the subject of him having 'competition,' so a couple details wouldn't hurt. "And anyway, it wasn't a guy, it was a girl."

Brandon's smile got even bigger, and I regretted informing him more than he needed to know. "I can roll with that. What was her name?"

"Mandy."

Brandon stared at me for a moment. "Does that mean you were the one with a hurt ACL? Did you play a sport or something?"

"That's beside the point."

"You did, didn't you?" Brandon must have found me playing a sport entertaining because I had never seen his smile so wide. I pretended not to notice the heavy heat in his eyes.

"I didn't get an incomplete tear from basketball."

I refused to tell him anything else. I would never inform him that I was a cheerleader. I would sooner die. He'd probably ask if I still had the uniform or if he could watch me do some cartwheels in a skirt.

"What did you get it from?" His curiosity would get him killed one day... by me. Very soon. With a shovel. "I'll find out somehow," he proclaimed. My silence made his impatience even worse. "Why won't you tell me? Was it embarrassing?"

"For me, yes. You'd probably love it."

"I'm sure I would. I have loved everything I've seen from you so far." The kindness in his voice made the thought of fake dating him seem less terrible.

"Um, I have a favor to ask of you... I-I wanted to ask you if... If you would..." God, this was painful.

"Yes, I'll be your fake boyfriend to make Jake jealous."

"What?" There was no possible way that he could have known I would ask that. How did he—

"That's what you were going to ask, right?"

"I mean...but I'm still not sure about it. I feel like it would be using you."

"Then use me," he said, like it was no big deal.

"What?"

His face moved closer until it was centimeters away from mine. It was difficult to keep eye contact without going cross-eyed. "Use me." His minty breath on my lips made me feel light headed. "Any way you want. I want you to get what you want and if you want him, I'll help you."

"But I thought you—"

"I'd do anything to spend more time with you. Of course, I'll help you. And, if you're my fake girlfriend, you can accompany me to those yoga lessons and fend off my fan girls. We both get something out of it then."

"I don't know…"

"Friends help friends; and we're friends, right?"

I suppose we were friends. I mean, I did not exactly like him as a person, but we were going to be stuck together for a while. "I guess."

"Wow, try to sound less happy about it."

I waved my hands in the air and squealed, "We're friends!"

He laughed at me, but I didn't care. I loved his laugh. I loved the happiness in his eyes…Brandon Gage was addictive to talk to, to look at, and to laugh with.

All of which made him dangerous. I couldn't let him distract me from my plan. I loved Jake and I would not give up on him right when he started showing interest. Even if Brandon made my skin tingle, my heart skip, and my smile spread so wide it hurt.

"Then it's settled. We're in a fake relationship."

Chapter Nine
Lessons For A Fake Girlfriend

Brandon

Michael smiled. "You plan to fake date Blondie?"

"It's about time," Lucas teased and threw me the football.

We were on the open field in front of their apartment building. Because of the injury, I'd not been able to practice and was dying. I *needed* football. It treated me well, other than causing an injury to my knee. It was my hobby, my passion. Without it, I contemplated between doing homework or staring at a white wall in complete boredom. Football kept me sane.

Thank God, the pain was just in my leg and occurred only when I ran. I could still throw and catch while standing still. Walking was all right. The main concern was if I pushed too far, the ACL could worsen and tear. I could not afford that. Agents scouted players for the big league during the later games of the season. Missing a chance to be scouted was not an option. My stats were already messed up because of the first game I missed.

"I can't believe she likes Jake. He's such a jerk."

I threw my hands up and caught the ball. "I know, right?"

Michael caught the football after I launched a perfect, hard spiral at him. "If she likes you too, then we'll know for a fact she has bad taste in men."

"Whatever. This way I get to show her how amazing I am."

"But you still don't want to be her real boyfriend, right?"

I remained silent for a second longer than I should have. "I don't know. I mean you know how I feel about girlfriends…but I also can't let Jake have her."

"So, this is like a competition for you now."

"No. I don't know. At first, I just wanted her—"

Lucas grinned—wider than I had ever seen him grin. That guy was such a romantic. "And now you want *all* of her?"

"I've never met anyone like her."

"Considering you've never had another female say 'no' to you about anything, that makes sense."

I did not let the subject go. "It's more than that. She…" Everything felt warmer with Mandy around. Talking to her filled my black hole feeling of not being able to play football. I did not need to slow down because she was always there to match me in whatever I said or whatever I did. No one challenged me the way she did. "She fucking lights me on fire."

Michael fumbled the ball because he was too busy watching two hot girls wave as they passed us on the field. "Sounds painful."

"I've never met anyone who I want to talk to and touch more than Mandy."

"Oh man, you're starting to sound like Lucas."

"What's wrong with sounding like me?" Lucas pouted. Two of the passing hotties yelled and blew kisses at him. Girls were just as obsessed with him as they were with me. I would be jealous if I cared about anyone else other than Mandy liking me.

"You sound whipped."

I threw the ball to Michael a little too hard. "Whatever."

Damned if I'd ever be whipped.

****

"Let me guess," I said into my phone to my father. "You're not angry, you're disappointed." I answered his call once his attempts to contact me reached into double digits. Ever since my injury pulled me out from playing, he had pestered me.

"I'm both," he responded. "Don't forget that the only reason you're at Arden is because you need to be scouted. You can't afford to miss a month of football, it'll mess up your stats."

After two minutes talking to him, I was exhausted. "I *know*."

"Do you? Do you know? It's my money that is—"

"I fucking know, okay?" I took a deep breath. "I can't do anything about it. Coach won't let me play again until the doc says I'm healed."

"Can't we do something to quicken the process?"

"They told me if I play too soon it could lead to permanent injury."

"Exactly, *could*. That's a chance I'm willing to take."

I kicked at the entrance door to the library, where I needed to enter to meet Mandy as soon as the call ended. "I'm glad you're so concerned about the well-being of your son."

"Your well-being is you playing football."

"I'll do the best I can."

"Hopefully, that will be good enough this time," he

barked and hung up on me.

I released a heavy sigh and unclenched my fist that had formed. This was supposed to be a good day. I was supposed to see Mandy.

After about ten minutes of cooling down, I found her in the study room of the library where we agreed to meet. I attempted to be light and humorous like usual, but focusing was hard. My father was right. Football was my only path to success. If I missed out on a scout's visit or making a few spectacular plays in a big game, my future would be nonexistent.

Mandy's bright gaze scanned my face. "Are you okay?"

I gave her a smile. *Act normal. You have work to do. Clear everything else from your mind.*

"Sorry, where was I? Oh yeah. Step one of being in a fake relationship with me." Mandy had agreed to meet with me to discuss our plan. I called it: OSMWSSJAEUWM. Operation Seduce Mandy While She Seduces Jake And Ends Up With Me. The acronym was too long for her to guess, so it worked for the time being. "You need to learn how to flirt."

She toyed with a strand of her silky blonde hair. "I know how to flirt."

Her awkward reaction led me to believe that she, in fact, did not know how to flirt. Damn, the idea of teaching her excited me. I pushed football far from my thoughts. "Sure you do, but shoving boys in the sandbox and sharing your fruit gummies doesn't work in college. In fact, I don't even know how it worked for you in high school."

"You make me sound like an abusive child."

"All I know is you're always hitting me and

pushing me away."

"Because you are always being ridiculous." She slapped at my arm. "I'm not flirting with you."

"Okay, sure, Blondie."

"Why do I even need to learn how to flirt?" She looked down at her hands and weaved her fingers together. "I'm supposed to be in a relationship with you, right?"

"The end game is to get Jake, right? You need to be able to reel him in and keep him hooked. Plus, no one will believe that we're going out if you're not flirty and acting like one of the sexiest girls on campus."

"Gee, thanks."

"Not what I meant. You're already sexy. It's just that you get shy and blush whenever I say something inappropriate. People won't believe we're together if you act all uncomfortable around me."

"I guess that's true."

"Okay, so let's go through the levels of flirting." I counted them off on my fingers. "First, eye contact; second, body language; and third, talking."

"How can you flirt with someone through eye contact?"

I looked into her fire blue eyes and thought about the first time I saw her in that trench coat... The desperate sounds she had made. The way her lips deepened the kiss out of instinct. I knew molten heat would be in my expression. Her wide eyes stayed locked onto mine. I moaned when a slight whimper escaped from the back of her throat and a seductive look washed over her face as well.

Her lips trembled and I couldn't tear my gaze away from them. They would taste so good. I still had not forgotten that kiss from the first time we met. Fuck, I wanted to drag her across the table to kiss her again.

Then I remembered we were in a very public library.

"Uhh," I cleared my throat and tried to calm down by thinking about all the old things in the library. Shakespeare. Oscar Wilde. The old librarian who was as wrinkled as the first editions. "I—I think you're good for now. Um, we can practice that later."

She nodded. "Okay."

"Okay, um…" What had we even been talking about? "Now, what we need to work on with you is that every time you feel awkward or don't know what to say, you lose all your confidence and start spouting random things."

"Um, excuse me, but that is so not true."

She looked angry, but I ignored her. "Blondie, I'm sorry but it is. You have a serious case of foot-in-mouth disease." I raised a hand to hold off any protest on her part. "Don't worry; it's not terminal. I can cure it."

She dug her hands in her hair and put her head on the table. "You make me so mad."

"See, you're embarrassed, so your first instinct is to hide." I brushed a couple strands of hair away from the side of her face. "You need to learn to remain calm and think before you speak."

She glared at me. "Thanks."

"Don't get me wrong, I love the way you get nervous and say whatever you're thinking. Like when you said you'd love to straddle me."

"I meant strangle and I get it. Geez, just tell me what to do."

I helped her with improving her ability to think on

her feet by practicing responses for questions like "when did you two start dating" and "how did that happen." After a while, her eye contact improved and she sat straighter.

Time to move on to body gestures and movements.

I told her to always point her feet at whomever she talked to in order to show interest. She also learned to touch someone on the arm, hand, or leg. I was happy to be her guinea pig for the touching portion. And finally, the hardest one of all: how to flirt while talking.

"Are you sure you're ready for this?" I asked, because I wasn't even sure if I was ready to teach her anymore. Sure, it was nice to have her practice on me, but it got harder and harder knowing that I taught her for Jake.

"I want to at least learn enough for the party tonight; I can listen to the rest later."

I wanted to test her out at a party that my friend was throwing at a fraternity house. It was the perfect place to show up as a couple because Jake would be there as well. "Okay, you need to combine everything you've learned so far, flirting with your eyes and movements, and add talking."

She fiddled with her thumbs. "The talking is the one part I'm worried about."

"Let's see how you are already." I leaned back in my chair. "Try to flirt with me."

She looked around the room, like flirting was scandalous and illegal in college libraries. "Here?" I did not inform her that, in actuality, *way* more scandalous practices happened in college libraries. "Now?"

"Here and now. Show me what you got, beautiful."

She shot me a stressed look but moved her chair

closer to mine until our knees tapped against each other. She leaned in to make better eye contact. "Hello," she said in a strained voice that resembled a thirty-five-year-old smoker. We had a lot of work to do. "Um, so you, uh, play sports?"

"Wrong. Wrong, wrong, wrong." I shook my head at her. "Your voice is shaking and not in a sexy way. Be more confident. You need to sound like you *know* you have my attention, not that you're asking for it." She nodded at the critique like it was helpful, so I continued, "Also you need to capture my attention. Put your hand on my arm or something in order to make me focus on you. And Blondie, I know this is going to be hard but try to cut down on using 'um.' Think about what kind of conversation you want to have, then decide what to say."

"Okay, can I try again?" The determined look on her face made me want to kiss her. Hell, everything about her made me want to kiss her, but instead I just smiled and nodded.

She leaned in even closer to me until her chest brushed against my arm. Whoa, way better than the touch of a hand. "Hey," she said in a deep, husky voice that took all the blood away from my brain.

"Hey," I answered, enthralled in her spell already. She hypnotized me with that sensual look in her eyes. What the fuck? She was a fast learner.

"I love your letter man jacket." When she stroked a finger down my chest, I almost jumped out of my skin. "You play a sport?"

My mouth went dry. I licked my lips. "Football."

Her lips formed the perfect O and I attempted to think of anything but where I would love that cute mouth to be…wrapped around the member of my body that hardened with every passing second. "So…you like playing with balls?"

For a second, I froze, then erupted with a howl of laughter so loud people raised their heads, hearing me through the glass door and wall of the study room that separated us. "Oh, Mandy." I nearly cried from laughing so hard. "You had it but then you ruined it."

She giggled. "Should I have said, 'I like to play with balls, too?'"

Damn, I was so glad she had not said that. "That, uh, that probably would have been too much."

"Oh, okay."

I was still laughing. "Great job before that, though."

She smiled up at me and my heart *melted?* Gross. Maybe I was whipped and it was all because of Mandy.

"I think you should be fine for tonight. I'll be there to help you the whole time. The party starts at nine o'clock so I'll pick you up at nine thirty. Also, be ready to practice not being uncomfortable around me because no one is going to believe we're dating if I don't have my hands all over you."

****

A knock sounded on the door as I sat at my desk in my dorm room, working on a class assignment. Grateful it wasn't Jake, because he would not have knocked, I paused to look through the peephole. Shit. Natalia.

"What are you doing here?"

I had not seen her since the football game where she kissed me in front of Mandy. Her smile sent an uncomfortable chill up my spine. Sure, Natalia was hot, but she was also crazy. She never took 'no' for an answer. That used to turn me on, now it annoyed me. "I came to see you."

I spoke loud enough for her to hear me through the door because no way would I open it for her. "Why?"

Her hands went to her hips and I inwardly groaned. That was the first sign of planting herself where she was. "I never needed an excuse before."

A shadow moved up behind her, then a form blocked the peephole. Dammit, Jake always had terrible timing. The door muffled their voices a bit but I was able to make out most of it.

"I need to grab my textbook. Does he have it locked?" The chime of him rifling for his keys sounded through the door. "You here to see Brandon?"

"Why else would I be here? I'm not here to see you." Natalia had no interest in Jake. If only I could convince Mandy to feel the same.

The door opened from the other side and I stepped out of the way.

"Think you two could give me a minute before you start jumping each other?" Jake asked.

"I'm not going to sleep with her."

Natalia glared at me as they both entered the room. "What's up with you? You've been acting weird lately. You don't even answer my texts."

"I've explained to you before that we are over."

"You think you can just sleep with me and walk away? I'm not one of your whores!"

"Whoa," both Jake and I exclaimed. Even though we slept around, neither of us used the W word.

She threw up her chin and growled, "You think I don't know about this new blonde you've been spending all your time with?"

"She's none of your business." I took a step closer in hopes closer proximity would help drive my words home. "Stay away from her, Natalia. I mean it."

"Oh, you 'mean' it? You mean it? I could destroy both of you without even breaking a nail."

"Wow." Jake had the audacity to chuckle at my situation. "I didn't know you had so much girl drama going on."

"Shut the hell up. And Natalia, don't think for a second that your words have even an ounce of more power than mine. Remember who my dad is? He employs half the state. Leave Mandy alone."

"Remember who *my* dad is," she countered. "The coach of your favorite NFL team. The one you want to be drafted for. Remember? If I see you around that blonde again, I might just have to give Daddy a call."

Her threats didn't work. "I'm not scared of you. Mandy and I are dating, and there's nothing you can do to stop it. Put the claws away and get out of my room."

She sent me a vicious look before she strutted out.

Jake shook his head and laughed. "Dude, you just pissed off Natalia McCallin. Do you know what you're doing? Is Mandy worth that?"

The next words I chose would decide whether Jake went after her. If he knew how much I cared, it would be a challenge he'd have to take; his last chance to prove he could best me at something.

If I said 'yes,' he'd try to take Mandy from me. If I said 'no,' he'd walk away and Mandy's plan of making him jealous would never work because he'd know I wasn't serious about her. Mandy was mine and there was no way he would win her over me. Let him try. My competitive side took over.

"She's worth everything."

****

I was at Mandy's door by nine twenty-two. Was knocking the appropriate thing to do or was I supposed to wait? Would I seem over eager showing up early? I had counted down the minutes until I could leave to see her again since we left the library. I needed to see her, look at her, re-convince myself that I had a solid chance with her, especially after the run-in with Jake and Natalia, my two least favorite people. Her door opening made the choice for me. It revealed a girl who was not Mandy.

I recognized her as Jake's sister and Mandy's friend. "Ashley, right?"

She nodded and smiled at me like she knew all of my secrets. "That's right, Brandon Gage."

"You can just call me Brandon," I said when she pulled me into the room. "Wow, you're strong—"

"Oh my God, Ash! I'm still changing," Mandy announced from the other side of the room and I caught a glimpse of her bare skin before she dropped down to hide behind her bed.

"Oh please, like he hasn't seen you half naked before."

I heard the click of Mandy's jaw dropping at Ashley's comment and I laughed. Now I understood why they were friends.

"Ash," Mandy groaned.

"Fine, we'll be outside the door," Ashley said and pulled me out of the room, closing the door. The rest of her statements she yelled through the door. "Open it when you're finished and don't you dare pull the top of that tank top up. It's meant to go down, stop trying to fight gravity."

She then turned to me. "So, Mr. Gage. How do you plan on seducing my Mandy and how can I help?"

Chapter Ten
Seductive Strawberries

Mandy

I feared Ashley might hyperventilate and pass out. "Ash, calm down."

"Sorry, it's just... I didn't think you would do it. You are fake dating Brandon Gage! I'm so excited. What are you wearing tonight? It better be sexy. No one will believe you two are dating if you don't look super sexy."

"He pretty much said the same thing." I pouted. "Am I not normally sexy?"

"What? Of course, you're sexy. Just not 'the first girl to ever date Brandon Gage' sexy in what you're wearing, that is. A worn out t-shirt and jeans don't make someone like him stop and stare, you know what I'm saying?"

"Between you and Brandon, you're both knocking me down today."

She kissed my cheek and gave me a hug. "We do it 'cause we love you."

I recoiled. "Brandon doesn't love me."

As usual, she ignored my negative spirit. A perpetual bundle of joy, she let every frown bounce off her. "But he will."

"I don't want him to. I want Jake to love me."

"And Jake will too... And then you'll be in the

middle of a love triangle. Oh, how fun would that be?"

"That does *not* sound like fun."

"Whatever. What time is prince charming picking you up?"

"Nine thirty."

"Hah, of course he has to be fashionably late. Okay, so I'll start your make-up first, then we can decide on what you should wear."

"What would I do without you?" I sank down onto the seat in front of Ashley's desk which was meant for schoolwork; instead magazines and make-up covered the entire surface.

She pulled the hair band off of my ponytail and brushed my tangled hair in rapid strokes. "You would be getting ready by yourself and we both know that would not be ideal."

I swatted her away from my sensitive roots. "Ow!"

"Beauty is pain," she announced and came at me with a stick of eyeliner so fast that I didn't even have time to scream.

"Do you think Brandon likes strawberry or orange better?" Ashley asked half an hour later as she lifted two different flavored tubes of lip gloss.

"I like orange," I offered.

"But that wasn't the question, was it?"

I sighed. "No."

She pinched my cheeks like she was my mother. They were alike after all. "And what was the question, sweetie?"

"What would Brandon like?" I sighed. "You know, maybe I don't want to live my life according to what some guy wants. Maybe I want to wear orange because *I* like it."

"And you totally can." She grabbed a concealer brush and danced it over my face once more to even out my skin tone. "But not on your first fake date with the hottest, most unobtainable guy at Arden University."

That made sense. "I'd guess strawberry."

She grabbed my chin and tilted up my head. "Strawberry it is."

"I can apply it myself, you know," I mumbled.

"Stop talking or I'll mess up."

I shut up. Ashley was a make-up queen. I was surprised she didn't go to cosmetology school instead of Arden. Though her mother did not support her dream of becoming a movie make-up artist, I believed she had the ability and skill to achieve it.

Ashley helped me pick out a sheer, shiny gold top that dipped low in the front. Once I put it on, I told her that I needed something to wear underneath it. She gave me a tank top that did not help with covering up my chest, but at least made me feel a little bit more comfortable. She said the color made my hair look like sunshine, which reminded me of Brandon calling me "Blondie." She didn't stop yelling at me, though, after I yanked on the material to block some of my cleavage.

She then picked up a fake leather skirt with pleats that made it look like a mix of a private school uniform and a biker girl. This would be one of the last warm nights of Fall before the chill made anything but pants unbearable. I needed to remember not to bend over tonight or people would see a lot more of me than I'd like. Since Ash hid all my normal cotton underwear, I had to wear a lace pair that my mom had bought for me 'just in case.' My mother was weird.

I was in the middle of changing when Ashley

opened the door and let in Brandon. She took him back out so I could finish changing, but not before I contemplated if it were possible to die from embarrassment. A quick glance in the mirror revealed the skirt was even shorter than I had thought. Great.

'More skin is showing than fabric,' I thought as I made my way to the door. When I opened it, Brandon's jaw dropped and his eyes darkened.

Geez. Did the room get hotter? Feeling over heated seemed impossible due to how little I wore, but sweat still dampened my palms. Neither one of us spoke as we took the other in. He wore dark jeans and a tight black shirt that did nothing to hide his muscles. Wow. How would anyone believe a guy who looked like *that* would date me?

"Okay," Ashley exclaimed and shook both of us out of our trance. "No drooling on the tile floor." She reached over and closed his jaw. "You two need to practice being a couple. After all, Brandon, I don't know if you've ever actually *dated* anyone before, and, Mandy, it's been a while for you, too. Would you both like some pointers?"

I stepped closer to him. "I think we know how it works."

"Eh, I don't think so," she said. "The least you can do is humor your best friend who wasn't invited to the party full of hot guys."

Playing the guilt card made me fold. "Fine."

"Great." She led Brandon and I back into our room and pushed us closer together, so we faced each other. "Now, practice kissing."

"Ash." I was more shocked than surprised when Brandon reached out to pull me flush against his body.

His head dipped and, a moment later, his lips molded onto mine. Electricity ran through my veins. He knew exactly what to do with his lips, tongue, and hands... Good *God.* I suddenly understood why people referred to him as the 'king of campus.'

His top lip sucked in my bottom one and the tip of his tongue touched mine in the most erotic way imaginable. A hand raced up the side of my bare leg, disappearing under my skirt and eliciting another moan from me. We continued to kiss until I pulled away in order to breathe. We ended with a long slow kiss that had both of us out of breath.

"Jesus," Ash said, bringing me back to reality.

I jumped out of Brandon's embrace. "Jesus," I repeated.

Brandon touched his bottom lip and I wondered if I had bitten him. "Fuck." He closed his eyes and groaned. "You taste like strawberries..." His eyes darkened as they met mine. "I fucking love strawberries."

Another shiver raced down my spine. I felt a pulse between my thighs. Was there anything this boy could do that would not either piss me off or turn me on?

Ashley cleared her throat again in order to get our attention. "I don't think you guys need to practice kissing anymore. Maybe you should both just head out to the party."

"Yeah."

Brandon nodded, the heat from our kiss still shining in his eyes. "Yeah."

"Have fun," Ashley said as we walked out of the room.

"So..." Brandon began, but stopped, so I filled the silence.

"Jake will definitely be there?" I asked and his warm eyes turned to cold stones.

He ground his teeth and looked angry as he walked me out of the building. Did I do something wrong already?

****

When we got closer to the fraternity house, my hands grew slick and butterflies bombarded my stomach. The kind of butterflies with sharp wings, like mechanical blades of a blender that chipped away at my intestines.

"Remember," he said. "We're dating. Try not to flinch when I touch you."

"No promises."

I elbowed him playfully, and he caught it and held on for a second longer than necessary. He then trailed his hand down the rest of my arm until he grabbed my hand and weaved his fingers through mine. Powerful sparks raced through my body when he held my hand. The feeling was new and exhilarating.

Two of the best-looking guys I had ever seen—except for Jake and Brandon—blocked the doorway of the frat house. One of them shouted and waved at him, slapping his hand as a greeting when we made it to the entrance. "Brandon, man." He reminded me of a wolf licking his chops before he pounced. I felt violated just from his gaze. "And who is this delicious lady?"

"This is my girlfriend."

It was like time stopped. The shocked expressions of the boys were comical. The one guy thought he had misunderstood. Poor thing. I'm sure this was a huge surprise but their reactions were pretty over dramatic. "Your... Your what?"

"My girlfriend." He put an arm over my shoulders and pulled me through the doorway. "Excuse me, gentlemen, but my date needs a drink."

When we were out of earshot, I leaned in close. "You'd think you had just told them you were an alien."

"That might've been more believable. After all, I'm so perfect, it's almost inhuman."

"Whatever." Fighting the smile forming on my face was impossible. "You're so full of it." He tipped his head down to mine and, before I knew it, he kissed me. My blood ran hot from the small, simple peck. "What was that for?"

"You're my girlfriend." He pressed his lips against mine once more. "I should be able to kiss you whenever you are being too cute to handle."

I fought to find the right words. "You really are full of it." He moved in to kiss me again but I pushed him back. "I need a drink."

"Alcoholic?"

I contemplated how tense I was. "No." Alcohol with a nervous stomach did not sound like a good combination. Plus, Ash would kill me if I forgot something and left out a detail.

"Okay, I'll grab you a soda. Stay here."

I stayed standing in the corner of the room after Brandon ran off, hoping no one would approach me. I did not want to stress out about what to say to a total stranger at a party. But then, fate never liked me anyway.

"What are you doing here?"

It was Natalia, the cheerleader. *This* was the kind of girl Brandon was used to. Flawless. Fantastic.

Be confident. "I-I'm here for the party."

She smirked but still looked beautiful. "But you're not popular...or rich."

Dang it, Brandon, where are you? "I'm here with someone."

She looked me up and down as if the boy who brought me had stamped his initials somewhere on my body. "Who?" Odds were she already knew who I was here with but chose not to accept it.

Another voice came from behind me. Finding Jake as the owner delighted me. "Me."

"Jake," Natalia said, "oh, you two would make a much cuter couple. Do you know where Brandon is?" She pouted but the edges of her lips twisted up into a smile. "I think I forgot my scarf on his dresser when I came over today."

Natalia was in their room today? When? Why didn't Brandon tell me? Had something happened? Questions flooded my head so fast, the dizziness suffocated me. It was like a flashback to Eric.

"I think I saw him around here somewhere," he said.

She took off, no doubt to troll for Brandon.

"What are you doing here, Man?" Jake asked.

I attempted to remain calm. I should not have worried about what may or may not have happened between Natalia and Brandon. I was at the party for Jake. *Jake.* Forget Brandon. We were *fake* dating. I should not like him in the first place. I did not like him.

Okay. What were the steps of flirting again? Eye contact. Body language. Confident discussion. I took a deep breath. Here we go.

I took a step closer to Jake, looked him straight in

the eyes, and made sure to droop my eyelids a smidge for extra effect. "Brandon invited me."

His gaze dropped to my lips before he looked into my eyes. "Brandon? And he just left you by yourself? Sometimes he can be insensitive—"

"Talking about me, Jakey?" Brandon appeared and wrapped an arm around my waist, pulling me toward him and away from Jake. "Here's your drink." He handed me my soda and turned back to Jake. "Which reminds me, why did you tell my girlfriend that I was dating Natalia?"

Jake's gaze moved from the arm around my waist and back to Brandon's face. Back and forth, maybe seven times, before he released a breath. "Girlfriend?"

"Yup. I just couldn't let her slip away." Brandon pulled me even closer before Jake's attention focused on my outfit. If such a small amount of clothing could be called an 'outfit.' "It's funny actually, I never would have met her if it wasn't for you." Brandon laid it on thick. "It's almost like you set us up."

"Almost." Jake turned to me. "We said we'd hang out soon and we haven't yet. Are you free sometime this week?"

"I—"

"We'd love to," Brandon answered for me.

"So…a double date then?"

I jumped into the conversation. "Sounds delightful."

Jake was about to walk away when he stopped. "How did you two meet again?"

Brandon squeezed his arm around me a bit tighter. "You know, classic story of boy meets girl, girl talks to boy, boy asks girl out. That sort of thing."

More like girl mistakenly lets boy see her in almost nothing but a trench coat, boy stalks girl, boy gets hurt, girl must help him heal, boy helps girl win her dream guy. That sort of thing.

Jake's eyes narrowed. "Kinda vague."

I faked a laugh, which of course came out creepy and unnatural. "Brandon is just being weird."

"I am weird."

"We met in our philosophy class," I said.

Jake gave us a stiff nod like he still did not fully believe us. "How about tomorrow night for the double date? Seven o'clock. Our room. I'll rent a movie."

"Great," I responded.

He smiled and leaned in to kiss my cheek. "See you then, Mandy."

My mouth hung open as he walked away.

Brandon looked as dumbstruck as me. "He just kissed you."

"On the cheek." My fingers trailed over the side of my face. "I guess our plan is working."

"I guess."

Because the idea bothered me more than it should have, I could not keep my mouth shut. "Was Natalia in your room today?"

He stiffened, then nodded and shrugged those great shoulders. "Only to try to seduce me and threaten our relationship like any other psychotic ex."

I felt sick. "She seduced you?"

Brandon was not like Eric, but him being known as a Casanova still bothered me. Why would he give up his promiscuous ways in order to be my pretend boyfriend? And he was my pretend boyfriend. *Pretend.* Why did the idea of him with Natalia make me feel uneasy? I shouldn't develop feelings for him. He wasn't the guy I wanted to end up with. I would never let myself end up with someone like him.

"*Tried*, Blondie. Only one girl has ever seduced me and she was a different crazy chick who showed up to my room in nothing but a trench coat."

It was hard to feel like I could not trust him when his eyes gazed into mine as if they had no interest in looking anywhere else. His words caused a flutter in my chest. Why did his small touch at my back spark something inside of me? Why, when he moved closer to me, did my eyes have a hard time not dipping down to stare at his lips?

Why did it hurt so much to think of him with someone else?

"Now that he's gone, should we leave?" I asked.

"Do you want to leave?"

"Parties aren't really my thing."

He took my hand and led me to the exit, pushing through the mob of sweaty people grinding with sloshing red cups. "You don't like drunk college kids throwing up on you?"

"Not particularly." What I did like was him holding my hand. "Let me guess, you're a big party guy."

"More big, less party." He laughed at my mock scrunched up expression. "I used to like parties, but after a while they feel a bit repetitive. I don't drink much because of football. Without alcohol, the deafening music and hot rooms with strobe lights are a lot less fun."

We made it outside and the fall air chilled my warm skin. "Then what do you do for fun?"

His smile faded. "Football." He opened the car

door for me to climb in and then got in on the driver's side. "What do you do?"

"Paint."

He chuckled. "Between the both of us, it sounds like we barely have any fun."

"I don't have time for fun."

He started the car and the engine roared to life. "What about right now? What would you want to do right now?"

An answer came to me. "You won't like it."

****

"You were right, this is terrible."

I shoved him and he grinned.

"This is what you thought of when I said fun? Looking at weird sculptures."

The arts building featured beautiful works hanging on the walls; a part of me had always wanted to explore it with someone. Guiding a guy like Brandon through an art exhibit had never occurred to me. I expected to give critiques and use big words like 'Terracotta,' but with him, it was easy to stand back and enjoy it all.

"They're beautiful," I defended the pieces of work. We stood in front of a copper piece depicting a crying woman, bent into a crouched position. It always took my breath away when I spent any time looking at it.

"You're beautiful. These are just okay."

My smile grew as I pulled him over to a painting on the far wall. This was what I wanted him to see. His reaction was small, but evident by a widening of his eyes and his breathless sound of surprise.

The black and white painting showed a girl's young face melting into a wrinkled old one.

"Beautiful," he whispered and stared at me. "You

painted this, didn't you?"

"It was one of the pieces in my portfolio that got me accepted here."

He gazed at it for another full, long minute before turning to me again. "You are utterly amazing."

A pause.

A shift.

And I kissed him.

Chapter Eleven
A Stripper Named Oregano

Mandy

"Okay, so how many times did you guys kiss tonight?" Ashley wasted no time to quiz me once I walked into our room. "Don't be shy. He's Brandon Gage. I know he kissed you."

I sank onto my bed. The clock read two in the morning and my eyes burned enough to make me question needing eye drops. "It was all for show."

She bounced down next to me on the bed. "Sure it was. Now, tell me every little thing that happened."

Even though exhaustion plagued me, I told her about how we talked and how we made plans with Jake for a double date for tomorrow night. I told her about how Brandon kissed me and always had his arm around me. I didn't tell her about how he made me smile, laugh, and feel…wanted.

All of a sudden he had become one of my favorite people to be around. This attraction to him was dangerous. Jake used to be the only guy who got my heart racing, but now…

I groaned into my pillow. "I just feel so confused."

She petted my hair until I passed out from thoughts about two very different guys. "I know, sweetie."

****

Jake smiled and ruffled my hair. "Happy New

Year, Man." I tried not to flinch at the nickname he gave me. "What's your New Year's resolution?"

That was a good question. A resolution? There was plenty to choose from: getting an A on my AP history exam, Jake no longer calling me Man, losing ten pounds, becoming beautiful, and then the main one: experiencing my first kiss. Of course, I'd sooner die than tell him any of those.

"Um, I want to learn how to, uh..." I strived to think of something that wouldn't sound idiotic. My struggles only led to my idiocy manifesting itself into my sentence. "Kiss." My inner thought slipped from my mouth, resulting in blood rushing to my cheeks so fast, I went dizzy. Would he laugh? Frown? Think I was a freak? Why couldn't God just strike me down with lightening when I wanted him to? This was too much for my fifteen-year-old heart to take.

He shot me an incredulous look. "You want to learn how to kiss?"

I wondered if a person could quite literally die from humiliation... Apparently not because my heart continued beating.

"I, uh, um, I meant—" What's another k word? Oh God please, what was another word starting with the letter k? "—kill." Kill? I was about ready to kill myself after all the mortification.

His lips curved into a smile. "You meant that your New Year's resolution was to learn how to kill?" I amused him. Great. I contemplated if it was better to be trapped in eternal friend zone or be thought of as a clown.

I nodded, knowing I'd made my bed and now I had to lay in it. "Yup, I want to learn how to kill...spiders.

They're tricky bastards, you know, always webbing around and such."

Jake stared at me and made a noise that most closely resembled a laugh. "You're pretty strange, Mandy."

My breath caught.

He had called me Mandy. Not Man. Mandy.

"What's your New Year's resolution?" I asked.

His blue eyes caught mine and my heart stopped for a moment. It was like staring up at a cloudless sky on a sunny day, beautiful and blinding.

"I want to teach a girl how to kiss."

I shot up in bed from the dream and sighed. High school Mandy was no longer who I was. She had loved Jake. He was her first kiss. Yet, I had changed a lot since then and Jake had as well. Was he still what I wanted?

'*Yes*,' I told myself. Jake was the guy I needed. The double date with him was hours away. My plan was finally working.

Still, I found myself walking with the speed of a cheetah to the philosophy class I shared with Brandon like my feet knew where they wanted to be: near him.

He sat in the seat next to my normal one and grinned at me when I sat down next to him. "Why, hello there, girlfriend."

I did not correct him with a 'fake girlfriend' comment. "Fancy seeing you here."

"Did you have fun last night?"

I smiled as I remembered how much of a good time I'd had with him. "Yeah, did you?"

"Definitely." He bumped his knee against mine under the long table. "Listen, I was thinking we should go over a few things before the double date tonight."

"Like what?"

"First off, Jake seemed pretty suspicious last night. I think he might try to ask us questions about our relationship. Moment of truth... What's your favorite color?"

"Are you serious?" I scoffed. "He will *not* ask us that."

"I once told him that I would never be with a girl whose favorite color was red."

I would have questioned his sincerity if he had not said it with such a straight face. "You are such a douche. Why is red so bad?"

"Because it's a sign that she could be a serial killer."

"Ashley's favorite color is red."

"Ashley is crazy so it makes sense," he said, and I laughed at him. "Now before we get side tracked again, what's your favorite color?"

"Blue."

"Then this was meant to be because I also love the color blue. Specifically, the color of your eyes." My cheeks warmed at his compliment. "Okay, what else...he might ask what you like best about me."

"Eh, I doubt he'll ask that."

"Come on, tell me." He poked my side with his finger and whined like a spoiled little boy who had been told 'no' for the first time. "Tell me."

"What do you like most about *me*?"

"Hmm... It's a tie. I love the way your eyes sparkle when you're happy, but I also love the way your cheeks turn a deep red when I say something that makes you uncomfortable." He leaned in closer until he was inches away from my face. "What about you?"

His dark coffee colored eyes distracted me. "What about me?"

"What do you like about me?"

I tapped my chin in fake deliberation and thought. "I don't like to think that hard." I laughed when he put on his best pouting face. "Okay. I like your big—"

"Mandy!" He put his hands over his ears and even had the decency to blush. "How inappropriate. How crude. How…did you know it was so big?"

"You ass." I slapped his shoulder and looked around the room to make sure no one had overheard us. "I was going to say your big brown eyes."

"Ah, I see; you like me for my looks." He feigned being hurt. "I don't know which one is worse."

"Fine, I also like the way you can always make me smile even though I feel like every time I'm around you, I'm visualizing punching you."

"As long as you don't mentally hit my face. It's the money maker."

Other students trickled in but we continued to talk until the professor appeared. Class went by the slowest it ever had. Brandon kept looking over at me as I pretended to watch and listen to the professor, so he would not catch me looking back at him.

At one point, I took notes without knowing what words I wrote down. He kept knocking his good knee against mine and every time we touched, a wave of heat washed over me. When class ended, I let out a long breath I had been holding.

"Want to go to lunch together?"

I nodded yes because I had barely eaten any breakfast. We continued to talk about what different things we needed to know about each other until we got to the cafeteria. The conversation died down as we sat at a table and ate. He started tossing his food at me when the silence threatened to become awkward.

I swatted at them. "Don't throw gummies at my face."

"I'll throw grapes at your face."

I sighed. "Will you throw college tuition at my face?"

"Is it that bad?" He tossed one of the grapes into his mouth and chewed. "Your loans?"

"Let me word it this way: I might have to start stripping for college money, but I'm not attractive enough to be the main showing, so I'd have to be the understudy. Like for when Cinnamon breaks her ankle."

He laughed. "Cinnamon?"

"It's the first spice that came to mind."

He chuckled again. "Not all strippers are named after spices."

"You would know."

"What would you name me if I was a stripper?"

I took a second to think about it before answering. "Oregano."

He titled his head and narrowed his eyes at me. "Why?"

"Because I personally find you tasteless, but everyone else seems to like you."

Brandon laughed, choking on his soda.

"What would you call me if I was a stripper?" I asked, ignoring the way the fire in his eyes made my stomach turn to knots.

He looked me over, taking his time to examine

every part of me that was visible, like he imagined it, until he smiled. "Trench Coat."

I shook my head at him as I attempted to suppress my lips from curling into a smile. "I expected better. I'm disappointed."

His grin made me blush and my heart beat harder in my chest. "I'm not."

****

My art teacher stumbled when he looked at my new painting in class. I sat on my stool and mixed more yellow into white paint as he moved closer to analyze it. "You're using yellow." He acted astonished. It was understandable. He had only seen me use black and white. "What brought on this change?"

Something had felt different in me. I was lighter, brighter...and in my mind the yellow became what I needed for the painting to transition with me. "As I was getting all my stuff set up, I looked at the yellow and before I knew it, I'd added it to the white."

"I have to say whatever is changing, I like it." Mr. Stratten touched his chin and tilted his head to better examine the canvas. "There's more...life in it now."

I tried not to beam at the first compliment he had ever given me. "Thank you, sir." His approval had the ability to affect my future as an artist. Continuing to impress him meant I could have a real chance at the New York internship he ran every year.

"Do you think this is the first step to you using more colors?"

"I'm not sure. But...I might be more open to it."

****

"I can't believe you talked me into this," Brandon said as he stared at the sea of yoga mats and bedazzled water bottles.

"Technically, you talked me into accompanying you." I followed him to one of the empty mats in the back corner of the room. "You should go to yoga because it will help heal your ACL, not just because I agreed to go with you."

"It smells like pumpkin spice and floral perfume in here."

The room was located in the Recreation Center of Arden University, across the hall from the sauna and one of the main workout rooms. It had a mirrored wall in the front, where the female instructor talked to a couple girls in hot pink sports bras and leggings. The dim lighting gave off a more spiritual and meditation vibe than normal yoga, and a speaker played mystical piano notes mixed with nature sounds.

Brandon sighed. "There are only two other guys in here." The number of females had to be over twenty five as well.

"Scared for your masculinity?"

Through the reflection of the mirror, recognition lit up some of the girls' expressions when they noticed Brandon. One of them pulled down her green camisole to show more cleavage and walked over to us.

"Brandon Gage?" Her voice was husky and sexy. Displeasure leaked into my at-ease posture.

"Yes."

"I just wanted to say—" She inched closer to him until she laid a manicured hand on his chest. "—the football games just aren't the same without you. You're still hurt?"

He pulled her hand off of him and took a step closer to me. "Yup."

"Anything I can do to help? I've been told I have magic hands—"

He positioned his body behind me as if using me as a shield from Ms. Doesn't-Understand-Physical-Boundaries Brunette. "This is my girlfriend. Her hands are actual healing magic because she's a PT assistant."

Her lips sneered at the mention of 'girlfriend.' "Really?"

"Sure," I said.

"I suppose two sets of hands are better than one though, right?"

Was she proposing a threesome? Those happened in real life?

I turned to see Brandon's reaction, half expecting him to give me a thumbs up and make some asinine comment, but instead he stared at her like she was a burned batch of brownies. No interest and a bit sad for her. "Sorry, but I'm good with one set." He grabbed one of my hands to show to her. "Especially, when they're so perfect. Look at it."

She frowned at my hand and strutted away from us, to the front of the room where the instructor set up to begin.

"You weren't kidding about how girls act around you."

He gave me a 'duh' look. "Why do you think I was so surprised by you acting like you had no interest in me when we met?"

"I wasn't acting." I stood on the yoga mat. "I had no interest in you."

"Had? Interesting use of past tense."

We smiled at each other, but the spell broke when the instructor clapped and called everyone to attention.

"We'll first start with a downward dog."

"Sounds like a sex position," he muttered.

"An uncomfortable one."

He gaped at me for making an inappropriate joke and laughed. It radiated through the room and heads turned to look at us. "Sorry," we whispered in unison.

The rest of the session was more intense than I had imagined a beginner's class to be. My flexibility helped me through out, but Brandon struggled after close to an hour of stretching his leg.

"Want to leave?" I offered. "You shouldn't push yourself too hard."

He nodded and followed me out into the hallway. Pointing to the sauna sign, he raised his eyebrows. "You want me to go in a sauna with you?"

"We said we'd do more fun things together." His eyes lit up with excitement. "This would be fun and different."

I looked through the fogged up circle window of the door. No one was inside. "I've never been in a sauna before."

"Is that a yes?"

Chapter Twelve
Sauna Steam And Broken Dreams

Mandy

"I feel like I'm being baked in an oven."

"You've never had the *Hansel and Gretel* fantasy?"

I leaned back against the wooden wall behind us and took in a deep breath of the steam. "You mean being eaten by a witch? Can't say I have." I swiped a slick hand behind my neck. "I'm sweating."

He chuckled. "That's the point of a sauna."

I crossed my legs in an effort to get comfortable on the wooden bench. "I thought the point was to be relaxing." In the movies, steam filled the saunas like majestic hot tub sitting rooms. This wooden box of a room was more full of heat than it was of any form of water. "Instead, I feel gross."

His dark gaze scanned every inch of me. "If it helps, you don't look gross."

The room must have jumped an additional ten degrees hotter. "I bet I smell gross."

He leaned into me, his damp, bare chest sliding against my arm. "Actually, you smell like oranges and strawberries."

"I sound like a fruit salad."

"Mm," he grunted. "You look as edible as one."

I gestured to my sweaty, messy self. "You think I

look good right now?"

"Yes."

"I'm wearing baggy shorts and a sports bra, with no makeup and my hair in a bun. You're lying."

His eyes narrowed. "I don't lie. You look like an athlete and I find that sexy. Whenever I compliment you, you think I'm lying or joking. I'm not. I will never lie to you. Ask me anything and I'll answer honestly."

Now that interested me. "I can ask you anything?"

"Try it."

"When you first saw me, did you want to sleep with me?"

He snorted. "You should ask something you don't already know the answer to."

I stared at him. His pinkie finger hovered over mine as our hands laid on the bench. "When you started pursuing me and showing up everywhere, did you only want to sleep with me or did you really want more?"

He lifted his hand to cup my cheek. "In the beginning, I just wanted to sleep with you, but you made me curious. The more I saw of you, the more I talked to you… It became more. I don't know when it changed but after a week or two of knowing you, I never wanted to stop."

In my experience, boys were not honest. Not my father, not Eric. This new openness thrilled me. "Why did you really agree to help me with Jake?"

"A mix of reasons." He paused. "I'll tell you two of them. One, because I liked you and wanted to spend time together. Two, because without football, I don't know what to do with myself. I was going a bit stir crazy and I needed a distraction."

"It really bothers you." I touched a strand of his

wet brown hair and pushed it off his slick forehead. "Not being able to play."

His chuckle was low and hoarse. Hurt. Broken. "Imagine breaking both your hands and losing the ability to paint."

I blinked. "I didn't realize—"

"This injury has pressed pause on my life and threatens to hit the power button every day."

The seriousness of his tone stunned me. He'd let on that he missed it, but I did not know his feelings were so intense. "What does that mean?"

He bent over and dug his hands through his hair. "It means, every practice I go to, I have to watch my friends run and play, while I am glued to the sidelines watching it all. It means, the more games I miss, the less likely I am to get scouted for the big leagues, AKA my dream and only dream." He glanced up at me. "You at least have a back up. Even though the medical field isn't your passion, it is still an interest. The only thing that has ever held my interest is football." He touched my hand. "And you."

I squeezed his hand. "It's not like you'll never be able to play again. Your leg gets stronger every day. That means you're healing."

"But I'll still miss the rest of the season?" A flicker of hope shined in his eyes as he wished for 'no' to be my answer.

"You should miss the rest of the season. Even if you heal and your pain lessens, you shouldn't jump back in right away. An incomplete ACL tear may be minor, but what if you get hurt again and it turns into a full tear? Those lead to career ending injuries."

He closed his eyes as he inhaled deeply, letting

steam fill his lungs. "Sometimes I feel like my career is already over."

I grabbed each of his cheeks and forced him to look at me. "Don't say that. You have so much left you can do. You're healing more and more. And if football doesn't work out—even though I'm sure it will—you can spend your time trying to find other interests. I'll help you."

"How?"

"I don't know. We could go out and try new things together. There are free cooking classes every Friday in the student union. Plus, there is a club for every interest ever. What about fencing? The motions aren't the kind that directly affect the ACL like football does."

"You want me prancing around in a white body suit holding a fake sword?"

We laughed at the image. I gave him a quick, light kiss on the cheek to show him I cared. "I want to help you like you've helped me."

"Football is all I know."

I pulled him closer to me, nestling into his chest. "Then you'll learn."

****

The last time I was in Jake's dorm room, I had been practically naked. Being back in the medium sized room had me wondering how different these past few weeks would have been if I had never shown up in that trench coat. I would not have met Brandon. After the sauna, we had gone our separate ways to shower and attend classes, before he picked me up and drove me to his dorm building for the double date.

Jake pulled me from Brandon's arms and gave me the longest hug he had ever given me in my life.

"Hi." I grinned at how excited Jake was to see me. Was I dreaming? He had never been in such good spirits over my presence. Making him jealous had been the key all along to gaining his attention. Why did that not feel as good as it should have?

"You look amazing." His cobalt gaze scanned my body. I wore a pair of leggings and a tank top with a sweater. "How are you doing?"

"Good, how are you?" I asked.

Brandon wrapped his arms back around my waist and led me away from Jake. "Great, now that you're here."

My knees went weak. *Calm down. You're supposed to like Brandon.* Fake like him.

"Here," Jake said. "Come meet my date." He gestured to one of the most beautiful girls I had ever seen. "This is Carly."

She was model thin yet had the curves that every boy drooled over. In comparison to her short, bright blonde hair; mine was a long, unkempt dirty blonde that lacked shine. The outfit she had somehow gotten herself into looked like a scuba suit, it was so tight.

"It's Carleigh. With a 'g-h,'" she corrected and wrapped her manicured fingers around Jake's muscular arms. "Wow, what an interesting sweater." The tone of her voice suggested that my interesting sweater was not interesting in a good way. "Is it cotton?"

I glanced down and rubbed the material between my fingers. "I think so."

She smirked and took a step away from me. "My cousin says if you wear less than fifty percent polyester, you get AIDS."

This girl was the type who gave blondes a bad

name. "Yes, Carly. That's exactly how sexually transmitted diseases are spread."

"It's Carleigh." She frowned, like I was stupid for not remembering the correct pronunciation of her name, 'Car-Lay.' "With a gh."

I looked at Brandon who appeared to be holding back either a cough or a laugh. "Isn't that what I said?"

Jake put an arm around Carly—*Carleigh*. "Mandy, how's your art class going?"

"Great, thanks." I beamed at how he remembered my major. "Soon, we're going to be using live models to come into class."

He nodded and smiled. "That sounds cool."

"Cool." Brandon's smile twitched and a darker emotion filled his cheerful eyes. "When you say models..."

"I mean models," I repeated. "Most of my paintings and drawings are of people."

"Male people?"

"Some, why?"

"I don't like the idea of you being around naked male models, Blondie."

"First off, no one said anything about me using nude models, and secondly, naked female models are fine then?"

"I mean..."

He wrapped both of arms around my waist after I pushed at him. "You are such a guy."

"You're right. From now on *I* should just model for you."

My mind flooded with inappropriate images as my voice cracked. "You would want to model for me?"

"I'd do just about anything to keep you away from

male models."

"If your class needs models, I could volunteer too," Jake suggested.

I grinned at him. "Thanks, that would be a huge help. My teacher has been looking for people but hasn't been able to find anyone yet."

"Great, just text me the details." Jake smiled while Brandon glared. "Anyway, you girls excited to watch the movie?"

Carleigh squealed. Literally. Honest to God, squealed. "I haven't watched a movie in so long. My roommate doesn't even have a TV. She doesn't believe in technology." She lowered her voice to a whisper, like it was a secret, "It's cause she's Irish."

"You mean Amish?" I questioned.

Carleigh flipped her hair. "Whatever."

This was Jake's date? He liked her? I had been in love with him for years and he was busy dating girls like Carleigh? This sucked. My jealousy flared up as she clung to him.

"Should I get HD or SD?" Jake asked when we all sat around the TV and he was about to stream download some kind of horror movie. "HD is three dollars more."

Just as he clicked on SD, Carleigh jumped in with her oh-so-important opinion. "Get HD." She gestured to herself. "Do I look like an *SD* kinda girl to you?" She wore a low cut top and the shortest jean skirt known to human kind.

"You look like an *STD* kinda girl," I murmured without thinking.

Brandon choked. Ms. HD looked at me with horror. Luckily, Jake had not heard my slip up. I had never met one of his girlfriends, so I had never experienced such jealousy before. The words escaped my mouth before I could stop them.

The movie hadn't been playing for ten minutes before Carleigh, cuddled against Jake, began making little gasps or squeals whenever something in the movie scared her. After the twentieth breathy intake, I was ready to make her stop breathing in general.

Brandon wrapped his arms around me and pressed his mouth against my ear. "You're not allowed to kill Jake's date."

"But I want to."

About forty minutes into the movie, the characters started dying off.

"Do it. Kill her," I said. The annoying blonde sorority character reminded me of Carleigh. Finally, I was able to use the movie as an outlet for some of my aggression.

She gaped at me. "You can't cheer for the ghost."

I had been raised on action and horror movies. They were my normal. "The idiot chose to run upstairs instead of running out of the house. I can't wait for her death scene."

Brandon's grip tightened. "You're a little scary, Trench Coat."

"Call me that again, and I'll become a ghost and haunt you," I shot back and returned my attention to the screen. I didn't mean to sound rude, but I became increasingly more agitated with Carleigh. This was the kind of girl Jake and Brandon chose to be with. Why?

She was not even Jake's type. Or at least what his type should be. Why had he begun to notice me only after I started dating Brandon? *Fake dating* Brandon. I confused myself.

A couple minutes later, I cheered again. "You're going to have to run faster than that."

Brandon laughed into my ear. "You sound like my dad during a football game."

The movie ended up being lame and not scary at all. That did not stop Carleigh from jumping onto Jake's lap and forgetting to jump back off. Once the movie was over, Brandon took my hand and walked me back to my dorm room, but not before Jake said goodbye.

"I can't believe it's taken so long for us to spend time together without my crazy sister around. You're so cool." He ruffled my hair and kissed my cheek. "We should hang out more. Wanna play hoops this week?"

Another reason why I wanted Jake: he knew me. He knew I liked my mint ice cream without chocolate chips. He knew my favorite and least favorite songs. He even remembered that I played basketball in high school. "That would be awesome."

After a night of watching him super-glued to Carleigh, I'd about given up on him. But hearing those words gave me hope. Brandon may be more intriguing every day, but he was not the type of guy I'd imagined myself with romantically. Would Brandon be better than Jake at helping me heal from everything Eric put me through? Could I trust him? I had known Jake my entire life, I *knew* him.

Wasn't it better to *know*?

Chapter Thirteen
The War of Love

Brandon

Mandy was addictive: her taste, her voice, and her laugh. It drove me insane that I could touch her, kiss her, and yet it was all for show. Sure, her moans sounded real, and her eyes held real heat when we kissed, but it was not enough. She still wanted Jake. Fucking *Jake*. She had known him her whole life but, damn, she didn't really know him. He was as sick and twisted as me, except for the fact that I liked her. Really fucking *liked* her.

Jake just saw her as a way to compete with me. He had done this before; shown interest in girls after he knew they interested me. It was like a game to him; before, I had not cared because it had been a game to me too, but Mandy was not a game. I had almost ripped his arms off when he devoured her with his eyes, right there in front of me. Did I look like that much of an ass when I gaped at her?

She still liked him. That much was obvious. The whole night whenever Carleigh touched him or made one of her weird noises, Mandy cringed. Still, she did not to let it get to her; she was a strong girl. I liked Mandy. *Really* like her. I liked how she talked during movies. I liked how she always had something witty to say. I liked how warm she was and how she smelled like strawberries. I just liked her.

It made me furious that Jake pulled her along by a string. A part of me wanted to ask him if he knew how much she cared for him. He had been all over Carleigh tonight, but spent most of the movie watching Mandy. Did he like her back? Was he going to make a move? For some reason, happiness did not fill me that our plan was working.

When Jake scanned Mandy's outfit up and down during the movie, I wrapped my arms around her and shot him a dangerous look that he chose to ignore. The thought of him or any other guy touching, even looking at Mandy, for too long sent a wave of jealousy through me. It was silly to feel that way though. Her endgame was Jake; so why did I feel my heart cringe every second she spent not smiling?

When we left my dorm to walk toward hers, she sent me a sad smile. "That Carleigh is something."

"Did you see her? 'Hi, I'm Carleigh with a g-h.' You'd think her last name was 'with a g-h'."

"Last time I checked, Carly was spelled C-a-r-l-y."

"Her parents must have loved vowels."

This time when she laughed, my heart skipped a beat. Jesus, what was wrong with me? Guys did not act this way. She nudged me with her elbow. "Thanks for doing this."

God, she was beautiful. Long pale blonde hair and bright neon blue eyes. I could not get over how amazing she was on every level.

"Because I'm walking you to your dorm? I know you think I'm a horrible human being, but sometimes I can be a gentleman."

She smiled. "I don't think you're horrible..." My

heart imploded. "Anymore," she added cheekily and I wanted to kiss that grin off her pink lips. "And I was going to say thank you for helping me with Jake. It's very nice of you."

I squeezed her hand, ignoring the sparks. "I just don't want you to get your hopes up."

"I won't. Anyway, I think it's working; he said I'm cool and he likes spending time with me."

"I like spending time with you."

"But you don't think I'm cool?"

"I think you're better than cool." I raised my hand and stroked her cheek. "I think you are phenomenal."

She stared at me for a moment before kissing my cheek. "You're pretty amazing, too." She waved and started to walk away. "Goodnight, Brandon."

"I'll see you tomorrow, Trench Coat."

She groaned and rolled her eyes. "I hate that nickname."

"You have plenty to choose from: Trench Coat, Blondie, Strawberry Shortcake, Goddess Healer... Pick one."

"Why can't you just call me Mandy? Like normal people."

"Normal doesn't fit you and me. We, my darling, are so much more than that."

That night I dreamed that Mandy and I were really dating. No Jake. No problems. I dreamed that I got to kiss and hold her whenever I wanted. That she wanted me to always be around her, the way I always wanted her around me.

Waking up from that dream felt like walking on glass and, as my alarm clock beeped, I decided to make that dream come true. I would get Mandy to fall in love with me if it was the last thing I did.

****

The next day, I received a cryptic text from Ashley telling me to go to her and Mandy's room at one o'clock. When I arrived, the door swung open before I even had the time to knock.

"He's here, ladies," she exclaimed to the two other girls in the room.

"Um, where's Mandy?"

Ashley pushed me inside. "She's in class, silly." I gave a small, awkward wave to the other girls who I assumed were Mandy's other good friends, Rachel and Elizabeth. She mentioned them from time to time. "This is the secret 'plan how Brandon Gage wins over Mandy' club. Come in, welcome."

Being surrounded by Mandy's closest friends without her there intimidated me. Then again, it was nice to see I had people on my side. "A club, huh?"

Ashley clapped as if the sound meant it was time for the secret meeting to start. "We know you have done pretty well on your own because of how much she has warmed up to you so far, but we think we can help you win her over."

"She just needs to realize that Jake isn't who she thinks he is, and that you're not another Eric," the girl, who I guessed was Rachel, added. It bothered me that Mandy compared me to the guy who had cheated on her and broken her heart. I understood that we had similar pasts but when I was with Mandy, I could not even see anyone else.

"And how do I show her how much of a jerk Jake is?" I asked and then looked at Ashley. "Sorry, I know he's your brother."

"No offense taken. He once cut off my ponytail while I was sleeping. And, basically, what we were thinking is that you just need to keep showing Mandy that you are the better choice, showing her how trustworthy you can be. She grew up around Jake, her 'love' for him is a lot like idolization. She has built him up to be the perfect boyfriend for her in her mind. You need to be the attainable guy."

"Also," Rachel said, "Jake has always been nice to Mandy but he's never challenged her the way you do. You need to continue to match her step by step. Push her out of her comfort zone. Go out and have fun together."

"But here's the most important thing," Ashley continued and I suddenly regretted not having a notepad and a pen at the ready to take notes. "Sure, Jake has been nice, but he's never tempted her the way you do. Play on how *talented* we all know you are. I think we've both seen how you light a fire in her."

"Seduce her and she's yours," one said.

The other added, with a smile, "Break her heart and we'll all kill you."

****

"Have you been doing your exercises?" Mandy asked during the next therapy session. I came in only two times a week now because my knee had healed faster than expected. "Your leg seems a little stiff today."

"That's not the only thing that's stiff." My goals were to make her laugh and find a way to kiss her before the end of the day.

"I thought we were past this."

"This, what? This is my personality, Trench Coat.

141

Take it or leave it."

She pulled my leg, resulting in me falling back onto the blue medical bed. "I have no other choice but to take it."

"Mm, I love a girl with no other options."

She rolled up my pants leg to examine my knee. "You're so weird."

"I'm weird? You're the art major. You are in the same profession as a guy who cut off his ear."

"Maybe I'll cut off yours instead."

My blood rushed between my legs. Damn, why did her threats turn me on so much?

She led me out of the private room, the one I had come to think of as ours, to the exercise machines. She pointed to the treadmill and I got up on it while she fooled with the speed setting. Since the pain in my knee had decreased over the past week, she needed to test it.

I took this to be the perfect opportunity to take my shirt off and let her see my abs again. Mandy took a step back after starting the machine and focused on the clipboard. In an attempt to get her attention back on me, I tossed my shirt at her and almost tripped when she caught the shirt and pressed it against her face.

I half laughed and half felt blood rush to a body part it should not have. "Did...did you just smell my shirt?"

"W-what? Of course not." She threw my shirt back at me and acted like she was not openly staring at my bare chest with a reasonable amount of heat in her eyes. "Shut up."

"I didn't say anything." I struggled to keep my voice normal and to not start panting, as I jogged on the treadmill and my thoughts turned to inappropriate images of her. Images I should not have been having while running on machinery. "What do I smell like?"

She hid her face from me behind her clipboard. "Have you been doing your at home exercises like I said?" She was adorable when she nervously tried to change the subject.

My knee bent at a weird angle. "I— Ow!"

She stopped the machine and slid down on her knees in front of me. I all but fainted from the lack of blood in my brain. Damn, what a position— *Don't think about it*. Mandy peered at my injury and flexed my knee at a strange angle. Pain flared down my leg.

"Okay, I think you should double your stretches." Her expression filled with worry, but it was hard to concentrate with her on her knees in front of me like that. She guided me back to our personal physical therapy room and had me sit back down on the bed as she typed some data onto the computer. "You should be okay to participate in some light practice soon if you continue to stretch and rest it."

"How soon? Because I have a game—"

"No. I told you, you could be out for the rest of the season."

"Blondie…I need to play, okay? I can't sit on the sidelines another week—"

"I'm serious. If you tried to play and you weren't fully healed, then you could get hurt even worse. We talked about this."

"Without football, I have so much free time, I might resort to studying," I whispered, scandalized. "*Studying*." I reached for her hand. "You said you'd go do things with me to keep me distracted and find other hobbies. That was a week ago. Stick to your word. If you don't come have fun with me and I'm forced to spend my time staring at the dots on the ceiling, you'll be held responsible for my spiral into insanity."

"How is this my fault?"

"I got hurt because I was distracted over why you left the game." The words came out before I could stop them.

She gaped at me. "I...I didn't know."

"I was just joking—" I rushed to correct myself. "—about it being your fault. I don't think that. It was my bad to think of other things on the field, another reason why I didn't do girlfriends."

"Don't do," she corrected me.

"What?"

"Technically, you still don't do girlfriends. We're just fake dating."

A pain arose in my chest, but I ignored it and changed the subject. "When are you going to show me more of your art work?"

"Are you trying to distract me?"

"I am also interested in your talent."

She glided her chair over to her tote bag and pulled out a portfolio looking thing. "Our conversations give me whiplash."

I opened the folder and forgot to breathe.

They were all in black and white except for a small painting of a crying woman looking out a window. Yellow streaks faded over her face like the sun itself tried to wipe away her tears.

"Your work is almost as beautiful as you are."

"Thank you?"

My heart stopped beating when I looked at the next drawing. It was a rough sketch of Jake. It was done well because it only took me a second to recognize him. I handed it back to her. "Eh, this is my least favorite."

"Why?"

"The technique is off; there needs to be deeper shadows around him and on his face." Specifically, shadows all over his face until it was completely covered and unrecognizable.

She stroked her sketch and appeared a little saddened that I did not like it. "What do you know about shading?"

I tried to lighten the mood by speaking in a bad Italian accent and moving my hand in the stereotypical Italian motion. "What can I say? I'm an art critic. My stick figures are—" I kissed my fingers to add dramatic effect "—perfecto."

She giggled, making my favorite sound in the world. One of my favorites. Her moaning topped the list as well. "Anyway, I want you to be stretching and resting your leg more. The sooner you heal, the less I get to see you."

"Rude," I whined. Her fake tough expression was easy to see through. She liked seeing me; I knew it.

A knock sounded on our door before Mrs. Sweet walked in. "It's been an hour and a half, so it's time for Brandon to go."

"All right." I sat up and grabbed my water bottle before I walked out. "See you later, Trench Coat."

"I like Blondie better."

She stuck her tongue out at me and I laughed. God, she was beautiful; I had to see her blush at least once before I left.

I moved as close to her as possible and leaned in so Mrs. Sweet would not hear. "Next time you stick your tongue out at me." I discretely nibbled her earlobe for good measure. "It's mine."

When her cheeks turned red and she started coughing, I grinned and left the room.

Mrs. Sweet followed me out into the hallway. "How has your physical therapy been going?"

"Great, I think I'll be able to play soon."

She frowned at me and shook her head just like Mandy had. "I don't think—"

"I'll make sure to get permission before I try to go back and play. I'll wait for you guys to sign whatever you need to sign to declare me as healed."

"I don't want you jumping back in until we know that you're ready."

"I do have a question for you though."

She lit up with excitement to help me. "Sure."

"You once said that Mandy had treated an ACL before. What did she do to injure herself?"

"Her original injury came from basketball, but she ignored it and continued her cheer leading, which ended her up in a cast and months of physical therapy."

Thoughts of Mandy doing cartwheels in a short skirt and crop top flooded my mind. "Wait, wait, wait. She used to be a cheerleader?"

She smiled and led me to the door. "Yup."

Teasing Mandy about cheer leading was something that would last me for weeks. "Mrs. Sweet, thank you. This is the greatest news ever."

She waved as I opened the door to leave. "I don't know why, but sure. Glad to help."

****

When I got back to my room, Jake was there. We nodded at each other and a bit of an awkward silence followed before he ruined my day by talking. "You and Mandy, huh?"

"Yup."

He looked me over like he was sizing up a threat. "I don't get it."

I sat at my desk. "What do you mean?"

"You two don't really make sense to me. I mean she's so—"

"She's amazing," I growled, my fists clenching at my sides. If he dared to say a bad word about her, then I would make it so that he could never say another word again.

"Oh, I know; good kisser, too. Been there, done that."

"Excuse me?" I had never truly contemplated murder before that moment but damn, I thought about it now. He had been her first kiss, which made me hate him even more.

"I'm just saying, you're Brandon Gage. She seems a little beneath you."

"Say one more fucking thing and I'll—"

"Whoa, man." He put his hands up in surrender. "I don't mean it as an insult. I'm just saying that Mandy isn't your type."

"Maybe my type has changed."

He leaned back and raised his eyebrows in a challenge. "Maybe mine has, too."

"What about Carleigh?"

He laughed. "You know how it is. I'm interested in someone else."

"What are you trying to say?" I already knew his answer; that asshole was going to try to win over Mandy. He was going to ruin my plan.

"I'm saying that whoever loses, no hard feelings, right? All is fair in love and war."

I narrowed my eyes. "You don't believe in love."

"No." He grinned and jumped onto his bed. "But I believe in war."

Chapter Fourteen
Beautiful Bed Sheets

Mandy

Brandon melted me. My reservations, my troubles…and my heart.

I'd gone crazy over the past few days, trying to decide my true feelings for him. Sometimes I wanted to slice and dice him. Sometimes I wanted to be his best friend; the one person he went to when he needed to talk or wanted to laugh. He made me want him just by the way his muscles wrinkled his shirt in certain places. I wanted to kiss him until I couldn't breathe and wrap my legs around his waist, feeling him hard against me. He made me crazy. Jake did not make me crazy.

I'd loved him since I was fifteen after he kissed me on New Year's Eve at the stroke of midnight. He was sweet and funny; every time I went to Ashley's house he made it a point to say hello and ask how I was. Was it crazy to think he might feel the same way about me?

He was the only boy who ever paid attention to me before I lost weight and discovered that makeup could change everything. I daydreamed about Jake. I imagined a life with him. Could I imagine a life with Brandon? Could I imagine a life without either of them?

I woke up to a text message that took me a couple views to realize whom it was from.

—Good morning, beautiful.—

Jake had called me beautiful. He had texted me good morning. Was the world ending? This had never happened before. As I contemplated what to send back, my phone buzzed again with another text from someone else.

—Wakey, wakey, Blondie. We're having breakfast together.—

The word Blondie told me exactly whom it was from, no caller-ID needed. I texted Brandon back.

—What if I'm not hungry? Don't just text me demands.—

I texted Jake.

—Good morning, hope you have a great day!—

My phone buzzed several times. I opened Brandon's messages first.

—Blondie, you're always hungry.—

—Rude.—

I did not have the time to feel embarrassed about my quick responses because he texted me back at the same lightening speed.

—Is it still rude when it's true?—

I rolled my eyes then checked Jake's message.

—Want to go to breakfast this morning?—

—Yes!—

I was so shocked that he wanted to hang out with me, I sent it without stopping to take off the exclamation point. *Damn it, don't sound too desperate.*

My phone buzzed. Brandon texted me.

—Are you dressed yet? As good as you must look in your silky see through pajamas that resemble lingerie, you need to change so we can go to breakfast. I'm starving.—

—My pajamas are sweatpants and a tank top.—

—Mm, bra or no bra?—

My jaw dropped at his message and I looked around my empty room as if to make sure no one saw the crude statement glowing on my phone.

—I seriously hate you.—

I opened the other message from Jake.

—Great, see you soon.—

I went back to Brandon's messages.

—And I hate that my girlfriend makes me wait so long for breakfast because she sleeps in.—

—Fake girlfriend.—

—My hunger is very real. Now hurry and get ready. I'll be outside your door in ten minutes.—

I then realized I had agreed to go to breakfast with both Brandon and Jake. *Kill me now.*

I texted Ashley and told her about my predicament. She had left for breakfast early, so I prayed she would be willing to help me and sit at the same table. She responded and told me to have fun with my two boys. *Gee thanks, Ash.*

I rushed to get ready, but I was half dressed when a knock sounded on my door. Brandon always showed up early. "Honey, I'm home," he said through the door.

"This isn't your home."

"Are you ready yet?" he asked as I struggled to pull up my pair of skinny jeans. I fell into my dresser when I lost my balance, making a loud thud. "You okay in there?"

I ran a brush through my messy hair and put it up in a long ponytail. "Fine, give me another minute." After applying some mascara, I grabbed my key and opened the door. "Good morning."

He must have taken a shower because his hair was still wet, and he smelled fresh and delicious. My mouth watered.

"Your hair is short." He pulled on a strand and tilted his head. "You got a haircut last night?"

"No, my hair just naturally shortened itself."

"Ah, there's my cranky, tired girl." He leaned in and kissed me before I could push him back. Once his lips met mine, I forgot why I would push him back in the first place.

Kissing Brandon ignited something inside me. The muscles below my stomach clenched as heat flooded me. One of his hands tangled itself in my hair when he pulled me against him. His lips slowly released mine as he took a small step back.

"What was that for? Practice?"

He shrugged and grabbed my hand. He did not let go of it until we arrived at the Diner and parted ways in order to hold our trays and get food. "Why did you cut it short?"

"My hair was getting long and...when I saw that Carleigh had short hair—"

He flinched. "You cut your hair for Jake?"

It sounded bad when he said it that way. "Not really. I just felt like a change."

"You shouldn't feel the need to change for anyone but yourself." His expression became serious. "If he's the one, you won't change *for* him, he'll change you. In a good way. I mean... When you meet someone, the way that person makes you feel will change the way you think and— Gosh, I'm bad with words right now."

"I think I'm rubbing off on you."

He stared at me. "Exactly."

The intensity of his eyes had me sweating. I changed the subject. "To warn you, I also invited someone else to eat breakfast with us." My shoulders tensed at the prospect of telling him that the mystery guest was Jake.

We sat down at a booth and he handed me an extra orange juice that he had carried for me. "That's fine. I love Ashley."

"Um, it's not Ashley." I opened a small carton of orange juice and took a quick drink. "It's Jake." I jumped in surprise because he laughed. Not the reaction I had expected.

He continued to chuckle until he saw my frightened face and froze like I had told him the world was about to end. "You're not joking?"

I shook my head and he took a deep breath, appearing to be in pain that his roommate would eat with us.

"Why him?"

"You know why him. He texted me this morning and asked, so I said yes."

"He texted his roommate's girlfriend to have breakfast with him? What a nice guy. Definitely has a strong sense of loyalty. Do you not see anything wrong with that?"

I bit my lip, mulling it over. Brandon was right; it was weird for Jake to act this way, knowing that Brandon and I were dating. "Maybe he's just jealous. That was the plan, right?"

"That was the original plan."

"How is your leg feeling this morning?"

"It still hurts but it's been feeling a lot better. I may even be able to play soon."

"Brandon." I used my warning voice to make him understand how serious the injury could be. "I told you, you can't play. You need to heal. What happens if you go out too soon and hurt it worse enough to be out all of next year, too?"

Jake appeared like a ghost in front of our table. He slid into the side of the booth and sat next to Brandon. "I see the old ball and chain is trying to keep you off the field."

"I am not a ball and chain," I said in defense. "I'm trying to make sure he stays safe."

"Trust me, I'm stronger than I look," Brandon said.

"The stronger they are, the harder they fall," Jake pointed out.

"Exactly." I nodded and tried to get both of their attention, but they would not look away from each other. "The more you overwork yourself, the longer you'll take to heal."

"Yeah, Brandon, no need to *overwork* yourself. I'll be happy to take on Mandy's needs for the time being."

"What?" I asked, confused.

"I think I can service her needs enough for the both of us," Brandon growled. They weren't talking about... Of course not. Jake would never say something like that. He was too mature.

"Anyone want to inform me on what's going on here?" I questioned them and their odd behavior. I did not want to be self-centered and think it was all because of me. Maybe it was a roommate problem.

They both met my gaze for the first time since Jake had sat down. "What?"

"Why are you at each other's throats?"

Brandon scowled. "Jake thinks he can take

whatever he wants without regard to who it belongs to."

"Maybe what I want would rather be with me than him," Jake shot back at him.

"I still don't get it. Is this a roommate quarrel?"

"Sure, it's about my sheets." Brandon stated through clenched teeth, "They don't belong in his bed."

"I think that's fair. If they're your sheets—"

Jake cut me off. "But what if I had them first and gave them to him."

"Bullshit!" Brandon exploded, a fire in his eyes. "You didn't give me anything because they weren't yours to begin with."

"Okay guys, I know you're men, so it's all 'rah, rah, testosterone, rah, rah,' but I think this is getting pretty heated over a simple conversation about bed sheets."

"She's right." Jake nodded at Brandon but he was still on edge. "We shouldn't fight. Whoever gets the sheets, gets the sheets."

"I'm gonna fucking get the sheets," Brandon grumbled under his breath.

"How about we have a normal conversation now?" I offered and strived to think of a topic that wasn't lame like the weather or the red color of the booth we sat in.

"Mandy." Jake saved me from spouting out something random. "I wanted to eat with you this morning in order to invite you to a party tomorrow night."

"We'll be there," Brandon said at the same time that I asked, "What party?"

"It's in the delta pi frat house."

"Why do we always have to go to parties at fraternity houses?" I made a face. "They always smell

155

like beer and cheap cologne."

Brandon reached over the table and ruffled my hair, while he smiled at me. "That's the natural scent of most college boys, Blondie."

"Anyway, I wanted to invite you. Ashley said she might be coming too, so you can hang out with her before I find you."

Brandon pointed to himself with a fierce expression. "Or she could hang out with her boyfriend." I hoped the rest of breakfast would not continue to be full of hostile statements and passive aggressive voice inflections, so I was happy when Jake changed the subject.

"I'm supposed to just meet you in front of your class today for the modeling thing, right?"

"I'll be there, too," Brandon said. They had both agreed to be models for my art class after I told them that my professor struggled with finding people to pose.

"Be at the room I texted you yesterday and I'll introduce you both to the teacher."

"I can't believe we get to be models today," Jake said. "What type of stuff are we supposed to do?"

"I'm not sure yet, but this will definitely be interesting."

****

Mr. Stratten greeted me as soon as I walked into class. Inside the room, easels formed a giant circle around the platform designated for where the models would stand. The dimmed lights made the classroom feel more intimate and helped put the focus on the models.

"Mandy, thanks so much again for finding us two thirds of our models for the day. You're a lifesaver."

"Of course. I just wish I could have found a girl who was interested; sadly we're stuck with all boys."

"There will always be other opportunities." Mr. Stratten waved off my concerns and looked around. "Where are your boys?"

"They should be here soon." I pointed as Brandon walked in. "There's one now."

Mr. Stratten followed the direction of my finger. "Look at that chiseled jawbone; you should draw it in charcoal to get the best dimensions. I'll go finish setting everything up, we will start soon."

Brandon glanced around before finding me and striding over. "I'm here before Jake, huh? Cool."

"You two are so competitive, it's crazy."

My criticism failed to dampen his mood. "Blondie, haven't you ever heard not to insult a model?"

"Oh, look, Jake is here, too," I said after he walked over to us. "Okay, so you guys go stand on that platform and I'll be sitting over here, okay?"

"Okay," they spoke in unison before glaring at each other. They followed my directions and joined Mr. Stratten and the other model.

I sat on the stool in front of my easel and placed my black and white paints and brushes on the small table next to me. The tube of blue paint at the bottom of my bag caught my eye, and I picked it up and put it on the table as well.

"All right, everyone, we're going to start," Mr. Stratten said. "First, let's thank today's volunteer models. This is Joel, Jake, and Brandon." The sound of whispering from the female students increased at Brandon's name. My fingers twitched. "Boys, please strike a pose using one of the chairs we have here or not, it's your choice. Artists, begin once you have chosen a model and found your inspiration."

I held back a laugh as Jake and Brandon both looked at the other model to see what to do. Joel sat down in the chair and crossed his arms. A standard pose that did not interest me enough to want to paint. I waited to see what Jake and Brandon would do.

They both crossed their arms and glanced at each other before they uncrossed them. Brandon flexed his muscles and there was an audible sigh from the crowd. Jake dropped down in a pushup position and held it. Brandon frowned at him and bent down into the classic football set stance. The way he crouched somehow made him appear even more attractive, like a Greek god. The slight wince that played across his face at the pain worried me.

Jake sat up and rolled up part of his shirt, revealing his abs. Every girl in the room made a sound. As great as they were, they were nothing against Brandon's. He seemed to sense this because he threw off his dark blue t-shirt and showed everyone just how fit he was.

"Um, boys…" My teacher said, "Taking off your shirts is not needed. Please just choose one pose and hold it, so our painters can get started."

Jake and Brandon glared at each other and settled into a stance. Jake sat on the floor and Brandon got one of the chairs and sat on it backward, his legs spread as he hugged the chair back. His eyes locked onto mine.

I smiled at him but his gaze never wavered. The power in those eyes trapped me.

After a minute, I dipped my brush in the—not black or white paint—but the blue. My right hand moved the brush against my canvas.

I had my inspiration.

****

When I got back to the dorm after classes and dinner, Ashley, Rachel, and Elizabeth were there. Ashley asked me how the breakfast from Hell and the art class went. I explained to all of them how torn I felt.

Ashley made a noise and sat on the edge of her bed. "At least I'll be there at the party tomorrow to be your wing woman."

Rachel pouted. "We want to go, too."

"You both still need to meet Brandon. Sometimes I feel like he thinks my only friend is Ashley."

Ash flipped her hair. "I mean…"

I threw a pillow at her. "Shut up."

Rachel jumped up and down with excitement on Ashley's bed, while Ashley flailed about. "You can't tell us at all who you're leaning toward choosing?"

"I don't know…the ways they both make me feel are so different from each other. Brandon makes me feel wild and Jake makes me feel…comfortable."

"Boring," Rachel and Ashley whined, and groaned at the same time while Elizabeth laughed at them.

That night I received two texts messages.

—*Goodnight, can't wait to see you tomorrow*—

—*Sleep well, Strawberry shortcake. You're going to need your energy for dealing with me all day tomorrow.*—

I texted back one of them, but I thought about both of them for hours before I was able to fall asleep. I needed to make a decision.

If Brandon did like me, then I could not keep stringing him along. If I really did like him, then I had to give up Jake. Whatever happened, someone would end up hurt. I just needed to talk with both of them and then make a choice.

I'd decide tomorrow.

Chapter Fifteen
Shots, Shots, Shots, Shots.

Brandon

I was so close to killing him.

I would not let Jake steal my girl right out from under me. Tonight, she'd admit that she loved me. The frat party was my last chance to shut him out of the competition. I was Brandon fucking Gage. I never lost. Mandy was mine.

Yet, there was also a chance she would be his. Ashley texted me after my PT session and informed me Mandy planned to choose between Jake and me during the party. It made me crazy. In a few hours, she would either be my real girlfriend or I would lose her to someone who did not really care about her.

No matter what happened, tonight would be the last night that I was her fake boyfriend. I'd be damned if I went down without a fight. I would kiss her every chance I got and convince her that I was the best choice. She was no stranger to the rumors of my womanizing and, though they were true, she had changed me. I wanted to be with her.

"I just want to say no hard feelings about who wins." Jake tried to create a bro-moment before leaving for the party. "I think it's best if the loser leaves the other one alone to be with Mandy in peace. For instance, if there's a sock on the door, come back later."

Did he really think I would let him sleep with her in our room after he talked about her like she was a game?

I scowled at him until he broke my fierce eye contact. "I can't wait to see you lose."

"I'll see you tonight." Jake smiled at me. "I wonder if Mandy still tastes like apples…"

Must. Fight. Instinct to tackle him. "She doesn't."

"Hmm, I guess I'll find out." He shut the door behind him.

****

When I picked her up, I almost had a heart attack. She planned on wearing *that* to the party? It barely covered her. "Mandy." I took a moment to swallow in order to make my throat feel less dry. "What, my darling, are you wearing?"

"Choose your words carefully, Gage." Ashley said from behind her, "That's one of my outfits she borrowed."

I had trouble keeping my eyes off her chest in general, but in this… '*I am a gentleman, I am a gentleman,*' I repeated in my head. But damn, I wasn't a fucking gentleman.

"Can she at least have a hoodie? You know, to cover…everything up?"

Mandy looked offended. "Excuse me?"

"Never mind, you look gorgeous. It's just that you're going to be very distracting." I worried about her looking down and seeing me grow harder against my jeans. Erections normally freaked girls out so I dreaded her reaction.

"Oh." She licked her lips and continued to look down at me. God*damn.* My pants became uncomfortably tight. "Maybe I should bring a jacket."

I nodded. "If you think that'd be best." I may have betrayed my Y-chromosomes by having her slide into a hoodie, but who was I kidding? I still found her attractive when she wore an over-sized sweatshirt. "Ashley, am I driving you, too?"

"Please and thank you, Brandon Gage."

"You know you can just call me Brandon, right?"

She nodded and walked out of the room to wait for us in the hall. "Yup, I do."

Mandy chuckled and pulled me out of the room to start heading out. "Are you excited for the party?" she asked me as we walked with Ashley to my car.

I took her hand in mine and interlocked our fingers. "I'm excited to hang out with you."

"Aw!" Ashley interrupted us and made kissing noises. "You two lovebirds are so cute."

"Shut up," Mandy and I said in unison.

I drove them to the party and tried not to crash while glancing over at Mandy's long, legging encased legs. Once we got there, even the bouncer at the front door had a hard time not staring at her. My arm glued itself to her waist. Ashley, however, left us the first chance she got, disappearing into the crowd.

"Could you get me a drink?" She had to yell for me to hear her over the blaring music.

"Sure, what do you want?"

"Maybe a wine cooler." She sounded nervous and she kept tapping her foot against the floor, so I assumed she wanted some alcohol to help her calm down. I didn't want her to drink because I wanted her decision to be made with a clear head, but I also did not want her to stress all night, so I agreed.

"Okay, I'll see what they have. Make sure to stay here so I can find you."

I rushed through the crowd and into the kitchen, so that I would be back to Mandy as soon as I could. Ashley was also in the kitchen, wine cooler ready.

"How did you know?" I questioned her.

"It's all she drinks. Our girl is weak when it comes to alcohol." My heart warmed when she said 'our girl.' I loved that Ashley liked me better than Jake; having the best friend approval would be an immense help. "Keep an eye on her tonight," Ashley added. "She gets drunk easily and I don't want Jake taking advantage of that. He once convinced her to have vodka in high school and she was about to play strip poker before I stopped her."

"He knows that she has a low drinking tolerance?" That was a piece of information someone like Jake would abuse.

"Whose idea do you think it was to play strip poker?"

"I've got to go find her." I took the cup from her and made my way back to Mandy.

"You like parties, babe?" Some douche bag had gotten close to her while I left to get her drink. Leaving her alone for less than a minute was impossible. "Wanna join the one in my pants?"

"Step away or I will literally break you," I growled at him. His eyes bulged out of his head in fear like a cartoon character. He ran away just as fast as one, too. I handed her the wine cooler. "You should wear a bright neon sign that says 'taken.'"

She raised an eyebrow. "Why don't you pee on me too while you're at it?"

I smiled, the tension in my neck calming. "Didn't know you were into that type of thing."

"You're the one who should wear a sign." She patted my chest. "Girls swarm you."

"I only care about one girl." I took her hand and held it. "Thanks for coming with me tonight. I know you don't like parties."

She drank from her cup. "You're lucky that I'm willing to do something I hate for you."

"I think I'm just lucky in general. I guess you more did this for Jake since he invited us."

She gazed up at me with her big, innocent eyes, but not all innocent because, damn, no innocent girl could kiss the way she did. "What do you normally do at parties?"

"Eh, party-me wasn't that good of a guy." I would hate for her to find out how I acted at parties. I drank with girls, danced with girls, and… Damn, I would hate for her to find out how I was at parties.

"I already knew that," she teased and gulped down more of the wine cooler.

I ruffled her blonde hair until it looked messy. She looked so sexy that way. "My little smart ass."

She kept looking over to the room where the loud music poured out and drinking her cup quickly as if she wanted to free up her hands. She tossed back the last of it and set the empty cup on a table. "Want to dance?"

I nodded and she took my hand, pulling me to the living room where most of the dancing occurred. If 'dancing' was the right word. Bodies grinded against each other and people made out on the couches.

She wrapped her arms around my neck until her body pressed against mine. Her chest pushed against me and I bit back a groan. She was so soft and, damn, she really did smell like strawberries. We swayed from side to side until she frowned. "I don't think we're dancing the right way."

"I think we are the only people *actually* dancing." I laughed but stopped when she rocked her hips against mine. "Damn, this is dancing, too." She smiled at me and got even closer, her body working against mine. "Shit, yeah. This is definitely dancing."

I was tempted to pick her up and wrap those seductive legs around my waist in order to feel every bump and grind to the fullest. Instead, I settled for grabbing her hips and pressing her even harder against me. She breathed into my ear and my heartbeat raced.

"Mandy."

My head fell back in defeat after hearing Jake's voice. Would I ever have this girl all to myself?

She stopped dancing with me and smiled at him. "Hi."

"How are you guys doing?" He asked her, "Do you want me to get you a drink?"

I started to say no. "I don't think that's a good—"

"Sure, I'd love a drink." *Damn it, Mandy.* I was just trying to help her. A little assistance would have been nice.

"Awesome." Jake grinned at her and she looked dazed by it. Whatever; he wasn't *that* good-looking. "Want to come with me? I don't want to leave you here with drunk strangers."

I glared at him but he didn't even look my way. "I'm here."

He grabbed her hand and pulled her out of my arms. "Come on."

I trailed after them, steaming. Ashley was still in the kitchen. I made hand gestures to her that resembled pouring a drink and turning on the sink. It took her a while to realize that I wanted her to water down Mandy's drinks.

If Jake's plan was to get her drunk, then we would make it as hard as possible for him. Ashley followed my instructions as Jake grabbed a beer from the fridge for himself and turned to Mandy.

"What do you want to drink, gorgeous?" he asked.

"Um, anything is fine." She sounded sleepy and a bit too carefree. Was that wine cooler really giving her a buzz already?

"Here." Ashley appeared in front of her and shoved the drink in front of her face. "Your favorite."

Mandy took a sip from it and made a face. "This tastes like one of those fruity water things."

Ashley had added too much water. Jake took it from her and drank a little bit. He met my eyes over the rim of the cup. He understood what she and I had done.

"Here." Jake opened the fridge and pulled out a tall pink bottle of vodka. "I'll get you a *real* drink."

"Pretty," Mandy muttered and stroked a finger down the bubble gum colored bottle.

"I know." Jake grinned at her. "Do you remember last time we did shots together?"

"I don't."

"What?" he asked, incredulous. "But it was so much fun."

She appeared confused, like she was trying to think back to that night but came up blank. "It was?"

"Totally. You know what, it's decided. We have to do shots tonight."

I wanted to kill him.

"No," Ashley shouted before I could. "I don't think that's a good idea. You don't want to get drunk, Mandy."

"She's not going to get drunk, she's just going to have fun," Jake said. I itched to get her away from him. "Don't you want to have fun?"

When she grinned, Jake grabbed three shot glasses and poured. He placed one in front of himself, Mandy, and me, then started the count.

"Okay, ready? One, two, three." We all tipped back our glasses. She swallowed and made a sound at the aftertaste. Jake filled up the glasses again before I even had the time to tell him no. "One, two, three."

She drank hers faster than the first time and I left mine on the table.

"Man, why do you have to ruin the fun? Drink your shot."

I narrowed my eyes at him. "No, thanks." If he thought he'd get me drunk on fruity vodka so I would not be watching over her all night, he was crazy.

"Someone has to drink it. Mandy, he's your boyfriend; you can have the honors."

She nodded. "That makes sense."

She grabbed the shot glass before I could stop her and had it up to her lips before I could say 'no.' I did what I could with the time I was given. I slapped the glass away from her mouth and caught it before it shattered on the floor. Sadly, some of the liquor spilled on her sweatshirt in the process.

"What was that for?" She took off her hoodie and I had forgotten what was underneath. When she revealed her low cut top, her chest almost completely visible,

Jake took in a sharp breath.

"Shit," he whispered, eyes nowhere near her face.

Kill. Him.

"What?" Mandy's speech slurred and she stumbled when she handed the jacket back over to Ashley, who had an expression full of dread.

Jake shot me a huge grin and I was seconds away from punching that smug look off of his face. He had done it. She was drunk.

Chapter Sixteen
Sexy Nurse Or Sexy Doctor

Brandon

I woke up when her weight shifted on the bed as she turned to look at me. She had an extreme case of bed head and her lips were somewhat swollen from kissing me last night. She was gorgeous. She smiled and held her head, so I assumed that she dealt with a major migraine from her hangover.

I grinned at her and petted the top of her head. "Good morning, Blondie."

I would never let her drink that much ever again. Ever. Again. She was a crazy drunk. By the end of the night, I'd been about to drive her home when she said she felt sick. She gave me one option: carry her to the closest bathroom and hold her hair back.

I offered to drive her to her dorm but she didn't want to move, so I let her rest in one of the bedrooms of the house. The fraternity had tried to get me to join before and left an empty room for me to move into any time I wanted. An advantage of everyone being so obsessed with me. She fell asleep on the bed. I took the spot next to her, to relax and take a deep breath.

She winced. "Morning."

"Head hurt?"

She groaned and held it between her palms. "Like a bitch," she responded and motioned toward the bed and me. "We didn't…"

"Trust me, if we did, no matter how drunk you were, you would remember it."

"You're so full of yourself."

Drunk Mandy may have revealed how she felt about what Eric had done to her, but sober Mandy still had her walls up. It made me want to protect and comfort her even more. I would not bring the hurtful subject up for her to think about, so instead I planned to spend the day trying to make her laugh.

I shrugged, which made her smile. She had a beautiful smile. "I know what I'm good at." I nudged her. "Are you happy with your decision?"

She tapped her chin in concentrated thought, as if she really had to think about it. She then frowned like she had regrets. She broke her dramatic expression and grinned at me. "Yes."

"You little…" I tickled her, which made her laugh and gasp for breath. "Think you can make me sweat like that?"

She wiggled her eyebrows at me. "Maybe I want to make you sweat while doing something else." Was she still drunk? Who was this girl using sexual innuendos? "That was a joke," she said.

"You can't joke about such dirty things. Now I'm thinking about—" She interrupted me with a kiss that ended up lasting longer than she probably meant it to. "Now I'm thinking about it even more." She kissed me again and rolled me over until she pressed against me from chest to toe. I only wished that we wore less clothing, so that I'd feel her soft skin and curves to the fullest. "Now this is all I can think about."

She sank down and sucked my bottom lip to show

me that she was not playing around. "Stop talking and kiss me, idiot."

I kissed her nose. "Maybe if you were nicer and didn't call me an idiot."

"Who would have thought that *you* would be the one to interrupt making out in order to talk? I'm disappointed. Aren't you supposed to be a womanizing bad boy?"

"Whoa. You're going to hurt my feelings, babe."

She captured my lips again and I groaned when her tongue seductively met mine. We kissed until we couldn't breathe and then we kissed some more. Being close to her, holding her, tasting her, made me feel complete, as if I had been missing something in my life before I met her. I loved our witty banter. I loved the way she smiled at me. I loved her.

She smiled up at me and wrapped her arms around my neck. "We're dating."

I nodded, tightening my grip around her. "For real this time."

"I wonder what will change."

"The first thing to change is that I will have a girlfriend for the Halloween party next weekend." I kissed her and said with an enthusiastic voice, "We absolutely *must* wear matching costumes."

She did not appear as excited as I was. "Must we?"

"We must. I want everyone to know that we're together and that you're mine."

"And you're mine," she pointed out.

My heart filled with warmth. "Exactly."

"Explain to me again why Arden celebrates Halloween in early December."

"Because everyone celebrates Homecoming in

October." At Arden, Homecoming qualified as a major holiday because it involved one of the biggest football games of the season. Plus, it was the fraternities and athletes who threw the late Halloween parties.

"But why move a holiday?" She did not understand the importance of Homecoming. I guess being a football player made me a bit biased.

I gave her a playful tap on the nose. "To throw a huge party, of course."

"What's up with you? You're so happy this morning."

"What is there to *not* be happy about?"

"World hunger," she commented.

"Damn, woman. Way to bring me down."

"Sorry, my stomach is growling and when you said that, it popped into my head."

I chuckled and helped her up, off the bed. "Breakfast time?"

"Please."

We continued to talk and laugh as we drove to the dining hall closest to her dorm. Apparently, they served a particular kind of pastry on Saturdays that was Mandy's favorite. Once we got our food and sat at a table, I brainstormed possible Halloween costumes. She would make an incredible sexy vampire or sexy teacher.

"So, costumes." I smiled at the idea of her dressing up. "What can we do about matching? What were you last year?"

"I didn't go last year."

I booed her. "Why?"

She acted as if it wasn't a big deal. "I don't really like Halloween that much." How could someone not like Halloween? Candy, costumes, music…it was a close second for best holiday, right behind Christmas.

I grinned at her and handed her a muffin. It was her favorite kind and her tray had been full, so I carried it for her. "Well, now you have me as your boyfriend so it'll be your best one yet."

The edge of her lips twitched like she tried not to smile. "I almost forgot how self-confident you are."

"My mom calls it optimism." I swallowed a bite of pancakes and continued, "I was thinking you would make a fantastic sexy nurse. No, wait, sexy doctor because women can be doctors, too."

She laughed. "I don't think the 'nurse versus doctor' was the sexist part of your statement. Did you know that there is such a thing as a non-sexy woman's Halloween costume?"

"But what's the point behind those?"

She sighed at me the same way that my mother did when she gave up trying to fight me on something.

"You know I'm just kidding. You could be dressed head to toe as a nun or something, and I'd still find you attractive."

"I feel like that was your way of saying you have a thing for nuns," she teased. "What do you want to be?"

"What do you want *me* to be?"

"I've always had a thing for pirates…" She gave me information to store in my brain for forever. Pirates? As in eyeliner, leather, and a sword? Oh, Mandy…Kinky.

"Then I shall be a pirate. What's a matching costume to a pirate? A sexy parrot?" Though Mandy would look cute in a costume made of feathers, I did not want to sneeze every time I got close to her.

"How about a mermaid?" she offered.

I pictured her in a skintight tail and bra. "Damn, you in a bikini top. Yes. I am totally okay with that. Yes. Let's do it."

****

"Congratulations." Michael grinned and slapped my back with pride. I had told them that I was finally dating Mandy for real.

Lucas freaked out. "I'm so happy for you. Big ole Brandon is all grown up and in love." Lucas stretched back on the couch in the study lounge that we were in, working on a project together. "Does she have any friends you could set me up with?"

I chuckled at the idea of Lucas and Ashley together. "Her best friend is pretty interesting."

"Wow, meeting the friends. Soon you'll be meeting the parents." Michael nodded his head at me with an impressed expression. "It seems like just yesterday you didn't even want a girlfriend."

"I'm surprised by it too, but Mandy… She's too good to let go."

Michael released an amused breath. "Pfft, you are so whipped, man."

"I'd rather be whipped than without her."

"That's the exact statement of what a whipped man would say."

"I think it's good that Brandon has a girlfriend. He slept around too much before."

Michael smiled. "Now there's more for me."

Lucas threw his pencil at him. "How do you think things with Jake will be now?" Lucas asked me, concerned. "Kind of hard to escape your roommate."

"I have no clue. Eighty seven percent of the time I

want to kill him."

"And what about the other thirteen percent?"

"He's the brother of Mandy's best friend so I have to act civil."

"He should be better now though, right?" Lucas took a drink of his soda. He called it 'pop' due to his southern ways and Michael always made fun of him for it. "I mean she chose you."

I held up my water bottle as if to say cheers to his words. "Here's to hoping."

****

When I walked into my dorm room, Jake was there. Michael and Lucas hit the nail on the head about it being weird living with him after everything. We used to talk when we were around each other, but now a constant silence deafened the room. I was just happy that it was all over.

Mandy was mine and she always would be because there was no chance of me letting her go. I'd sooner die than see her cry again. Ashley was still Mandy's best friend, so I would have to deal with Jake no matter what. "No hard feelings, right?" I repeated Jake's own words back to him.

He sneered. "You know what they say, 'Losers make promises they often break. Winners make commitments they always keep.'"

"And what does that mean?" I wanted him to clarify his statement because his smirk screamed that he hid something. "Since you are the loser."

"I might have lost," he said, "but I'm not going to keep my promise to stay away."

Fucking. Bastard.

Chapter Seventeen
Artist vs. Cheerleader

Mandy
I can't believe I got that drunk.

I recalled small bits of the party, but my drunken state had wiped a good amount of the memories away. I remembered dancing and laughing, but a lot of that night was a blur. Waking up beside Brandon made it okay. I had expected to feel disappointed over letting go of Jake, but joy filled me when his brown eyes stared into mine that morning.

Ashley continued to pry. "Is he…you know… *Good*?" Convinced that Brandon and I had sex after the party, she refused to believe me when I said her assumption was wrong.

"I wouldn't know," I said for the third time.

"But you slept with him."

"I didn't."

"You did."

I groaned at her annoying persistence. I loved her, but she acted like we were back in high school. "No."

"Yes."

Of course, she would be this difficult. I fell back onto my bed to at least relax while being pestered with questions, or rather the same question again and again. "If it happens, I'll tell you."

"You mean, if it happens again."

I threw a pillow at her face, which she caught with ease. "If it happens," I stressed, but she was selectively deaf to the word 'no.'

She threw the pillow back at me. "If it happens a second time."

"Sometimes you're as annoying as him."

"But you love us anyway?"

I rolled onto my side, away from her. "Whatever."

Did I love Brandon? After knowing him for almost a month and proclaiming my hatred for him during a good amount of that time, did I love him? Of course not, not yet anyway. Impossible. Improbable. Right? He made me smile so much that I felt wrinkles forming on my face. Around him, I laughed until my voice went hoarse. How long did it take for someone to fall in love? Brandon couldn't love me yet. He had never really had girlfriends anyway. What if it was an infatuation? What if once he had me...

Shut up, Mandy.

****

Before Brandon showed up for his PT appointment, I freaked out about my clinic uniform. It was fine to wear when we weren't together but, geez, it was so plain. A white shirt and jeans covering everything. Wearing jewelry or make-up broke Mrs. Sweet's rules on the 'natural healing' theme of the clinic, however her dictates only covered the physical therapy and rehabilitation areas. The staff in other departments, like the nurses and patient care aides, got to wear scrubs or actual uniforms.

Brandon's world consisted of girls constantly on their A game with mascara and eyeliner, cheeks contoured, and whatever the latest craze was in makeup. What if he figured out I wasn't good enough? Butterflies filled my stomach like a beacon, telling me he arrived.

"Are you ready to fix me for good, Healing Goddess? I have this new super hot girlfriend who keeps trying to jump my bones and I need my leg to be fully functional for everything I have planned."

I fought back a smile as I led him to our private room and pointed for him to sit next to me on the bed. His grin triggered inappropriate thoughts for a professional setting.

He sat down almost on top of me. "You naughty girl, are you touching my butt?"

"You literally just sat on my hand."

He leaned in so close; I struggled to maintain eye contact. "I missed you."

I backed away from him a bit. "You just saw me hours ago."

He moved in until his breath touched my lips. "Mandy."

I tried to make any noise that wasn't a moan or a squeal at how close he was. "Mm?"

He pressed his forehead against mine and gave me one of his flirtatious smiles. Then he kissed me. Heat hit my body like a train. My breath hitched as he nipped my bottom lip, teasing me. His lips were cool to the touch like kissing a peppermint. His cinnamon scent warmed me and eventually I lost control of my breathing from the way his lips turned scorching against mine.

One of his hands latched onto my waist and played with the pant's waistband. I forgot where we were. The room faded around us. We were alone together until my loud moan broke the silence and the spell. I pushed him back. "We can't do this here."

His eyes had darkened and his heavy breathing matched mine. "Where can we do it?"

"You're never going to be healed if you keep distracting me."

"Are you kidding?" He leaned in and kissed me. "I'm feeling better already."

I pushed him away again. "Have you been doing your exercises at home?" I tried to remain professional but damn, he looked so good. Why did he always look so good?

He huffed at my obvious professionalism and leaned back on the bed. "There's something I'd rather be doing at home... Or should I say someone." He flinched. "Wow, that was bad."

I touched his cheek. "You need to do them; they help stretch your muscles. It'll take longer for you to heal if you don't do them."

"I know, babe. I've been doing them. Trust me, I'm doing everything I can to heal so I can play soon. The pain has already lessened." He bent his leg and showed me the range of motioned. "Watch."

A strange scene flashed through my brain.

"Watch me."

Jake threw the small white ball and it landed into the first beer cup in the triangle. A couple people at the party cheered.

"Wow." I grinned at him and jumped up and down in excitement. Dizziness swarmed me from the alcohol so I stopped jumping. "You did it!"

Brandon threw a ball on the other side of the table and it landed in one of Jake's cups. "Me too."

"Mandy is on my team." Jake handed me one of the balls. *"Go ahead and try it."*

I did. The ball did not land anywhere near the cups. In fact, it bounced right off the table. I frowned at my evident lack of skills. "Damn." It was possible that seeing double the cups affected my aim.

Brandon chuckled. "Looks like I'll be winning this game."

I crossed my arms and his gaze dropped down to my cleavage before shooting back up. "You're going down."

"Really?" Brandon raised his eyebrows at me and appeared amused. "Trash talking after missing the cups entirely?"

"It was my first try. I'll do better."

"Sure, you will," he teased me.

My skin warmed at the challenge.

I rubbed my forehead, shaking off the flashback. "Did we play beer pong at the party?"

Brandon nodded.

"Did I win?"

He laughed. "You won me."

"Consolation prize, huh?"

He smiled and pushed a piece of my hair behind my ear. "Have you remembered anything else?"

"It comes back in pieces. All I know is, I'm never going to drink that much again."

Without warning, another flashback hit.

"I'm never letting you drink this much again," Brandon told me as he supported me while the room spun.

"I don't feel well."

He picked me up. "I'll take you home."

181

The spinning stopped when I clung to him and wrapped my arms around his neck. "I don't want to get in a car." Even the idea of motion sickness gave me motion sickness.

He stared down at me with concern. "Then what do you want?"

Jake ruined the moment by appearing and pushing a cup in my face. "Mandy, I got you another drink."

I cringed away from it. The vinegar smell coming from the cup caused another moment of nausea to consume me.

Brandon did not let me go from his hold and instead took a step back to create distance from Jake. "Leave us alone. I won't ask again."

Jake scowled at him. "It's a party. I'm just making sure she has fun."

Brandon's low and threatening voice gave me chills. "Does she look like she's having fun?" Brandon growled at him, "You got her drunk, congratulations. You're not going to take advantage of it. Now leave before I punch you in the face."

I needed a bathroom. Stat.

"Please, like you don't like her better this way."

Brandon whispered, "Hold onto me," and took one arm out from under me, tipping me a bit. A loud thwack *sounded and someone groaned...*

I gaped at Brandon. "You punched Jake!"

He made a guilty face. "I was wondering when you would remember that."

"I can't believe you did that."

"I can't believe it took me this long to do it," he said, mischief in his eyes. "Do you remember what happened after that?"

"I remember you rushing me off to a bathroom."

"Think hard." The laughter in his eyes scared me. "Right after the punch, right before me running you to a toilet."

I closed my eyes before mortification gave me a heart attack. "Please tell me I did not throw up on Jake."

"I honestly think it made me love you more. He went down from the punch and then you just let him have it."

I hid my face in my hands. "Gross."

"I know you're embarrassed, but you shouldn't be. He deserved the effects of your drunkenness."

After a minute of reminiscing and regretting, I lifted my head up again. "I do remember you holding my hair back that night. Thank you for that."

"Taking care of you is my job."

"Anything else mortifying happen?"

And the hits just kept on coming . . .

During the middle of the night, I woke up and opened the front button of Brandon's jeans while we laid beside each other in bed. "Mandy?" His eyes opened and his voice cracked as my hands wrestled with his jeans. "What are you doing there, honey?"

"I'm—" I struggled with the button. "—gonna have sex…" I opened it and traveled to his zipper. "With you." My slurred speech decreased the effectiveness of my seduction.

He put his hand over mine. "Stop." I squeezed him through his jeans, resulting in a moan escaping his lips. "You-you're still drunk."

"Yeah." I giggled and tried to kiss him, but instead banged my head against his. "Ow," I whined and

cupped my forehead. He used my distraction to roll my body on the bed until I was beneath him and he could restrain my arms over my head. "Oh." I wiggled my eyebrows. "I get it. Mr. Gray will see me now."

"What? Not Gray, honey, Gage."

"You don't get it." I pouted, puckering my lips, then relaxed back onto the bed. "Are we doing this or what?"

"Doing what?"

"It. The deed. The big S. Sexsexsexsex," I chanted, and he put a hand over my mouth to silence me. I licked his palm, and he pulled it away. "I want you."

"You are also still drunk, so that's not happening tonight."

My voice became serious as I wrapped my legs around his waist. "I may not be very good at it since Eric started sleeping with somebody else, but I swear I can get better." Tears prickled my eyes. "I'll be good for you, just...let me try before you leave."

A tear fell down my cheek and he wiped it away with his thumb as he cradled my face. "I could never leave you. That guy was a jerk." The edge of my lips twitched up and he continued, "A stupid jerk. We don't need to have sex. You don't need to feel like that's all you have to offer me. You are better than good enough. I don't care about that anymore, all I need from you is a smile. You are all I need. You're fucking everything."

I blinked and reached for him. "Thank you."

For a second, he appeared flustered by my show of emotion, but when he leaned back and stretched out his leg, his backpack toppled over and a card fell out of the front pocket.

I picked it up. Bright colors spelled out the words

Get Well Soon. "Aw."

Brandon's hand shot out and snatched it from me, but not before I read the short message inside. "Get well soon or else?" My eyebrows furrowed. "Who would write that?"

"My dad."

"Was it a joke?"

He let out a noise. "Not a funny man, my father."

No wonder he kept asking when his ACL would heal and be approved to play again. It wasn't just missing his teammates. He had pressure coming from home as well.

He must have sensed the change in the atmosphere because he lightened the conversation the way he always did. "Why didn't you ever tell me you were a cheerleader?"

Now that subject distracted me. "Who told?"

"Can't say. I signed a confidentiality agreement."

Good lie, but it didn't work. "Oh really?"

"Really. Tell me, Blondie, can you do a back flip? Do you still have the uniform? Do you remember any of your cheers?"

I still wanted to ask him about his father but I did not want to pry. "How about we do this... For every exercise you complete, I'll answer a question."

"Done, what's first?"

"Twenty squats."

He stood and did as I instructed. "How short was the skirt?" Brandon pestered me with questions during the reps. "How high did you raise your leg?"

"Me being a cheerleader in high school really turns you on, huh?"

"You have no idea. I've always had a thing for

cheerleaders."

"Oh, I know." My tone conveyed the jealousy that I tried not to reveal. "I remember Natalia."

"I wish you didn't. She's crazy and not worth your time." Brandon finished the squats before walking over to kiss me on the nose. "I don't remember anyone before you."

"How many times have you used that line?"

I handed him two twenty-pound weights, and he sat down and lifted them as I examined his knee. He needed to continue his usual routine of lifting weights to counteract the lack of over-all toning due to the forced inactivity while his leg healed. I tried not to stare at his muscular biceps as he went through the arm curls.

"Thrice... That's three times, right?"

I laughed at him. "Correct."

"But it's never been true until I met you."

"Uh huh, and how many times have you used that?"

His grin reminded me of a little boy hiding a cookie jar. "Twice, but the only person I can ever imagine wanting in the future is you." His eyes appeared sensitive and sincere, as he lowered the weights. My heart skipped a beat. "And that was the first time I have ever said that."

Feelings overwhelmed me. "Good, now um...choose a question for me to answer since you finished your exercises."

"But I have so many." He pouted and whined, "How can I choose just one?"

"I have faith that you'll choose the worse one that pops into your mind."

Brandon ignored my comment. "I've got it. Can

you still do a split and or put your foot behind your head? This is valuable information because it can be used later on." He winked and added, "In bed."

"I got it, and to answer your question, yes."

"To which one?"

"I guess you'll just have to find out," I said in a low voice and laughed when he jumped on the bed.

"God, I lo—" He cut off and his eyes widened for a moment before he recovered from whatever thought he had. "I love that you were a cheerleader."

"I'm also an artist."

He kissed my nose. The temptation to pull his face down and give him a real kiss ate at me. "But, sweetie, that's less sexy."

"I'll have you know, paint and an uncertain income in the future is very sexy."

Chapter Eighteen
Sweet, Spicy, Sour, Breaded Bribery

Mandy
"Ms. Cross?"

"Yes," I said into the phone speaker after hitting answer to an "unknown number" call. Answering calls from strange numbers was a habit of mine. It came from hoping as a kid that someday on the other end would be my father's voice.

"I have a business proposition for you."

Telemarketer. "I'm sorry, but I'm busy—"

"Trust me when I say you don't want to miss this."

The low voice sounded familiar and I struggled to place it. I checked the screen again. "Do I know you?"

"No, but I would like to pay the rest of your tuition and settle the debt on your student loans—"

I dropped the phone on the carpet of my dorm room, then hurried to pick it back up to hear him out. "Excuse me?"

"I know you've been having trouble covering the costs. I'd like to help you."

I let out a silent scream, my mouth opening wide. "Is this a scam? I'm a very delicate person, please don't lie to me about money."

"It is not a scam. I'm not lying."

Was this a new type of charity? Giving money to struggling college students? "Who are you? Why would you do this? Not that I'm not grateful, I am, but, it doesn't seem realistic—"

"My name is Walker Gage."

My breathing stopped. Was Brandon behind this? "Are you—"

"I'm Brandon Gage's father. I believe you are the clinic assistant overlooking his physical therapy."

Where was he going with this? "I-I am." *Also his girlfriend.* But at the time I didn't think that was important information to share.

"I'd like to pay for your education if you agree to clear him to play."

I almost dropped the phone again. "What?"

"You're a smart girl." His voice sounded hard and unfriendly. This man raised Brandon? Happy go lucky Brandon? "I think you understand what I'm asking."

"You're bribing me?"

"I'm offering you help. The daughter of a single mother, drowning in debt—"

"I'm not—"

He cut me off. "I know your loans have become tricky lately. Rising interest rates and all. Seems to me you could use my help."

"Sir, I can't just clear Brandon. I'm only the assistant."

"I know." He huffed with impatience. "First, you sign off, then the physical therapist takes a look at him and signs off. Then he is cleared and good to go."

"Me signing him off wouldn't help. You'd need the therapist—"

"Don't worry about her, she's taken care of." It sounded like a line from a mafia movie. "She'll sign as well."

"Sir, Mr. Gage, Brandon is already doing better. He just needs more time. Rushing back into playing could extend the tear in the ACL, which could end his career in football. It's not worth it—"

"I'll decide what it's worth."

"You're risking causing him a serious injury. He may be cleared in several weeks anyway. Even then, he shouldn't jump back on the field. Can't you wait?"

"Are you saying no to my deal, Ms. Cross?"

I stayed silent.

"Think carefully. It's a lot of money you'd be refusing."

He had shocked me silent.

"I'm sure you know the right decision—"

I cracked. "How dare you bribe me to put your son in harm's way?"

He released an angry and disappointed noise. "Fine. You think you're protecting him but you're not. Understand one thing, football is all he is good at. It's all he knows. Without it, he is wasting his life."

"A few more games, maybe the rest of the season, that's all he will miss to stay safe. That's not wasting life, it's valuing it."

"Good luck with your loans, Ms. Cross. Call me back if you change your mind."

Before he disconnected, I said, "Your son deserves better than you."

I then texted Brandon.

—*You know how you said you needed a distraction/replacement for football? Are you free tonight?*—

—*I'm free every night when it comes to you.*—

****

190

"Damn it!" Brandon yelped and stuck his thumb in his mouth.

"How could you have possibly burned yourself?"

The free cooking class I had taken him to was pretty advanced. The director wore a fancy chef hat with lapel buttons from a variety of four-star restaurants he worked at once upon a time. I guess teaching college students did not interest five-star restaurant chefs. He spoke in a fake French accent while informing us on how to cook sweet and sour chicken.

The small room contained ten small kitchenettes which included a small sink, stove, and oven. Most of the people there were couples out for a date night. We fit right in except that Brandon had somehow managed to burn himself three times in a row while stirring the sweet and sour sauce.

He took his burned thumb out of his mouth. Such a baby yet such a babe. "Seeing you in an apron is very distracting. I stop looking at what my hands are doing and then something happens."

I gestured down to where the apron tied tight around my waist. "This is distracting you enough to burn yourself?"

He sighed like his ridiculous attraction to me was uncontrollable and inevitable. "You're like a siren, but instead of luring me to my drowning death, I keep frying my skin for you."

I looked at his hand. "Maybe I should take over the sauce, and you can keep checking the oven to see when the chicken is done."

He poked at me with a playful smile. "You just want to watch me bend over."

"You have a problem." I laughed and then quieted

191

when I remembered his father's call earlier.

He tilted his head. "What's wrong?"

To avoid eye contact, I leaned over to check the chicken. "Nothing." A cooking class was not the ideal place to tell Brandon about his father's bribe.

He wrapped his arms around me and pulled me close. His gaze on me had the same power as bright interrogation lights, causing me to sweat and weaken. "I don't lie to you, you don't lie to me. Deal?"

I sighed. "It's about your dad."

His smile dropped off the face of the earth. "I told you I didn't want to talk about that stupid card he sent."

I leaned my forehead against his. "It's not about that. He called me today."

He pulled back. "What? Why? How?"

"Three very important questions. He offered me money to clear you early so you could play in the next game."

His eyes clouded as he absorbed my words. "How much money?"

I gave his shoulder a light swat. "It doesn't matter. You need to go back the right way, when you're fully healed."

"So he didn't bother you?"

"His morals did, but no, not other than that."

A loud beeping noise came from behind us. "The chicken!"

I opened the oven and used a mitt to take it out. Half of it was burned.

"I guess neither of us has a future in culinary arts."

I sighed. "I'll stick to normal art-art."

Brandon picked up a spoon. "We can cover up the blackened part with sauce. No one will ever know."

I laughed. "We'll know when we eat it."

After dividing the meal onto plates, we sat down and ate at a table.

"Did my father say anything else?"

"Nothing worth repeating."

Brandon nodded and swallowed a bite of chicken. "He trash talked me."

I reached over and took his hand in mine. "Don't worry about him."

He stroked his thumb over my palm. "What should I worry about?"

"How bad of a cook you are. This sweet and sour chicken tastes spicy, which makes no sense at all. I expect better from a boyfriend," I teased him and a smile appeared on his face. "How are you going to wait on me hand and foot in the future when you can't even make chicken?"

"You're right. I need to apply myself more."

I leaned over and kissed him. His hand cupped my cheek and kept me from pulling back. What started as a simple peck ended as a heated embrace.

He whispered against my lips, "I bet you'll taste more delicious than anything I could ever make us."

"Cannibalism is frowned upon, Brandon Gage."

He laughed and yanked me in for another hot kiss. I flicked my tongue against his. He groaned while his fingers tangled in my hair.

A minute passed before he pulled back. "Blondie, you've got to stop smiling while I kiss you. You keep biting me."

"I'm hungry. Sue me."

****

During the next art class, the most amazing thing

happened.

"You are improving." Mr. Stratten motioned to my purple painting and grinned. "Have you thought about applying to the New York internship program I run?"

I bit back a scream of *yes*.

He smiled. "Ask me for a recommendation once you fill out the paper work."

I flew on air while walking back to my dorm. It took me a minute to notice Jake sitting under a tree and reading. The adrenaline pumping through me led me to run over, and apologize for Brandon's punch and my sickness.

"Hi, Jake."

The *Introduction to Sketching* book he held surprised me. "You never told me you liked to draw."

The way the sunlight hit his dark hair made him look like some kind of prince, but seeing him did not fill me with the same nerves I had when I saw Brandon. This discovery shocked me. It made me even more comfortable and happy with my decision.

"There's a lot you don't know about me."

I raised my eyebrows at his statement. I knew almost everything about him. After all, I had been in, what I thought was, love with him for years. "Like what?"

"Like...I like you."

My jaw dropped and I took a step back. "Jake."

"I'm sorry, but I can't lie about how I feel."

How could he say this now? "I'm with Brandon."

"But like I said, I really like you."

"I really liked you too, but I love him." The words fell out of my mouth before I could stop them. Love. I loved Brandon?

"You love Brandon?"

"I-I—"

Ashley's voice broke through the haze of my mind. "What are you guys doing over here?" She took hesitant steps toward us.

"I was just about to ask Mandy if she could help tutor me in art."

Ashley's face scrunched up and her eyes narrowed on him. "But you don't like art."

"I do," Jake said to her in a sharp tone. He got up and grabbed his books. "I'll see you around."

I waved, but he speed walked away. "Bye."

"What was that about?" Ashley inquired.

"I have no idea."

"You're hanging out with Brandon tonight, right? Do you think you two are going to…?" She whistled, clucked her tongue, and winked as if one signal was not enough. I didn't know what we would do other than hang out in his room. I did know what *I* wanted to do. "I can help you pick out sexy lingerie, if you want."

I contemplated the idea but shook my head. "Shut up, Ash."

Chapter Nineteen
Sexy Game Night

Brandon

My eyes strayed from my computer screen to the clock for the thirty-fourth time within a half hour. Soon, Mandy would be here. In my room. For a date. My left leg bounced up and down under my desk like a yo-yo. What the hell? I never got nervous, especially when it came to girls. But something about her made my stomach twist in knots and every molecule of my body vibrate like it was on a personal, eternal sugar high.

To calm myself, I took a deep breath, but my body still ran in overdrive. It was always like that now. Around her, I was on fire. Away from her, I fought a fire inside myself. She was the only one I wanted to see, the only one I wanted to talk to. She had become…everything.

My phone buzzed once and my entire being jumped in anticipation. I opened the text from Mandy and smiled.

—Here.—

A knock on my door accompanied the message and I sprinted to see her.

I grinned so hard that it hurt. "Blondie." A second later, I lifted her into my arms and carried her into my room. Her legs wrapped around my waist like it was a reflex of pure instinct. "I missed you." My lips met hers and every muscle in my body contracted with excitement when her tongue interlocked with mine.

A kiss had never been so hot and full of…emotion. Kissing girls didn't feel like this, only kissing Mandy did. She turned my world upside down. I whined when she tore her mouth from mine in order to catch her breath and giggle. Only she would laugh at me after such a hot kiss.

"You saw me like less than five hours ago."

"Too long."

I returned to kissing her and my body shook with arousal when a low moan escaped her. Her lip sucked mine, causing me to go cross-eyed for a moment. My right hand brushed the side of her breast and I swallowed a groan. I was torn between wanting to seduce her and saying something to make her laugh. I loved her laugh. "You know, I purposely turned the heat on high so that you could feel free to go shirtless tonight."

She released a short laugh that made my smile even wider. "I knew it felt warm in here."

"Just trying to make you more comfortable."

"If by comfortable you mean sweat, then job well done."

"I can think of a few other ways to make you sweat and I must say I'm mentally approving all of them for tonight."

Images of her naked body underneath of mine flooded my head and I bit my tongue to suppress a groan. We were dating for real. No more Jake, no more hesitation… just Mandy. Damn, that made me smile.

"Do you ever think about anything other than sex and football?"

I laughed at myself because hell yes, I did. I thought about *her* all the damn time. Since seeing her first take off that trench coat, she was all I thought about. All I ever wanted to do was see her, talk to her, make her laugh…and fucking kiss the hell out of her.

"Sometimes I think about food." I stuck my tongue out at her. My mind filled with thoughts of where I really wanted my tongue to be. "But then I just start thinking about licking some off your body and then it's back to sex."

"You are such a guy."

I could not resist kissing her cute nose. "We've established that fact. I'm glad you are aware of my body's anatomy." I pushed my hips against hers to reinforce what she already knew. "Because I can assure you that I am very aware of yours."

My gaze betrayed me as it scanned her body from head to toe, stopping when further time needed to be taken to appreciate specific body parts. Her cheeks grew pink and I was desperate to see where her blush continued.

"How are you so comfortable all the time talking about…it."

"Aw, is Ms. Trench Coat shy? I'm comfortable because I have it on good authority that I'm god-like at it and I have had a *lot* of practice with many, so— wrong thing to say. I am saying the wrong thing. Wow, you are so beautiful. Insert distraction here. My bedspread is blue like your eyes. Oh look—" I grabbed the remote and hit the play button so it would skip the commercials. "—I'm turning on the TV, so we can start the movie now before I say anything else wrong and awkward."

She stared at me, her fire blue eyes narrowing on me with suspicion. "What's up with you tonight?"

I swallowed. "I have no idea what you mean."

"You just seem…" Her eyes widened. "Oh my God, are you nervous?"

"Me? No way."

The excited, flirty sparkle in her eyes blinded me. "You are, aren't you?"

"Incorrect."

"Oh my God." She laughed again. "Brandon Gage is nervous."

I frowned at her. "I am not nervous. If anyone should be nervous, it should be you because I'm going to blow your mind." I tried to rescue my ego from her but she always found new ways to knock me down, which I kind of loved.

"Sound like empty words to me."

"Empty words, huh?" My heartbeat accelerated at the idea of showing her everything I knew. I knew how to make her toes curl with excitement, how to make her eyes roll into the back of her head from pleasure. "I promise you, Blondie, when you feel every muscle in your body spasm and ache with erotic bliss, you will never second guess my words."

Her breath caught and her face turned cherry red as my statement registered in her brain. My erection throbbed at the thought of proving to her how much I knew. God, I could not wait to feel her nails dig into my back. I couldn't wait to watch her fall apart in my arms while she screamed my name as passion overtook her. I wanted to show Mandy how much I loved her, and maybe that was why it felt different; I loved her.

My face was inches away from hers when she

whispered, "Are we going to watch the movie or…"

"Okay, Ms. Professional Mood Killer. I suppose we can watch the movie."

Her jaw dropped and she feigned the expression of hurt. "I don't kill moods."

"Your mouth always finds a way to say something that ruins the moment." I wasn't mad about it. I loved her mouth. I loved the way it didn't wait for her brain. I loved the way it felt against mine.

"I'll have you know, my mouth does nothing of the sort."

"Babe, we've been over this. You have foot-in-mouth disease."

"Babbling doesn't make me a mood killer."

"You're right. Next time I kiss you, and you tell me your lips are chapped and you just ate a donut, I'll remember that." She huffed like an adorable little wolf and I smiled. "It's okay, Blondie. I love your sexy, loose mouth."

"You make my mouth sound slutty."

"Mmm, I might prefer it that way."

She playfully slapped my shoulder and even at such brief non-romantic contact my body lit on fire for her. "Shut up."

"I have a better idea than watching a movie."

She bit her lip and I wanted to lick it better for her. "Should I be scared?"

I wiggled my eyebrows up and down, and my stomach twisted with new found excitement. "Not unless you don't like to play games."

"What kind of games?"

Her suspicion made my suggestion more fun. "Let's have sexy game night."

She laughed like it was not one of the hottest experiences she would have. Oh, would she learn. "And what makes game night sexy?"

"We start off with strip poker and then once you want to stop, if you ever do that is, we'll play sexual favor monopoly."

"Sexual favor monopoly?" Mandy questioned every one of my statements, but I had no problem giving her detailed explanations if she would go along with it.

"Instead of using just fake money, you can also bribe your opponent with sexual favors. Like if I buy Park place or I have a get out of jail card and you want it, you could offer a kiss on the lips, the neck…more *intimate* places." I grinned at her. "I'm always up for negotiations."

She blushed. "And what if I have something *you* need?" Her squeaky, breathless voice gave away her excitement to play. "What makes you think I'd want any of your sexual favors?"

"Hmm, well maybe the fact that when I kiss you, you moan like you can feel it everywhere on your body and when I pull you against me, you start rocking your hips like it's an instinct to be as close as possible to each other. Let's be honest, Blondie…" I leaned in and whispered on her lips, "We both know you want to play with me as much as I want to play with you."

Her eyes filled with heat. "And playing with yourself isn't an option?"

I went to my desk drawer to retrieve a deck of cards to start the strip poker. "I can tell you from experience, it's not nearly as fun."

Her eyebrow arched. "Are we still talking games?"

"Naughty girl. What else were you thinking?"

I dealt out the cards and placed the rest of the pack between us on the bed, where we sat opposite each other.

I wanted to see every aspect of her in front of me, so I could crack through her poker face, and find her telling ticks and tricks. Maybe the twitching of an eyebrow or the shaking of a hand would give her away. *She* would be the one losing the majority of the clothing tonight. That I would work extremely hard on.

Hard on.

Oh, the irony.

I was already painfully turned on while she sat there fully dressed. I swear she held some kind of mystical power over me.

"Trench Coat, do you know how to play?" I asked while watching her over my hand of cards.

"Of course." Her focused face revealed nothing but annoyance at my interruption of her concentration. "My mom taught me."

"Your mother taught you how to play strip poker? Because—"

"No, you idiot. Normal poker. I assume, however, that the rules are pretty self-explanatory. Lose a round, you lose an article of clothing."

"You almost quoted the Webster's Dictionary definition exactly," I joked.

She rolled her eyes at me and returned to focusing on her cards.

The first round ended with her biting her lip and losing. Her socks came off first even after I whined that socks were the cliché of the first piece of clothing to go. When she lost again, I convinced her that her shirt should be the next item. She took it off and a groan erupted from the back of my throat. Even though she wore a black tank top underneath, it still gave me a great view of her cleavage, a very distracting view of her cleavage. I lost the third round due to the magnificent diversion. She then got a great front row seat to my shirtlessness.

I held back a laugh as she ogled my bare, muscular chest. "You've got some wandering eyes there, Blondie."

"I didn't say anything when you were staring down my shirt."

"The word 'were' seems to falsely suggest that I stopped at some point. This is strip poker, it would be rude not to look."

"Mhm," she murmured through lips trying not to smile. Due to my naked chest distracting her, I won another round. She was left in a pair of shorts and a bra. "Maybe we should stop here…" Her voice sounded a bit nervous like she took discomfort in being vulnerable in front of me. I then lost on purpose and took off my jeans, so she would not be the most naked one. I hated myself that I did not change into less embarrassing boxers.

"Time for Monopoly?" I suggested, trying to bring her eyes back to mine. My arousal was evident from her view, her gaze glued to my boxers. I twitched when she licked her lips.

Her breathy whisper filled my ears and echoed there as I got out the board game. "Please."

"Okay, here we go. Also, every time you pass go, you have to kiss your opponent," I added as I set up the board in front of us on my bed.

"Why do I feel like you just made up that rule?"

"If you knew me at all, you would know I'd never say anything to try to get you to kiss or touch me in any way."

"You literally say nothing but that." She grabbed the shoe character and the dice from the box. "Who goes first?"

I nodded to her. "Ladies first."

Mandy handed me the dice.

For a second, I sat stunned until an unexpected chuckle came from my mouth. "You are so persnickety." I took the dice from her. "I'm choosing the race car so you don't keep second guessing my masculinity."

"Because men with sports cars don't seem to be overcompensating for something."

I rolled the dice and moved seven squares. "A chance card. This will be fun. I think we should make up each other's chances and community service."

"Do you want to move back five spaces and forfeit a hundred dollars?"

"No."

"Then take the chances the game gives you."

I gave a loud sigh and pouted. "And here I thought now that we're dating you would be nicer to me."

She shrugged. "I can't let us get stale."

I leaned in and kissed her cheek before she managed to dodge it. "Blondie, you could never be stale."

We played the normal way until each of us wanted something the other had.

"Please, give me Vermont. I just need one more orange property and I can buy hotels. Please. Please,

please, please," Mandy begged me, and I sat back and enjoyed the show. "*Pleasepleasepleaseplease.*"

"Didn't I tell you that this is sexual favor Monopoly? You're going to have to do better than offer a hundred dollars more than what it's worth."

She gasped for breath after her endless supply of 'please' ran out. "What do you want?"

My eyes raked over her as she sat on my bed across from me in her black bra and blue shorts. Her cleavage drove me insane and my hands itched to touch her soft skin.

"Make me an offer."

"A kiss?" she questioned.

"I can just wait for one of those when I pass go."

Her face turned to stone as she strategized. This was what made having an over competitive girlfriend amazing. She would do almost anything to win. After a minute of thinking, she smiled slyly and leaned in. "I'll let you take my shorts off."

"Done. Deal." I pulled her body toward mine by her hips and my hands slipped to the top of her waist where her buttons shined like little gold medals.

She kissed me as I undid her buttons and slid down her zipper. We both groaned as I pulled the tight fabric down her legs and revealed her bright, red polka dot underwear. For some reason, the fact that her lingerie didn't match made it even sexier.

"God, I love you." The words escaped my mouth like an inevitable embarrassing scream during a scene of a horror movie. "I-I mean…" I wanted to take the words back in an instant from the way her eyes widened.

Instead of freaking out, she grabbed the back of my

neck and pulled my face to hers. In a frenzy, her lips latched onto mine. Her bra rubbed against my bare skin and I was a bit embarrassed by my moan at such simple contact.

"How can I feel this way?" she groaned. "I've known you for less than a month. Feelings don't work like this."

We fell back onto my bed with her legs straddling my waist as she moved herself on top of me. If I had known telling her I loved her produced such a positive response, I might have done it earlier. I rolled us over until my body stretched over hers and I kissed down her neck. When my hands came into the picture, her mouth opened in a big 'O' and a loud moan escaped her.

"Mandy…" I whispered in her ear and pressed myself against her a bit harder. We were almost naked and, damn, I could feel all of her when she bucked her hips up like that. The heat building inside of me became unbearable.

Her voice was raspy and sexy as hell. Every fiber of my being clung to her words. "I-I want you—"

Jake swung open the door and made me seriously consider how to commit an unsolvable murder. "Man, at least put a sock on the door." I blocked Jake's view of her body with my own. "But I guess being roommates with Brandon Gage means walking in on many moments like these with many different girls, am I right?"

"Get out. *Now*," I growled, my tone colder than ever before.

"Rude. This is my room, too. I can stay if I want."

"Don't be a jerk, Jake," she commented from underneath of me. I swear my grin opened wide enough to split my lips. Good girl. Please realize that Jake is in fact a jerk.

"Yeah, don't be a jerk," I repeated her words in a more mocking manner.

"Brandon, you need to not be a jerk, too."

I turned my gaze back down to meet her eyes. "Babe," I whined, "You know I have no control over my jerk tendencies. I'm just being myself."

Her expression softened and I fought myself to not kiss her. "I know."

"If you don't want an X-rated show, then you'd better leave now," I warned him.

Mandy broke my heart and my arousal. "I think we should call it a night."

"We barely even got started."

"You almost got me naked on our first date, I think we should end here for the night." The sexy twinkle in her eyes made my body throb with awareness. "Maybe you'll finish the job tomorrow."

"First date?"

"I mean, technically, tonight was our first date."

I took one last look at her semi-covered body before throwing the bed sheet over her and grabbing her clothes so she could change under the covers. "I think it went super well."

Mandy frowned. "Until Jake showed up."

I nodded. "Until Jake showed up."

"Still here, but whatever." Jake sounded upset, which made this night even better for me.

Once Mandy was dressed, I walked her outside of the dorm as an attempt for a bit more privacy before our night ended.

"For the record, tonight didn't feel like our first

date. It felt like our fiftieth." I leaned in and captured her lips with my own. "We started dating the day I saw you in that trench coat."

Chapter Twenty
Give Me An H; Give Me An O; You're a Ho.

Mandy

I clicked the answer button to quiet my ringing phone. What time was it? My eyes strived to adjust to the darkness of my bedroom while looking at the bright screen. "How's my beautiful girlfriend doing this morning?"

I groaned. "Tired." Who had the guts to call and wake me up at six in the morning? "Brandon?"

"Sorry, babe. I forgot that you wouldn't get up for another three hours. I just wanted to say, I'm hitting the gym with my friends right now. Then I'll be at Bell field for unofficial practice when your class ends. I won't be able to see you until dinner time."

"Count yourself lucky."

"You'll forgive me for waking you up early once you drink some coffee."

"I don't drink coffee."

He gasped. "Excuse me?"

"I don't drink coffee," I repeated and rolled over to get comfortable enough to fall back asleep.

"Are you one of those hippy nut jobs who doesn't believe in the unending values of caffeine?"

I blew out a breath of impatience. "I just don't like it." Why did I think his ability to talk about anything all the time was endearing?

"Then how do you stay awake each day?"

"It's called sleep. Which I was doing until you woke me up," I snuck in one last word, "Ass."

"Okay. I get it. Mandy needs her sleep. I am kind of interested in this other side of you, though. Your voice is raspy and your words are aggressive. For some strange reason, it's turning me on."

"*Every*thing turns you on."

"Everything about you."

"I hate you."

The jerk laughed. *Laughed.* "Maybe after your class you could stop by and watch me practice? It'd be way cool if you met some of the guys. They're all pretty great, except for Jake. Plus, I may even be able to play soon and since we made it into the conference championship, we'll be playing games into December."

"I'll be there to make sure you don't hurt yourself. Remember that me saying you're fine to practice and work out a bit, does not mean you're ready to play full on, okay? The ACL could tear completely if you push it too far. Even if there are games in late December, you still shouldn't jump back into them again."

"Okay, mom."

"Call me your mother again and you'll never see me naked."

"I love you."

"Goodnight."

I didn't know why I couldn't say 'I love you' back. He did not seem to mind that I hadn't responded to it yet and that at least made me more comfortable to think over it all. My feelings for him were strong, but some part of me hesitated. What if this was just an infatuation for him? What if he dumped me once I slept with him?

I had thrown the word 'love' around since middle school when I first developed a crush on Jake, but until I met Brandon I had no idea how intense feelings for someone could be.

He was always there. In a hot stalker kind of way. When I wasn't around him, I thought about him. When I was around him, I thought about killing him but kissing him got in the way. I wanted to tell him I loved him. I loved him, yet for some reason the words refused to slip past my lips. Maybe I was just waiting for the best time…or waiting for something to go wrong and hoping my broken heart would hurt a little less if I refused to admit it.

"Dream of me, my future coffee addict."

Boy, did I love him. I ended the call and closed my eyes. It took me a bit longer to go to sleep because of my smile.

****

I hissed when Ashley's alarm clock roused me from my dream. I groaned and threw a pillow in the general direction of her bed without opening my eyes.

"Um, ow." She yelped and retaliated by throwing a pillow against my back. "What the hell?"

I grabbed the pillow she'd thrown back and used it to cover my head, to better mute and drown out her voice. "Sleep."

"Because of that, I'm going to open the blinds."

"No!" Bright white light filled the room, resulting in me learning what dying must feel like. "You've blinded me."

"With my beauty? Aw, you're so sweet in the morning."

"Brandon woke me up at six."

"Did he know you would take out your exhausted wrath on me?"

I opened my eyes to watch her as she threw books in her bag, a sign that I needed to get ready for class as well. My body disagreed. "Do you want to come with me to watch his practice after class?"

"You're asking me if I want to watch the most attractive guys at our university practice a sport that will probably make them sweat, and take off their shirts and spill water on themselves as I pretend it's all in slow motion?"

"Yes."

"What time and where?"

I smiled at her. She grinned back. All well in the roommate-best-friend world. "Justin Bell Field, one o'clock."

"You have art class today, right?" she asked as I dragged myself out of bed. "Don't you have some big project coming up?"

"It's some kind of surprise. The professor hasn't told us what it will be yet." In front of my dresser, I took out a fancy camisole and a pair of leggings, my go-to 'too tired for jeans and a real shirt' outfit. "I think he'll have us create a new portfolio."

"You should paint Brandon. I'm sure he would be into it. It could be a cool activity for you two to do together."

"I've thought about that."

"He could be your nude painting."

My cheeks heated up as an automatic response to imagining Brandon Gage naked. "Dammit, Ashley."

"Come on. You want to be an artist, don't you? You're going to have to paint a nude guy some time."

"That's incorrect. Maybe I'll just paint pineapples my entire life."

"You hate pineapples."

"Then I'll finally be a tortured artist."

"I've seen your artwork. You love painting people. The way you capture them... It's like you can see every emotion in their eyes." Her compliment warmed my heart. She'd been the first to tell me not to give up on art. "Imagine if you painted Brandon and you were able to show the way he feels about you in a painting."

The way his eyes lit up when he talked to me. The way his eyebrows twitched with amusement when I made him laugh...

I forced myself to change the subject. "I'll see you at one o'clock?"

"Unless I'm held hostage at gun point—and even then—I will be there."

****

"Does everyone understand the project?"

We were expected to create five new paintings, each one tied to the others in some way and due in one week's time. "On that date, we will have a mini art show for Arden students and teachers. I expect everyone to be finished on time, no excuses."

"What if my pet lizard eats my sketches?"

Professor Stratten glared at the random smart ass. "Since most paints would be toxic to animals, you'll fail this class as well as your pet."

Deadlines on creative projects were the worst. Creating a painting each day? I really was a tortured artist. I worried over the project during the walk to Justin Bell Field. Seeing Brandon would calm me down, that much I knew.

"Mandy, my love." Ashley ran up. "Do you have any idea how lucky you are to be dating Brandon Gage, and how lucky I am to be your best friend who is single and able to date all of his other hot friends?"

"You sure have a one-track mind."

"Thank you for complimenting my amazing ability to focus extremely well on one thing at a time. Also, just to warn you, the cheerleaders are practicing on the field, too."

Jealousy nibbled at me. "So?"

"So, that Natalia girl—the one we hate because she kissed him at the game—is here."

"If she has the nerve to kiss my boyfriend in front of me, then I have the nerve to shove her pom-poms down her throat."

"You really are homicidal when you don't get enough sleep."

"Tell me about it."

I scanned every inch of my surroundings, looking for Brandon, as we approached the field. As an unofficial practice, it was not located in the stadium. On the multipurpose field in front of the university, they planned to throw a ball around and play a couple scrimmages. The light brown grass resembled straw except for a few green patches the color of a watermelon rind.

When I found him, I had to remember to breathe. He ran around the field shirtless and the shorts he wore did nothing to hide the answer to what every girl at school wondered about.

Wait, why was he running full speed?

Once he saw me with my narrowed eyes and disapproving expression, he slowed down in his jog over. I tried to keep my eyes on his face but, damn, his body distracted me.

He panted a bit when he leaned in to kiss me. "Blondie."

"You better not run full speed for this thing. You said it would mostly be catching and throwing."

He smiled. "You made it."

My snarky side chimed in before I reined it in. "Apparently, so did the cheerleaders."

"I know, I'm sorry." Brandon's eyes shifted to the group of the pompous pom-pom posse. "Ignore her and she won't bother you."

"That didn't work with you," I reminded him.

"As my mom says, I'm special." He looked back over to his teammates and shot me a look that I knew well, like a dog begging.

"Fine, go play. Remember *no* hard running. Just catching and throwing."

He kissed my nose before heading back to where his friends threw a football.

Once he was out of hearing range, Ashley nudged me. "Is it just me or is Natalia trying to use some kind of psychic power to burn you by staring and glaring?"

I followed her gaze to the she-devil herself. Natalia's hatred full eyes made my body temperature rise. "She certainly doesn't look happy to see me." I gave her a small, sarcastic wave. She seethed. "Geez."

"Oh my gosh," Ashley squealed. "Is she coming over here?"

"Act like we weren't just talking about her."

"But acting like we *were* talking about her would be so much more fun."

"Say something so she won't think we're terrible."

Ashley stalled until Natalia neared us. "But we are terrible."

I elbowed her. "Hurry and say something."

She babbled, speaking loud enough for Natalia to hear right before she landed in front of us. "And then she said: those are my ruby red slippers." I wanted to hide my head in my hands. Really, Ash?

Natalia sneered. "What are you doing here?"

The morning crankiness, triggered by her hateful tone, returned in full force. "Let's see. I'm standing, breathing, and talking to my friend. Why are you so interested in my business?"

"This is a private practice. As in only players and cheerleaders allowed."

"That's weird," Ashley joined in. "Considering we were invited."

Natalia tilted her head as if she half cared about our answer. "And who do you seem to think invited you?"

"Brandon Gage."

Natalia gave me a judgmental scan up, then down. I suddenly regretted my tired, ten-second outfit. "Why would he invite *you* to a practice?"

"Maybe because I'm his girlfriend."

She laughed. "Brandon doesn't do girlfriends. Are you sure he didn't say 'I'm going to practice' and your stalker brain considered that an invitation?"

"What a bi—" Ashley started but a look from me silenced her.

"I'm sure I'm his girlfriend considering the fact he has repeatedly told me he loves me."

"He only said that to sleep with you." She fueled the fire of the fears and doubts already in my head.

"Weird, considering we haven't slept together."

"*Really*?" Her eyes narrowed into snakelike slits. "Then he must find you disgusting because Brandon Gage sleeps with anyone." Her smile turned sinister. "Anyone but you."

I hate her. I hate her. I hate her.

My hands went to my hips. "What's your problem with me?"

She got in my face. Up close, her makeup looked even more flawless. "You aren't Brandon's type. I want you to stay away from him."

"And what's his type? You?"

"Haven't you ever watched a movie before? I'm the cheerleader; he's the jock. We're perfect for each other."

"You certainly have the same size egos," I muttered. "And if being a cheerleader is all it takes to date him, I was head cheerleader in high school, so—"

"Not good enough to cheer in college?"

Her body language and words shouted 'challenge.'

"I could out flip you any day of the week."

I knew how many cartwheels and back flips I could still do. Natalia would stop after three for fear of messing up her perfect brown hair.

She stepped closer, enough for me to smell her powerful perfume. Mint and roses. Could something about this girl please be less perfect? "You think you can out cheer me?"

"Give me an H! Give me an O." I flailed my arms. "What's that spell?" I asked Ashley.

"Ho," she shouted back. People close by turned to see whom it was directed to.

Natalia glared at both of us before refocusing her attention on me. "Fine. Right here. Right now. Let's see

217

who's better."

She bent, grabbed her ankle, and lifted her foot as high as it would go. I matched her every move.

My leg cried as I pulled it up and behind my head. We held our position that way for forever or, more realistically, about two minutes.

When Natalia finally let her leg swing back down to the ground, I did the same. Then she dropped into a split. Damn. I spread my legs apart and slid down, trying not to think about getting grass stains all over my pale blue leggings. My muscles screamed as tendons and ligaments pulled. Boy, I regretted not stretching.

She smirked, stood, and did a cartwheel.

My time to shine.

I had been trained in flips as a kid. I pushed my body off the ground then soared through the air, re-lifting myself after each back flip and cartwheel. Once I became dizzy after doing at least ten of them, I stopped and met her gaze, knowing she didn't match me.

Never, ever had I seen anyone look so mad. Her tan turned an unflattering shade of fire truck red. And the twitch in her left eye concerned me.

Whistles and light clapping filled my ears, and I turned to see Brandon walking over to me yet again.

"This isn't over," Natalia growled. "You're just another girl. I'm the one he always comes back to." With that she sped away, shaking her hips more than any human female should.

"You forgot your broom!" Ashley shouted.

Chapter Twenty-One
Birds Were Once Dinosaurs

Brandon

After Mandy lifted her leg and put her foot behind her head, I no longer had the capacity to focus on the football coming my way. It hit my chest with a sharp blast but the pain did not even register. The way she held that position for so long took all my attention.

Natalia dropped into a split; no big deal. I'd seen her do that dozens of times. But my jaw dropped when Mandy copied the move. Damned if my thoughts took a turn to how I could get her to ever spread her legs that wide and fast for me. After the split contest ended, they both started doing these flip things. Natalia stopped after a couple but Mandy continued to soar through the air like gravity refused to touch her.

I had never seen anything so graceful. Funny how a girl, who often got so nervous she couldn't form a coherent thought was so comfortable flying and twisting through the air. Also funny how turned on watching her made me. I mentally recorded the memories for later.

What I did not enjoy, however, was the way my teammates watched Mandy. The heat in their eyes was unmistakable and I regretted bringing my beautiful girlfriend to one of my practices. I had wanted her to meet them, and now all I wanted was to take her away to a private place where she'd let me watch such tricks and not worry about other prying eyes.

Since everyone else stopped playing in order to watch them as well, it was safe to walk over to the girls. A benefit of planning an unreal practice was no angry coaches to complain about player distraction. I did not miss the way Natalia glared at Mandy or that she whispered something before strutting off.

"Damn." I pulled her to me until we touched stomach to stomach. A noise escaped my throat as I leaned my face against hers. "Do you think you could put your foot behind your head again...and maybe next time be wearing a skirt?"

She shook her head. "You have a problem."

"You're right. It's called being in love with you."

"Gage, are you going to introduce us to your girl already or what?" Michael asked.

Should I introduce them? The flirty looks in their eyes bothered me. Michael and Lucas knew she was mine, but some of the others didn't.

"What's your name, sweetie?" another inquired.

"Mandy," she replied. "And this is Ashley."

"Hi." She grinned and put a hand on her hip, flirting with her eyes. "Best friend of the girlfriend. How are you boys doing today?"

"Fine, sugar," Lucas responded with his heavy southern accent before any of the others had time to. He took her hand and kissed it, a steamy expression exchanged between the two of them. Mandy released an amused sigh.

Once Lucas released Ashley's hand, she made a fanning gesture with it. "It's pretty hot outside today. Are you sure some of you don't want to go shirtless? I just want to assure you that Mandy and I would be totally fine with you guys taking them off."

I made a noise.

Ashley tore her eyes off Lucas long enough to see that I disapproved of her flirting—and throwing Mandy into the mix. "Sorry, let me rephrase that: Mandy will get to stare at *her* boyfriend's naked chest and I would appreciate something to look at as well."

Wow, she put it all out there. No wonder she convinced modest Mandy to show up in my room wearing a trench coat and lingerie. Lucas winked at Ashley and yanked his jersey off. Watching them flirt felt weird. Her eyes devoured him the same way Mandy's always did to me.

She nodded at him and he grinned. "Mmm, ten out of ten."

"I'm an eleven out of ten, right babe?" I whispered in Mandy's ear and she blushed when she glanced down at my chest again.

"Isn't this a football practice?" she asked. "Shouldn't you guys be practicing football?"

Michael smiled at her. "We're just trying to meet the famous blonde healing goddess who Brandon talks so much about."

"He's lying," I said. "I don't talk about you a lot."

"You're an art major, right?" Michael brought up one of the details I had conveyed to them, proving my statement wrong.

She nodded.

"I think it's time we restart practice—"

No one listened to me.

"Has Brandon told you about how he's afraid of birds?" Michael continued, trying to embarrass me. I needed to get new friends.

"I'm sorry, what?" Mandy glanced at me just in time to see me blush. "Are you serious?"

"Excuse me, but birds are terrifying." I attempted to defend myself. "They were once dinosaurs."

She laughed. "Everything was once a dinosaur."

"But not everything has deadly claws."

I clapped and motioned for the rest of the team to head back to the main field to practice. My friends nodded at her and walked away. Lucas left after saving Ashley's phone number.

Mandy smiled and waved goodbye to them. Then her entire face changed. Emotionless. Stone. She froze right before my eyes. A chill moved through my body as I prepared to protect her from whatever or whomever had made the color drain from her cheeks.

A strange voice sounded behind me. "Mandy?" A tall guy with blonde hair and a big smile came toward her. She appeared to be in shock. "Mandy? You're never on the sports field side of campus," the new guy said. "What are you doing here?"

"I-I-I…"

"I've been meaning to talk to you. Have you been getting my messages?"

Ashley's cold voice threatened to give someone frostbite. "She blocked you."

"E-Eric?" Mandy blurted.

Eric? The guy who dated her for two years, then cheated on her? The guy my hands itched to strangle for making her feel so inadequate?

"It's been a while," he said.

"Mmhm." The noise came from Mandy, who only nodded and offered nothing more in conversation. She looked like she had shut down.

"Maybe we could talk—"

Mainly because I didn't like how this guy's being here was affecting her, I stepped in. "I don't think so."

He looked at me like a piece of old gum on his shoe, annoying but not concerning. "Is your name Mandy?"

She dated this dick? Worse, she'd felt bad after he dropped her?

Ashley moved to stand a bit closer to Mandy. "She doesn't want to talk to you."

"I think she can answer for herself." Eric met Mandy's gaze. "Mandy?"

She trembled slightly against me. "U-um, okay."

My temperature rose as Eric shot Ashley and me a smug look. He walked Mandy from the field, heading toward a tree-shaded picnic table.

"What the hell just happened?" I asked Ashley.

She released a heavy sigh. "Eric kind of has a power over Mandy. He was her first for, well, basically everything." My fingers clenched into fists so tight that the cracking of my bones was audible. "When he cheated… I mean it broke her. It took a year for her to even think about moving on."

Ashley and I stared at Eric and Mandy as they talked a couple yards away from us. He reached for her hand. She let him take it.

Ashley's eyes narrowed. "This is not good."

****

"Have you already gotten your mermaid costume?"

Mandy and I sat down in the Diner to eat. She had not told me what Eric said to her or how she felt about him showing up out of the blue. Each time I brought it up, she changed the subject. The best thing to do was act like nothing had changed, or at least remind her how good things were between us.

She looked momentarily confused. "My what?"

"We said we would dress up as a mermaid and a pirate for the Halloween party, remember? It's in two days."

She frowned. "I told you I don't like Halloween."

"And I told you that you've never had a Halloween with me, so all your past ones will never be able to compare."

"Brandon…"

"Why don't you like such a fun holiday?" I teased, needing to put a smile on her face. "Do you hate fun?"

Mandy rolled her eyes. "No."

"Do you hate candy?"

"Of course not."

"Do you hate dressing up super sexy for your amazing boyfriend?"

When her lips twitched into a smile, I knew I'd break her serious exterior. "Do you really want me to answer that?"

"Why don't you like Halloween?"

"I just…had a bad experience as a kid."

I lifted her chin up to have her meet my eyes. "Did someone steal your candy?"

Sadness registered on her face, making me hate myself for prying. "No. It was back when my dad started not coming around as much. He had promised to take me out trick or treating, and I spent hours getting ready…and he never showed up."

Her voice shook. Enough to make me want to track down her dad so he could give her an explanation. "I sat on my porch waiting for him for forever. Kids stopped ringing the doorbell; the houses stopped giving out candy… He never even called. It was like he forgot all about it."

All the men in her life had burned her. I wanted to soothe every wound. "I'm so sorry."

Her tone came out breathless as she tried to get a hold on her emotions. "It really sucked."

I reached over and took her hand in mine. "Let me change your outlook on Halloween. I promise, you'll have a good time. Think how fun it will be to see me dressed up as a pirate."

"That *would* be pretty fun." She gave me a timid smile. "Thank you."

I squeezed her hand. "Of course."

She spoke again before I had the chance to bring up the topic of Eric. "Are you doing something over Christmas break?"

I wondered where she planned to go with her question. "Probably going home, why?"

"Would you want to maybe come celebrate Christmas with my mom and me at Ashley's house?"

"Ashley's house?" What was her family like that she celebrated Christmas with her best friend?

"My dad left us when I was pretty young and my mom had a hard time always being there to raise me. In the end, Ashley's family practically adopted me because they lived next door. My mom joined in, too and it was like we became relatives. Now we always spend holidays together. That's why Ash and I feel so much like sisters." Her eyes softened when she talked about her family. "It's funny, my mom and Ashley are really similar."

"I can't even imagine a mom being like Ashley."

"If you stay with us for Christmas, you'll get to meet her."

"Meeting the parents, huh? Should I be nervous?"

"Only if my mother likes you."

"Don't I want her to like me?"

"My mother is a very special woman. If she likes you, she will never let you go."

"I'd love to come and meet your mother." I smiled and then my thoughts turned. "If you spend Christmas with Ashley and her family, and Jake is biologically her brother, does that mean he will also be there?"

She sighed. "I know you don't like Jake but he's my best friend's brother and your roommate, so I think you should try to get along with him."

"Blondie, he's my arch enemy."

Her lips twitched at my statement. "You are so dramatic."

"If I had to kiss, marry, or kill Jake Kane, Josef Stalin or the guy responsible for air filled chip bags, I'm pretty sure I'd still kill Jake."

"But who would you marry?"

"Whoever was richer," I replied with lightning speed, anticipating her question.

"Gold-digger."

"You better make good money selling your art, Blondie, or you might just lose me to Stalin."

"And the award for the weirdest sentence ever uttered goes to…" We laughed before she became serious again. "You were roommates before, didn't you two get along then?

"Jake and I enjoyed a very strange relationship. We competed with each other. It was like having an annoying brother whom I didn't have to like." Though I'd probably take Jake over Eric. I barely knew him and I despised the guy.

She cringed. "Sorry."

I squeezed her hand again. "It's fine. So…" I changed the subject. "Do you think you'll be able to get your costume in time for the party?"

"Ash can help me."

I grinned at her and took a bite of my pasta. My body vibrated with excitement at the prospect of seeing Mandy as a mermaid. I just hoped to God that her tail wouldn't act like a chastity belt.

Mandy smiled, a mischievous look in her eyes. "Speaking of Ashley, she's on a date with Lucas right now."

"What does she think of him?"

"She thinks she's in love." I smiled at the amusement in her eyes. "She says she wants him to call her his 'crisp, sweet, cinnamon, golden, mini apple pie,' in that southern accent of his. She spent an hour coming up with southern dessert nicknames."

"That's Ashley for you." I chuckled and Mandy nodded. "What did Eric say—"

"I already told you I don't want to talk about it." The light from her eyes faded. I hated when she was sad. "It was really nothing."

"It was not nothing. It's been bothering you. You haven't laughed much since you two talked."

"Maybe you're just not as funny as you think."

"Impossible."

"It was nothing."

Her pained expression led me to change the subject again. "I was thinking, Sunday night will be one of

Arden's last football games and now that you've cleared me for practices—"

"No."

"I'm telling you, I'm fine."

"I just want you to be safe, okay? You won't be safe to play until next season."

"Okay." But they were empty words. The pain in my leg no longer bothered me. I worried now that she refused to request a clearance for me because of her emotional attachment. "I don't want to fight with you."

She pulled off her sweatshirt and got her shirt caught in it on accident. I sucked in a deep breath as she mistakenly flashed everyone in the Diner her pink lacy bra, before realizing what she did and pulling it back down. I swallowed back a moan at the now burned image in my brain.

She looked mortified as she glanced around for witnesses. "Please tell me that did not just happen."

"Please tell me that will happen again."

"I guess there is no chance in us fighting when I ruin heavy moments like that."

I gave her a small smile. "I guess."

****

Jake walked into our room an hour after Mandy left. I decided to try to talk to him for the first time since he threatened my relationship with her.

"How's it going?"

He looked at me with a shocked expression. "Fine. How's Mandy?"

"Perfect," I responded.

He frowned as if he hoped I had gotten bored of her by now. "Too bad you won't be playing this Sunday."

"What do you mean?"

"I mean some NFL scouts are coming to watch the game. It's a shame you'll miss a once in a life time shot just because your knee hurts."

"My knee doesn't—" I stopped. "I'll be there."

"What?"

"I'm going to play on Sunday." My healed leg was fine. "The coach does whatever I say and he'll listen to me if I say I can play."

"And Mandy is okay with this?" Jake asked in a smug filled voice.

"Yup, by the way I'm spending Christmas with her at your house. Hope that's okay." We both tried to establish some type of dominance.

"Fine," Jake growled.

Everything between us was far from fine.

Chapter Twenty-Two
Mermaid Madness

Mandy

"It's been a while," Eric said once I followed him to the tree, away from the others at Brandon's practice.

"It has."

As attractive as ever, his hair shined in the sun and his eyes sparkled. I tore my gaze from him and glanced at Brandon. Between the two of them, there was no comparison. We stared at each other until Eric broke the silence. "I've missed you. Have you missed me?"

I had. Before. But now? "No," I said it as if waking up from a dream and realizing something.

"If it helps, Stella and I are still together."

I scoffed. "It doesn't help."

He stared at his shoes and kicked at a pebble on the grass. "I'm sorry." He looked up and took a step closer to me, then stepped back again. "I should have said it a while ago, but I'm sorry."

I met his gaze head on, not blinking or breaking eye contact. "It was a dick move."

His eyes widened at my words. It was the first time I acknowledged the situation as just his problem. A part of me had always thought I contributed to him cheating. Maybe if I wore makeup every day or dressed up more or shaved my legs in the winter, maybe he would have stayed with me.

I didn't see it that way anymore. He had not appreciated me. Brandon appreciated me.

"It was and I want you to forgive me."

Eric stood there, saying words I had waited a year to hear, and they did not matter. He apologized for how he treated me and... I didn't care.

We talked but the conversation wasn't important. The way he looked at me didn't make me feel small. The way he spoke to me didn't make me feel less than good enough. I was good enough. Not just good enough for Brandon, but good enough for me.

Eric was my past. Brandon was my present. I was my present.

Seeing Eric...messed with me, but it also reinforced what I already knew. Brandon was not Eric. He was someone I trusted. Someone I loved.

****

"I think I'm in love with Lucas," Ashley said with her usual squeal. "He uses words like sugar, darling, and sweet pea. Plus, sometimes he doesn't understand when I'm just joking, so he'll do the things I say. Like I told him if he wanted a good night kiss, he'd have to show me his abs again. He pulled up his shirt without any hesitation."

"Are you going to the Halloween party tonight?"

I laid the pieces of my costume on my bed. The light pink shell bra reminded me of a bubblegum sunset. The formfitting violet tail skirt reached down to my calves and flared out to the ground.

She went to her closet and pulled out her costume. "I'm going to be a sheriff, partly because I want to carry around a fake gun. I told Lucas to be a cowboy because men with hats and rope are sexy."

"I didn't know sheriffs exposed so much skin," I teased her. The skirt of her costume was so short, it looked like it had been made for a doll.

"Hush, I make the laws around here," Ashley attempted a southern accent, but it ended up turning British. "You and Brandon." She wiggled her eyebrows up and down. "Have you…"

"Not yet."

"Yet, huh? Interesting word choice."

"I was thinking maybe tonight—"

Ashley cut me off with a scream. "Ahhhhhhh!"

"Calm down." Tonight, I would tell and show Brandon that I loved him. I was ready. Seeing Eric again and getting closure showed me that.

"I'm totally doing your make-up." Ash pulled me back into the moment. "You're going to look the hottest you've ever been tonight."

"Thank you."

She bit her lip as if holding in a squeal while she patted liquid foundation on my face. "You love him, huh?"

"I think I have for a while. He just…stuck with me…through everything. He makes me so happy. Like so unbelievably happy."

"And you're going to make him happy tonight?"

My cheeks warmed. "I'm going to try."

"Anyone can see how he feels about you. You make him happy without trying."

"I just hope I'm enough for him, you know? Before we met each other, he was constantly with other girls and is way more experienced than me—"

"None of that matters when you're in love."

My nerves did not settle down. Ashley proceeded

in contouring my cheeks with powder, and defining my eyes with mascara and eye shadow. By the time she finished, recognizing myself was a challenge. My pale pink lips matched my shells and my wavy, curled hair resembled a mermaid's. I smiled in the mirror, feeling ready to face Brandon.

Ready to love him.

****

—Aye, are you ready yet, me lass?—

The text message from Brandon came in two minutes before a light knock sounded at the door. I opened it and gasped.

His pirate costume consisted of a scrap of cloth that barely covered his muscular chest and tight, black leather pants that almost made me have a heart attack. Black eyeliner lined his eyes, making his gaze all the more intense. Even his hat turned me on. Oh man, he would so get lucky tonight.

"Yo," he announced and then paused briefly before the second word. "Ho." He then proceeded to laugh at his own joke.

My eyes raked over him and took in every little attractive detail. "You're a pirate."

"And you are a mermaid. We've already discussed this. We were planning these costumes to match."

"I know but..." I swallowed, my mouth suddenly dry. "Damn."

"What?" He gestured to his body. "I look that sexy?" We both knew he looked sexier than any word in the English dictionary could describe.

"I mean...yeah."

"Should I be scared that the first time you have ever acknowledged me being attractive is while I'm wearing eyeliner?"

My hand moved on its own volition and stroked down his sculpted chest. "I think I have a thing for pirates." He let out a husky noise when my fingers touched the top of his leather pants. Brandon's arms wrapped around me and pulled me closer. Our warm bare stomachs pressed against each other.

Brandon's heated eyes devoured every inch of me. There was a lot on display. "I have a thing for you because geez, girl, you're going to kill me in that."

A seashell bra was all that covered my torso. The mermaid's tail skirt clung like a second skin, leaving nothing to the imagination.

"That skirt better not be difficult to take off."

I looked at him. "Think of it this way: once it's off, it stays off."

His head dipped to kiss me. "Agreed." His lips sucked mine in a new erotic way he had never done before. He had me moaning in minutes. "In fact…" Brandon's hands wandered to the waistline of my tight skirt. "How badly do you want to go to this party?"

"I spent two hours getting ready." I swatted his hands away even though my body screamed at me in disapproval for stopping him. "Don't think you can seduce me before we've had any fun."

"Babe, I promise it would be much more fun to—"

I poked at his chest. "No."

He grabbed my hand and held it to his heart after giving it a quick kiss. "What do you want to do tonight? There's a haunted house, plenty of dark rooms for you to take advantage of me. There's a fraternity dedicated to Halloween games, which you could play to try to distract yourself from how amazing I look. And then there's a place designated for dancing, if you find that you can't keep your hands off me."

I patted his chest. "You sure are full of yourself tonight."

Brandon opened the door for me, and we made our way out of my dorm and to his car. "I'm full of myself every night."

I shivered at the chill of the fall air and he pulled me closer to him. His warmth radiated through his costume. "Never has another statement been so true."

"What do you want to do first?"

"Halloween games sound fun," I commented. "I'm guessing they're not the standard games?"

"The pumpkin carving is probably the most normal thing they have, but then after you carve them, you get to race them."

I imagined how competitive such a thing between us could become. "That sounds fun."

"Plus, there's bobbing for alcoholic apples."

I almost laughed. "Alcoholic apples?" It sounded like the most frat thing in the world.

"Don't drink the cider. I know from personal experience what a light weight you are, so I shall protect you from alcohol and monitor everything you drink."

"Besides being full of yourself, you are also very controlling."

He wrapped his arms around my waist as we walked through the parking lot to get to his car. "Mmm, do you like that side of me?" Brandon leaned in to whisper in my ear. So sexy. Maybe the pirate thing made it even more dramatic. "You can call me master anytime you want, I hear that's the new big thing."

"I won't even call you sir."

"Shame. It would be pretty sexy if you did."

"You think everything is sexy."

"I don't think Jake is sexy," Brandon joked.

I grinned. "What do *you* want to do tonight?" I asked him as we climbed into his car. Somehow being trapped in such an enclosed place with him excited me even more. Trying to sit down in the mermaid tail, however, was extremely difficult.

Brandon witnessed my struggles and chuckled. "What do I want to do? Let's see: talk to you, walk with you, dance with you, kiss you… Basically, as long as we're together, I'm good for the night."

"You're so sweet." I teased him, "What would your frat friends say if they heard you now?"

"They'd probably faint from shock."

"I can see that as a possibility."

We talked about Halloween and the different haunted houses we visited as kids. At a young age, Brandon was convinced his grandmother's house was haunted. As an adult, he still clung to the idea of ghosts being real. I told him about the time I went to a haunted house with Ashley and one of the actors pulled a chainsaw on us because Ashley wouldn't stop complaining about how 'not' scary she found the place. She then started talked about all her ex-boyfriends, rating them by ten. The guy with the chainsaw eventually ran away from *her*. He and I ended up laughing all the way to the frat house.

Brandon offered his hand to lead me and I took it. Holding his hand always made me feel better. "Halloween games first then?"

I cracked my knuckles like we were about to fight.

"I'm going to slay you at pumpkin carving."

"We'll see. I have many talents with a knife..." He stopped and frowned. "That came out a whole lot creepier than I meant it to."

"As long as you don't decide to carve me up and hide my body, then we're good."

"I could never hurt such a beautiful body." He kissed my forehead and walked with me into the large house. "There's the pumpkin station."

"First one there gets a five second head start in the pumpkin racing," I announced and rushed to the table full of pumpkins.

He laughed and easily caught up with me, but I pushed him into a wall in order to be the first one there. The wall, however, did nothing to muffle the "I love you," he muttered against it. I grabbed the largest pumpkin, my thinking based on the more it weighed, the faster it would roll. I did not remember much from my high school physics class, but I recalled reading that somewhere.

Brandon grabbed my waist from behind me and pulled my back to him. "I think you're the first girl to ever push me into a wall over a pumpkin."

"I'm not the first girl to push you into a wall in general?"

"You'd be surprised. My turn to pick. Let's see..." He picked up one of the tiniest pumpkins on the table. "This one looks good."

"That is literally the smallest one they have," I told him. "You'll never win with that."

"Hasn't anyone ever told you that size doesn't matter, Blondie?"

"No. In fact, you've been bragging about your size

since the first day I met you."

"Whoa, someone has a dirty mind this evening. I wasn't even talking about that, I was talking about the science of gravity. As long as I can push mine harder than you can push yours, I'm pretty sure I'll win the pumpkin race."

"What makes you think you can push harder than me?" I questioned him, moving my face threateningly close to his. His eyes darkened and I felt an answering throb between my legs. Wow, why was I so turned on by competing with him?

"Maybe the fact that my muscles have muscles."

His statement made my gaze drop down, just to further appreciate the fact that he was right. His muscular build was like something out of an erotic fairytale.

"But you're also easily distracted. For instance, let's say my shell bra just happens to get loose when you're about to roll your pumpkin..."

"You wouldn't."

I nibbled his ear and his groan made my knees go weak. "I'm very competitive."

"You know I wouldn't be able to look away."

I pressed my chest against him in order to first, emphasize my threat and second, to relieve some of the pressure I felt behind the shells. "Exactly."

He leaned into me, like he needed us to be as close as possible for what he planned to say next. My heart skipped a beat and my body flooded with heat in anticipation.

"Hey, guys." Jake's voice cut right through our sexual tension. "You having fun?"

"If you don't go away." Brandon lifted his

pumpkin. "I will literally throw this at you."

"Whoa, man. That's such a small pumpkin."

Brandon closed his eyes and took a deep breath before turning to me. "I will literally throw this at him."

Jake grinned at me and uncomfortable, I shifted under his gaze. "Relax. My date and I just wanted to say hi."

"Date?" I regretted asking it because of the way Brandon looked at me. I had to make it clear to him that I was far from jealous… I just had a curiosity problem.

"You know Natalia."

She appeared behind Jake wearing one of the most revealing costumes known to man. How could Jake meet my eyes while someone so attractive in so little clothing stood next to him?

"Hi," I said and she ignored me. "Great to see you again, too."

She had the audacity to shoot my boyfriend her 'bedroom eyes' look right in front of me. "Looking good, Brandon."

I put my hand on his chest. "He feels good, too."

"You don't have to tell me." She smiled at him like she relived memories of their past in her mind. "I know exactly how he feels."

The smug expression on Natalia's face shook me to the core. "Didn't anyone ever tell you not to flirt with someone else's boyfriend when she's so close to a carving table full of knives?"

"Whatever." She turned her attention back to him. "Why are you dating a freak? Is she that good in bed?"

He shrugged like it was no big deal. "Sex isn't the only thing to a relationship."

Natalia's jaw dropped. "Since when?"

"Since I met Mandy."

"Jake." Natalia's voice went shrill. "I'm thirsty."

"But I just—"

"Jake."

He huffed and left us to go to the drink table.

"This isn't over," Natalia snarled at me before trailing after Jake.

Brandon chuckled in my ear. "Well then."

"Nice gal, that one," I said. "Makes me want to rub sandpaper on my ears."

"She's his problem now. They kind of belong together."

"I guess they kind of do."

He took my face in his hands, a dramatic and serious expression on his face. "You know what we have to do now."

I giggled. "What?"

"Dance."

"Does that mean you no longer have the self-control to keep your hands off me?"

He looked down at my hand, which had been stroking his chest for at least the entire conversation. The scary part was that I had not realized my petting him. "Looks like you're having the same problem."

I swallowed hard at the heat in his eyes. "Dancing sounds good."

Chapter Twenty-Three
Sharp, Sexy Seashells

Mandy

We moved to the dance floor now crowded with other couples. The moment our bare torsos met and rubbed against each other, I was done for. I needed him. Every touch of his fingers against my bare waist, every moment I caught him staring at my shells, everything made me want him. Every moment of knowing him acted like some type of frustrating foreplay building up and waiting for this instance.

With each beat of the music, we pressed against each other harder and harder, my hips bumping against his. Closer and closer. His eyes darkened and my breathing became heavy. He held onto me when I stumbled. Preventing myself from complete collapse became even more difficult after he dipped his mouth to my neck and kissed right below my ear.

His tongue flicked the bottom of my earlobe and he whispered, "I want to touch you tonight."

"You are touching me."

His hands dropped low enough to cup my bottom in my costume. "I mean really touch you." He rested his forehead against mine and stared me down. "Touch you without the shells and the tail."

The song picked up in pace and we matched the fast beat together. I felt him, hard against me, just as caught up in the moment, and that knowledge turned me on even more. Brandon's hot gaze locked onto mine, piercing deep as if he could read my thoughts, see how much I wanted him. He thrust his hips forward and moaned as he rubbed himself against me.

"Is there anywhere we could go?"

He stiffened. "There are plenty of empty rooms here…" His hands squeezed my hips. "Are you sure?"

My doubts disappeared at the excitement and adoration in his eyes. "If I'm in this skirt for another five minutes, I'll—"

"Understood."

Lifting me in his arms and cradling me to his chest, he ran us away from the dance floor and up the stairs to a room. Once he found one, he swung open the door and quickly closed it.

He pushed me against the wall. The smooth painted wood against my back made it all feel more taboo. His mouth claimed mine and as a result, tingles swept through my entire body. My nipples tightened under the shells and a groan escaped my throat. As our kiss became urgent, hotter, scorching, his hands wandered over my body. My nails dug into his back from pleasure when he pressed against my shells.

"Ow." He pulled his hand away from my breasts. "Damn, babe, your shells cut me. Why did you have to be so anatomically correct? I would have been perfectly fine if my mermaid girlfriend was just wearing a bikini top."

I pouted. "I like the shells."

"I like them too." He nibbled my bottom lip. "But I also like touching you and they are making my life substantially more difficult."

The blazing fire in his eyes melted me.

"Maybe it would be easier for you to just take the top off me," I remarked.

His entire body jumped and he grew harder against my thigh, groaning on my lip. "Oh, yeah?" He was so breathless that for a second I thought he would start panting. Or maybe that was me; I could have been the one panting.

"Yeah." I tilted my head so he saw the thin straps wrapped around my neck. "All you have to do is untie a string."

The teasing look in my eyes had the desired effect. His grip on my hips tightened and he pushed our bodies even harder against each other. The knob of the door dug into my back but I loved it. Every inch of me touched every inch of him…in every delicious way.

"That sounds an awful lot like rocket science."

"I'll buy you a step by step instruction manual."

His eyes devoured me everywhere I was uncovered. I blushed as my shell bra slipped down my chest. Raising my hands up, I blocked his gaze.

He grabbed my wrists and pinned them over my head. "Don't ever hide yourself." He stared at my breasts like he had never seen anything like them before.

He licked his lips and I all but fainted from the rush of blood leaving my head. Even though a part of me loved the way he reacted and stared in awe, his direct, focused gaze on me made me uncomfortable with each second that ticked by without him making the next move or kissing me.

I attempted humor to lighten the mood. "My eyes are up here."

"But your nipples are down there and I think they just convinced me that there is something in this world more beautiful than your eyes."

I blew out an amused breath, relieved that he still wanted me even though I did not resemble the usual girls he acquainted himself with. "You're ridiculous."

"And you're gorgeous."

His lips crushed down against mine. The kiss lit a fire inside of me that I hadn't even known existed until I met him. The fact that he pinned me to the wall added to the heat of it all. He lifted me into his arms and walked us to the bed.

After we tumbled onto the mattress, he rolled on top of me. He palmed my bare breasts, his fingers knowing exactly what to do with my half nakedness. I clung to him when he ground his body against mine. I wanted nothing more than for him to rip my mermaid tail off of me, so I could wrap my legs around his waist and feel him hard right where I wanted him. It appeared that we had the same thought because a minute later, he tore my tail in half and threw the scraps across the room without a second thought.

Brandon fell against me and groaned. "You're not wearing any underwear."

"It would've shown through and made lines in my costume. The skirt was too tight."

His eyes pressed shut. "Oh, I know how tight it was." He took a second to look down at my bare lower half, before he closed his eyes again and released a ragged breath.

"You okay there?"

"I've never been better." His warm chocolate eyes surveyed every inch of me. His body practically vibrated with awareness. "God, you are so beautiful." His shaky finger trailed from my neck, down my chest, and then to rest on the inside of my thigh. "Like you were made for me." He kissed me deeper than before. "Love you."

He moaned as we rolled over and made out on the bed, getting closer and closer to what we both knew would change everything. "Fucking love you."

I had never been so turned on. I had never felt anything more intense than when his hands slid between my legs and found a part of me that made my eyes roll into the back of my head. I had never loved anyone as much as I loved him.

"I can't hold back tonight." His hands continued to work their magic between my legs as he spoke. My mind barely registered his words. I was ready for him. "I've got to have you; next time we'll take it slow."

"Okay." He could have gotten me to agree to anything with those fast, skillful fingers of his. My heartbeat thumped so hard in my ears, I hardly heard the sound of the condom package being ripped open.

"Are you sure?" he asked before moving to align his body with mine.

My back arched for more pressure, seeking him out. "Yes," I shouted for what had to be the ninth time followed by the thirteenth "Oh, God" as he, after slipping on a condom, pushed inside me.

"I told you, babe, my name is Brandon." He tried to joke, but sweat formed on his forehead as he thrust his body against mine. I fell apart at the way he rolled his hips. "Next time, we'll go slow and I'll kiss every inch of your body." His pumps sped up. "I'll take everything slow; every caress, every lick, every stroke, every goddamn thing. I'll make you burn for me before I give you what you want." Both of us were a mess of moans as we got close, so close. "I'll make you scream."

"Oh, God," I repeated again.

He took the time to slow his thrusts in order to tease me, then went faster than he had before. Dots of colored light formed behind my eyelids, dancing, as the pleasure and pressure took me over. He groaned as both of us reached a level never experienced before.

In, out. In, out. The force behind each of his thrusts added to the frenzy I felt. It was like someone squeezing a glass, the grip tightening with each second that went by until resistance could no longer exist. Like glass, Brandon and I shattered.

"Oh fuck, so good." His hips slowed and pushed against me harder with each word that flowed from his lips. "God, you feel so good." He dropped down against me and kissed me from my neck to my mouth. "I love you."

I wanted to say it back, but I struggled to catch my breath and my thoughts drifted into exhaustion. By the time I had the chance, the moment was gone.

****

I woke up slowly, each cobweb inside my head fading as I opened my eyes. We were still in the bedroom. Brandon's steady breathing calmed as he slept next to me, snoring. I squeezed my eyelids shut and thought back to last night. I had never fallen apart like that, never been *unraveled* like that. No wonder girls called him a God. My gaze shot down to his sheet-covered waist. The thin white fabric did nothing to mask the size of what lay beneath it. His erection was

ready for round two, or rather round four—if I wanted
to count the times we woke up during the night, his
hands unable to stop touching me.

He looked gorgeous while he slept, at peace. My
palm itched to touch him…his chest, his…other body
parts. I lifted the sheet off of him, revealing what I most
wanted to see. Biting my lip, I tried not to groan at the
sight of him. For some reason, the word exquisite came
to mind. It reminded me of admiring a Greek sculpture.
Glancing at his sleeping face once more, I moved closer
to his body.

My finger trailed itself from his muscled chest to
his cock, which already stood straight. He was
insatiable. I touched him and a sigh came from his soft
lips. A burning need to give him a real touch filled me.
I wanted to show him that I was worth his attention. I
had yet to say I love you. I would start by showing him.

Swallowing hard, I wrapped my hand around the
base of him. I smiled at the juxtaposition of his softness
and hardness. This man was an anomaly: both sexually
dominating and sweetly attentive. With a small stroke,
his breathy sigh sounded a bit louder than before, a
slight whine echoing in the back of his throat. His
reactions motivated me to go farther. I tightened my
grip and renewed my stroking to a slow pace. Small
sounds continued to escape him, but his eyes never
opened.

I wanted to make his eyes open.

Moving down the bed, I straddled his legs and gave
myself a better view. His eyelids twitched at each
squeeze of my hand, but they refused to open. I then did
something I had never done before. My tongue flicked
against the most sensitive part of him as I quickened my

strokes. His eyes shot open. Finally.

He groaned and moaned when he saw my mouth on him. "Mandy…" Brandon's body jumped and quaked so hard that I had to stable myself on top of him. "Damn, what a way to wake up."

I tried to talk but I had my mouth full.

"You never stop surprising me." His head fell back against the pillow and his fingers snaked themselves into my hair. "Perfect night. Perfect morning. Perfect week." My cheeks hallowed as I gave him a final big suck. He yelped at my efforts. "Fuck, that's enough." He pulled me off of him. "I don't want to come yet. You come first." He threw me back on the bed and climbed over me like a man possessed. With passion. "You'll always come first."

"No complaints here." My voice was already hoarse with arousal.

His lips claimed mine and I throbbed for him. His left hand cupped the swell of my breast while his other one slipped between my thighs. A finger entered me and I had no control over the sound I made. When his mouth captured one of my nipples, I melted even more.

"You're ready for me."

My breath caught at the powerful tremors wracking my body. "I am." I needed him. Badly. *Now.*

Another expert finger joined the one that curled and rubbed a spot that had me going momentarily blind. "You're always ready for me."

I would have said anything to have him continue. "Yes."

He grabbed for a condom on the nightstand and ripped it open with his teeth. Something about that made it even hotter. "We'll go slow next time."

I gasped when he pulled my legs up. "You said that last time."

He kissed the inside of my thigh. "Someday, when I don't feel like I'll die if I'm not inside you, we'll take it slow—" He positioned his hips over mine and I wrapped my legs around him like it had become pure instinct. "—but today is not that day." He pushed inside of me and my toes curled from the pleasure.

Words slipped from my mouth before they even registered in my mind. "I love you."

He froze inside of me and my hips bucked for him to move against me. "Say it again."

If he did not resume moving inside of me, I would cry. My body ached for him. "What?"

"Say. It. Again," he ground the words out through his teeth. Why did I find that so sexy?

"I love you."

His hips pounded against mine harder and faster than I thought possible. "Again."

My eyes rolled into the back of my head with each deep stroke inside of me. I screamed his name when his hand found its way between my legs to rub my clit. "I love you," I panted.

He would be the death of me. I felt so close to something. So close. On the edge—so close to falling. *So. Close.*

"Again."

"I love you!" Bright light erupted from behind my eyelids and every muscle in my body spasmed with release. I came and clenched around him, causing him to yell just as hard.

"You bet you fucking do." His hips pumped against me as he climaxed. Brandon took in a deep breath and rolled off of me. He then wrapped his arms around me and pulled my body against his.

"That's one way to get you to admit it."

I had never smiled so widely.

****

The next day as I walked back to my dorm after my last class, Natalia headed straight for me. Avoiding her became impossible when she stopped in front of me. "Mindy."

"It's Mandy."

"Don't care. Because you're not going to be a problem anymore."

I took a 'I'm not afraid of you' stance. "Uh huh and why is that?"

"If you don't leave Brandon alone, I'm going to make sure that he never plays football again."

"And how are you going to do that?" I held back a laugh at her dramatics. "Brandon already told me your dad is a pro scout. He also told me you've threatened us before by saying you'd get your dad not to recruit him."

"I'm not talking about the big leagues." She moved close to me, the wildness in her eyes scaring me a bit. "I'm saying if you don't leave him, he will *never* play another game again. Did you think his injury was just an accident? That other player had been told exactly how to tackle him to keep him out for the rest of the season. He was paid to do it."

The temptation to rip her pretty brown hair out was unbearable. "Are you confessing that you sabotaged my boyfriend's well being?"

She fluttered her eyelashes. "I'm confessing that I might be inclined to ask someone for a bigger injury next time."

"How can you act like you care for him when you threaten to destroy his future? Do you know what a bigger injury could do to him?"

"He might never play again. In fact, if it's a major injury, he might never be able to walk again. I wouldn't want to go that far though. When we're together, I don't want him in a wheelchair." She looked over her painted nails with a nonchalance that grated on my nerves. "If he thought he could walk away from me before, it might be fitting for him to lose his ability to walk again though." She released a dramatic sigh. "Sounds almost poetic."

I took a step back and stumbled over a crack in the sidewalk. "You're crazy."

"I'm dedicated. Brandon is mine. And if I see you with him again, a broken heart will be the least of his worries."

Chapter Twenty-Four
Colorful Changes

Mandy

Ignoring his calls topped the list of the hardest things I'd ever done. I finally got to the point of telling him I loved him, and then Natalia threatened his safety and his future. All Brandon wanted in life was to play pro football. He didn't want to think of other options. His knee bothered him, but the worst pain he'd been through the past few weeks came from watching his friends play while he sat on the sidelines. Brandon hated the sidelines.

How was I supposed to break up with the guy I loved more than anything? I'd had no clue how irreplaceable he was in my life until I admitted to myself how much I cared for him. He had become my everything. I vented to him, joked with him, worked with him, laughed with him, and loved him. If Natalia had threatened *me*, I could overcome it. But she'd endangered his safety and well being.

I would never let him get hurt because of me.

I looked over the messages he had sent me today. I had not replied to any of them.

—*Morning, gorgeous. How's it going?*—

—*Miss me already?*—

—*I miss you. I know it's been less than twenty four hours, but it feels like forever.*—

—I can't stop thinking about last night…and this morning.—

—Hitting five unanswered texts now and going strong.—

—Hello?—

—Did I do something wrong?—

—Blondie?—

—Mandy?—

It killed me. If I talked to him or saw his face, I would break down. When he showed up outside of my room about three hours later, I told Ashley not to let him in.

"Can you at least tell me what happened?" she asked.

My eyes prickled with unspent tears. "Please, just keep him away from me." I hugged my pillow and turned over in my bed as she walked over to answer the door. I tried not to listen in, but my ears acted like personal hearing aids tuned to his voice.

"What's going on?"

"I don't know what you did to her, but she doesn't want to see you."

"I don't know what I did either. All I know is everything was perfect and then she wouldn't pick up her phone all day. Is she okay?"

"Honestly? I've only seen her like this once before… She's broken hearted."

"I swear I didn't do anything." His voice got louder. "Can you hear me, Mandy? I didn't do anything. Please, come out and talk to me." The sadness in his tone tore me up inside.

"I don't know what happened but just give her time," Ashley warned.

The sound of him fiddling with the doorknob filled me with dread.

"Fuck that. We've spent enough time apart because of stupid drama and other peoples' agendas. I'm talking to her, and she's going to tell me what's wrong so I can fix it." The door creaked and a small sob escaped me. My back was to him but I *felt* him as he stepped inside. The entire energy of the room changed when he entered.

His warm hand touched my back and I cried harder. "Mandy…" He sounded as broken as I felt. "Babe, tell me what happened."

I swatted at the hand touching me without turning around to face him. "G-go away."

"Did…Did I do something?" How could he think that? He had always been perfect to me. *I* was the one who used him to make another boy jealous. *I* was the one who cut him off after saying I loved him.

I wanted to kill Natalia. She knew I would not let him get hurt again. "N-no."

"Then, Jesus, babe. Tell me what happened between this morning and now."

"I-I can't."

A weight settled on my bed and his arms wrapped around me as I continued to lie on my side, facing the wall. "You damn well can." He held me for a couple moments before his grip tightened. "I fucking hate it when you cry."

"I'll leave you two alone for a bit," Ashley said and closed the door.

"If you'd just tell me, we can get through anything," he said once we were left alone.

I gasped for breath in hopes to calm myself down.

His warmth against my back comforted me. "Not this."

"All right then, let's play a guessing game. Does it have to do with last night?"

"No."

His fingers threaded themselves through mine and he held my hand tighter than ever before. "Does it have to do with Eric or Jake?"

"No."

"Does it have to do with Natalia?" I didn't answer. He sighed against me. "Babe, whatever she said doesn't matter, okay? I told you, she doesn't have the power she thinks she does." I stayed silent. "Will you just turn over and look at me...please?"

My resistance wore down and I flipped over to face him. His deep brown eyes shined as he wiped away the tears that clung to my cheeks. "There, that's better, right?" His lips puckered and kissed my nose. "What did Natalia say?"

I touched his chin as I gazed up at his face. "She was behind you getting hurt."

"That was my fault." He nuzzled his forehead against mine. "I got distracted and messed up. She had nothing to do with it."

"She paid the player to tackle you."

He blinked and raised both brows. "That's...surprising, but I wouldn't have gotten hurt if I hadn't been watching my back out there. If I had been running full speed, he wouldn't have been able to touch me."

"You don't know that for sure. You're not indestructible. You could get hurt for real next time."

"Next time," he repeated my words and cupped my cheek in his hand. "Let me guess, Natalia threatened you that if you didn't break up with me, she would pay another player to hurt me even worse than last time."

"And she'll do it too." He refused to listen to how serious it was. "You didn't see the look in her eyes. She could affect your entire future."

He kissed my cheek. "You are my future."

I pushed at him. "Don't be stupid. You want to be a football player. That's the only thing you want to do. Us dating, risking your chances, your safety... It's completely illogical!"

"No, us dating is completely *magical*. Natalia can't just break us up with empty threats."

"Not empty." I stressed. "She's done it before."

"We can't live in fear. It's us. We have gone through so much to be here and I'm not going to let you walk away from everything because she scared you."

"I'm doing this for *you*."

"You're not. If you were doing this for me, then you would listen to what I have to say about it. I think you're doing this for you because we are moving so fast and that's scaring you. I love you more than I have ever loved anybody."

Stay strong. Stay strong. I had to do this. I had to. "I won't let you risk yourself for me."

He moved away from me and stood up. "And I won't let you walk away."

"You think this is easy?" I tangled my fingers in my hair and sat up. "I hate that I have to do this."

"You're giving up on us. That's it, plain and simple." Now Brandon sounded just as livid as me. "You're giving up over a couple words that could be lies... The worst part is how easily you've decided to break things off. Do you even love me?"

My blood boiled. "Of course, I love you. How can you even ask that?"

"Maybe because for most of the time I've known you, you've told me that you hated me and that you were in love with Jake. Now when we are together, you're fine with my psychotic ex breaking us up."

"Do you not see how I'm torn up inside?" My voice got louder as I stood up. "I fucking love you. So. Much. You drive me crazy." He stared at the ground, so I grabbed his chin and forced him to look at me. "You make me rethink everything. You make me feel like I'm on fire. I used to be cautious and then I met you, and now almost everything I do is impulsive. I used to paint in black and white, and then you kissed me and everything became brighter. My world was colorless without you and you goddamn blinded me."

I took in a deep breath and repeated, "You have blinded me, Brandon Gage."

He stood there with his mouth hanging open and his eyes wide. It was the first time I had ever seen him appear so surprised, so dumbstruck. We stood, staring at each other in silence for another minute before he broke it.

"If you knew what you did to me…" He wrapped his fingers in my hair and pulled my face closer to his. "You have changed me so much. I'm a better person because of you." He kissed me, his lips claiming mine for mere seconds before he pulled away. "You have brought me to life. Trust me when I say Natalia can't hurt me. She can't hurt *us*. If you think I can't take care of myself, then know my teammates will pick up the slack."

****

My grin did not fade for about fifteen hours. It was hard to sleep with my mouth so stretched. It had also been hard to sleep because Ashley had slept over in Rachel and Elizabeth's room so Brandon stayed the night in my room.

We discussed all of our issues, and now I felt free and open about everything. Natalia loved playing mind games and Brandon assured me he would be safe. Plus, I didn't have to worry about it because his injury would keep him out of at least a few more games, if not out for the rest of the season. By the time his senior year began next Fall, he would be fully healed.

My new excitement for art class surprised me. At first, my work had not impressed Mr. Stratten but I could tell that the more color I put into my paintings, the more he liked me.

"Your use of red is stunning," he commented on the piece I worked on. I still had yet to figure out what type of collection to paint for my final project, but I was more and more comfortable using color. Brandon truly had changed me.

"Thank you." I had painted two people in black and white. Different red lines and tints connected them to represent the many forms of passion. "I wanted to show the different sides to red."

"Love, lust, and anger. I see it, how…interesting." I didn't miss the way he spent more time inspecting my work than he did that of other students. "Have you been thinking about your final project?"

I bit my lip. "I'm not sure what I'm doing yet."

"Maybe make your theme whatever has caused this change in you and your art. Making me understand your uniqueness as an artist would be a great new realm for you to explore."

****

Michael opened the door to his and Lucas' apartment, and I practically ran him over as I sprinted and jumped into Brandon's arms. Thank God he was so strong or we would have both fallen down from the impact. My legs wrapped around his waist as he held me up and I kissed him with more passion than normal.

He chuckled against my lips. "I assume your day was good."

"Amazing. Mr. Stratten is really liking my work. I might even have a shot at that internship. How was your day?"

He lifted up one shoulder. "My teacher accidentally said cinnamon instead of synonym, so for the last thirty minutes of class all I could think about was apple pie."

He wrapped his arms around my waist and walked me into the kitchen where Ashley and Lucas ate the pizza they had ordered for our friend night. Michael joined Rachel and Elizabeth where they sat at the dining table.

Behind me, Brandon gasped at what Ashley and Lucas ate. "Did you guys drop that pizza on the ground outside? Why are there leaves on it?"

Lucas sighed. "Spinach is good on pizza."

"So is cheese and tomato sauce and pepperoni."

Ashley put a hand on her hip and used the other one to hold Lucas' hand. "Excuse us for trying to be healthier."

"You're excused. Now, where is our normal cheese pizza?" He checked a few before he picked up the box itself and ate from it as if it was a massive plate.

My hand moved to steal one of his slices but he shooed me away from his food. I rolled my eyes. "You can't eat that whole pizza."

"Challenge accepted."

That night we played pool, watched TV, and ate junk food. Our friends complained about how Brandon and I couldn't keep our hands off each other, but they all appeared happy for us. We sat around a table when Ashley announced she wanted to play poker, and I blushed as I remembered the last time Brandon and I had played together. I could tell that he remembered as well by the way his gaze smoldered as he took his seat next to me.

The high table hid his hand on my inner knee but it did not hide the way I sucked in a very loud breath at the contact. Everyone looked at me. Brandon fake coughed in order to mask his laugh.

"I, uh, I'm just excited to play poker," I said. Brandon grinned at me, his grip on my knee tightening.

"What do I get when I win?" Ashley asked us, and most of us laughed.

"Who says you're going to win?" Michael leaned back in his chair. "I'm great at poker."

Focusing on their words was hard to do when Brandon's fingers trailed up my inner thigh. I shot him a warning look, but he had on his innocent poker face and refused to look at me. I was no stranger to his teasing, but my hips still rocked into his hand when he moved closer to the real place I wanted him.

Once his fingers made it to between my legs, they retreated back down to my knee. Nice and slow. Sweat slickened my hands as Rachel dealt out the deck of cards for us to play. My face struggled to stay straight, but the muscles in my smile twitched when his hand moved back up my inner thigh.

He stopped again right before he got to where I ached.

"Mandy?" My head shot up at my name. "You feeling okay?" Ashley asked, concerned. "You look a little flushed."

"If you're feeling warm, you should take off your sweatshirt," Brandon added with another annoyingly innocent expression. It bothered me that he wound me up so tight and acted as if he wasn't affected at all by it.

I leaned over and put my hand on his knee, not missing the way his entire body jumped at my touch. "I'm fine, thanks." I sent him a heated look and his sinister grin widened. "Let's play."

I held up my cards to look at them but my focus centered on the circles his thumb rubbed so close to the junction of my thighs. Every small little stroke caused my inner muscles to throb.

He could do with some torture too. My hand squeezed his knee and then dragged itself up to where a very noticeable bulge pressed against the zipper of his jeans. *Hmm, not so innocent after all.* I gripped him and swallowed an evil laugh when a loud moan escaped him. I feigned a naïve expression when everyone's eyes shot up to look at him.

"Mmm, wow." Brandon waved his cards in the air to explain his outburst. The tension in his voice turned me on even more. I loved how responsive he could be. "I have a great hand."

"I fold," Rachel said and handed out new cards to people who chose to exchange them.

As his thumb's movement accelerated under the

table, Brandon leaned into me and whispered in my ear, "What about you? Are you ready to go farther or are you going to fold?"

My hold on his erection tightened and his eyes crossed for a second before returning to normal. "I bet I can last longer than you."

His thumb moved its circles to the spot I needed them over my sweatpants and he whispered in my ear again, "I bet you're throbbing for me."

I held back my whimper but he could see it in my eyes. My hand rubbed over his groin and his breathing became heavier against my neck. A few seconds passed until he looked at me again. Both of us close to breaking.

He stood up from the table, pulling me in front of him and picking me up in his arms. "Mandy's feeling a little warm. She needs to take a shower." He kissed me and walked us out of the living room.

****

The next night, I grabbed a book and read while lying in bed. My cell phone rang. It was nearly eight o'clock, which was pretty late for anyone to call me. Brandon had said that he would be busy all day, so it couldn't be him.

When I read that it was Ashley, I answered it. "Why aren't you home yet?"

"I need you to get down here. Now."

The serious tone in her voice scared me. "What's going on? Where are you?"

"I'm at the football stadium. Brandon is playing."

I froze. "He's what? Who cleared him?" Had Brandon's father gone around my authority and bribed the physical therapist?

"I'm scared he's going to really hurt himself. With what Natalia told you... You need to get down here."

"I'll be there soon." I rushed out of the room and didn't even stop to lock the door after me. I panicked. My heart raced faster than it ever had before. Sweat dampened my shirt as I ran to the stadium. It was located a couple buildings away from my dorm.

The loud music and cheers became clearer and clearer as I got closer. The only thought running through my head was that I needed him to be okay. He had to be okay. By the time I got there, the game was in progress. Brandon was on the field, playing. I pushed through the crowds in order to get a better view. I pushed through all the way to the front row seats that Brandon had shown to me at the first game he invited me to attend. I screamed his name but it was useless. He couldn't hear me.

The quarterback launched a pass and Brandon plucked it right out of the air, then ran toward the goal line, faster than a human should have been capable of...until the worst happened.

Someone fell and grabbed him by the ankle. Brandon's legs collapsed and gave way beneath him. He landed on the ground with an audible *whack.* The entire stadium went silent at the same moment.

The coaching staff huddled around him. One of the trainers made a motion, signaling for the emergency medical staff who raced onto the field, carrying a stretcher. Hushed sounds traveled through the crowd in waves as they moved Brandon off the field.

How could this happen? We were together just last night. I *told* him not to play.

In that moment, I did everything I could to get to

him. Only a railing prevented me from running onto the field. Without hesitation, my hands grabbed the metal bar in front of me and I pushed myself over it. Using the gymnastic skills that my mother had ingrained in me as a kid, after saying things like: it will be easier to find a husband if you're flexible, I flipped over and down onto the fake grass where the coaches and players waited. I ran after where they had carried him until a large man stopped me.

"Excuse me, miss, but this is off-limits."

"You don't understand." I was desperate. "He's my boyfriend. They took him in there."

"Only family or medical assistants are allowed."

"That-that's me. I'm his physical therapy assistant." Then I lied my ass off. "I'm the one in charge of healing his ACL."

He still seemed suspicious of me, but I slipped past him and ran after the two men carrying Brandon down the hall.

"Brandon," I shouted but the men did not slow down. They quickly got him into the infirmary and laid him down on one of the medical beds. "Brandon." I took my place beside him and squeezed his hand.

The men left to get the doctor.

From the corner of my eye, I saw Natalia slip into the room, but I didn't care enough to ask her how she got past the guard. All I cared about was Brandon opening his eyes.

"Honey?"

His eyelids flickered. When they opened, my entire body relaxed.

"You're okay. Thank God, you're okay. I was so scared." My voice cracked as my eyes watered like geysers. "Don't ever do something like that again, do you hear me? You are not invincible no matter how macho you seem to think you are."

He frowned, looking confused. I wanted to kiss the distressed expression off his face but I restrained myself. "I don't understand."

"Sorry, I know you want me to think you are a strong manly man but... I saw you go down. Your head... Never get hurt again, okay?"

Brandon continued to frown at me.

"What's wrong?" I joked, "I've never heard you stay silent for more than a few seconds before."

He stared at me for a moment with a blank expression.

"Babe. You're scaring me. What's wrong?"

The next thing he said utterly broke my heart.

"Do I know you?"

Chapter Twenty-Five
An Amnesia Affair

Brandon

The beautiful girl looked at me like my words were life altering.

She looked so familiar, sounded so familiar... Everything about her was on the tip of my tongue. A thought burned into my memory but drifted away at the last minute. Stunning, electric blue eyes pierced me. "W-what?"

"Do I know you?"

"It's me." The girl broke down in front of me. "Mandy. Your girlfriend."

"Girlfriend?" I would have laughed if she had not looked so heartbroken. I didn't do girlfriends. I was Brandon Gage.

Natalia remarked, "I guess you're not very memorable."

A man who most resembled a doctor walked into the room. "Excuse me, ladies, but you're not allowed to be in here. You need to leave while I look him over."

"Of course." The blonde's voice went completely stone-like. I shot her a questioning expression but her gaze of terror never wavered.

She and Natalia hesitated but left the room.

"Do you remember your name?" the man asked.

I scoffed. "Duh. It's Brandon."

The doctor raised my chin and shined a bright light into my eyes. "And what do you remember from tonight, Mr. Gage?"

I looked down at my body. From the pain in my leg, it was obvious I'd been hurt. "I assume I was playing football."

"I didn't ask what your assumption was. I asked what you remember. I think you sustained a concussion from your fall." He touched the side of my head and I winced. "What is your last memory before waking up here?"

Every thought seemed to move through a bowl of gelatin before making itself known. What was my last memory? I had a fight...at Thanksgiving dinner with my dad. I must have come back to campus...

"Thanksgiving."

"I see... In addition to a concussion, it seems you also have a case of amnesia. It's a normal side effect in your condition and should eventually fade with time."

"How much time?"

"That cannot be calculated. It all depends on you and how fast your brain will heal. It might be helpful for you to go back to your normal routine and see if anything triggers a memory. Most likely once one comes back, they all will."

"Will my teachers still make me take my finals even though I've missed half the semester?"

"Don't worry about that right now. First, we're going to get you to the emergency room in the University infirmary. You'll need a CAT scan."

I jumped down off the table and stabilized myself when slight pain shot down my leg. "My knee hurts."

The doctor nodded and moved to the corner of the

room for a wheel chair. "I'll order you an MRI as well. You'll need to be under observation for at least the next twenty-four hours."

I sat down and he wheeled me out into the hallway where Natalia and the blonde girl stood waiting for me. "I have amnesia," I told them.

"Jesus." She followed us as the doctor wheeled me to the exit. "He needs a CAT scan."

"Yes, I know," the doctor responded. "Girls, you might want to give him some space."

"He also recently healed from an incomplete ACL tear. The fall might have extended it." How did she know about my medical history?

"Yes," the doctor slowed down. "He mentioned his leg. Who are you?"

"I'm his girlfriend," the blonde said.

"She's lying," Natalia said. "This girl has been stalking you for a month now. She's probably trying to use your amnesia to make you think you two were dating. She's a loser. You know me, you know I would never lie to you."

"But you are lying," the blonde accused Natalia. "You're the one responsible for all this. I-I'm not—" She turned to me. "Come on, Brandon. Deep down you have to know that we're together."

The doctor wheeled me a bit faster, trying to get me away from the girl drama. I glanced between the two girls a couple of times before my gaze stayed and latched onto the blonde's. She really was something else. Her breath became heavy as she speed walked to keep up with us. Her fiery blue eyes were so hot they melted me.

"You…"

"You've got to remember me," she pleaded, her voice cracking with emotion.

I tried to find any prior memory of her. I tried hard, but I continued to draw a blank. "I'm sorry, I don't."

"You've been complaining to me about this girl stalking you for a while now," Natalia started again and I wanted to roll my eyes. God, she was such a bitch.

"I don't think I would complain if a girl who looked like her was stalking me…" In fact, it would be more believable if *I* stalked *her*. "I mean, damn…" My eyes raked over her. A light blush formed over her cheeks and for some reason it felt like it was not the first time I had seen such an adorable occurrence. "Let me guess, I slept with her at a party and Natalia, since you're so obsessed with me, you got mad or whatever." Nat was always getting jealous when I slept with other girls, but I had told her before that I didn't want a girlfriend.

The blonde shut her eyes and wore a pained expression.

"Look, I want to believe you, but I honestly don't have girlfriends. I just don't." I wanted to comfort her, but I ignored the impulse because I didn't waste time comforting girls. For some reason, conflicting thoughts kept running through my mind.

The doctor opened the door to the outside and the winter air shocked me. The harsh wail of an ambulance siren hit my ears. Once it parked next to the sidewalk, two men came over and assisted me into the back of the emergency vehicle.

"Isn't this a little much?" I asked the doc but he no longer listened to me.

"After his scans and some observation, you can

visit him," he informed the girls.

The blonde girl stared at me with shiny eyes.

Then the ambulance doors closed.

****

When stuck in a hospital bed, cherry gelatin tasted like heaven. Especially when the air smelled like bleach, baby powder, and burnt toast. I didn't like hospitals. Every move I made on the bed crinkled the wax paper beneath me. Every ten minutes or so someone out in the hallway yelled at a nurse loud enough for my roommate and I to hear through the wall. I shared the room with an old woman named Helen who I assumed to be an elderly professor.

She controlled the TV remote and kept switching the channel between five different soap operas. "This is a good one," she said in her grandmother voice. "Julio runs away with his brother's bride."

"Yikes."

She ate some of her green apple gelatin, her eyes glued to the screen. "That's what his brother says."

I chuckled. "You love drama?"

"When you get to be my age, you'll realize the most interesting experiences were caused by handing over the reins to passion instead of clear judgment. It makes these shows feel a little less unrealistic."

"That woman just fed her husband his favorite cat because he kissed someone else." I pointed at the screen showing a character crying on the shirt of her long lost twin brother. "You find that realistic?"

"Hell hath no fury like a woman scorned."

A female doctor walked into our room with a clipboard. She jotted something down and then looked at me. "Mr. Gage, you'll be happy to learn, your ACL is fine. Still sore, but no tear."

I put my plastic cup of gelatin down. "Okay."

"As you know, you have a concussion and a mild case of amnesia—"

Helen roommate turned away from the TV to listen in. "Oh!"

The doctor appeared confused, so I clarified, "She loves soap operas."

"Right." She gave Helen a tender smile and focused back on me. "To deal with the amnesia, all I can say is to dip your toes back in the water. Go about your normal routines; you might begin to remember something."

"The other doctor said the same thing."

"Everyone is different in their healing time. You'll have to stay here overnight and rest, but for now I wanted to ask if you felt up to seeing visitors. There has been a woman in the waiting room asking about you for hours now. She said she's not family."

The blonde? "Just one girl?"

"Another caused a scene and left earlier."

"Interesting," my elderly roommate commented.

"She can come in."

She smiled. "I'll go tell her."

My roommate grinned at me once the doctor left. "So who is this girl?"

"I don't know."

"Come on, you can tell me." Helen pressured me. "We're sleeping in the same room tonight."

"I've slept with a lot of women."

"I'll give you my next pudding cup."

That piqued my interest, but I had no real answer. "I honestly don't know. Amnesia, remember?"

Chapter Twenty-Six
Fate Hates Me

Mandy

"Did you do this?"

Natalia sat across from me in the waiting room of the infirmary. Her manicured fingernails dug into her chestnut brown hair. She did not respond.

I raised my voice. "Did. You. Do. This?"

She stared at me. I cracked a knuckle. She blinked. And caved. "No."

"Why should I believe you? You've threatened him before."

"I was bluffing." She leaned back in the molded blue plastic and grabbed her purse. She rifled around in it frantically as if to distract herself. I needed a distraction, too so I watched her venture through packs of gum, pieces of paper, and makeup. "I just wanted you away from him."

"You didn't pay someone to hurt him in the other game? When he hurt his ACL?"

"Do you think I would do that?"

Yes. "You've given me no reason not to."

She pulled a lip balm out of her purse. "I didn't. I was lying. It's what I do. I just didn't want you two together, okay?"

"Not okay!" I yelled at her. Others in the waiting room stared at me. "You're selfish and manipulative and… God, you got what you wanted, didn't you? He doesn't remember me. Are you going to throw a parade?"

She put down the lip balm. "You think I'll go after him since he doesn't remember you?"

"Won't you?"

She glared at me and stood up. "I'm nobody's second choice."

A bitter laugh escaped me. "If you cared about that, then why have you worked so hard to break us up?"

She tapped her shoe on the dirty tile floor and responded, "Because if he doesn't want me, he deserves to be alone."

No one deserved to be alone. "You are such a spoiled brat."

"A spoiled brat who knows she deserves better. Look, I came here because I care about him—"

"When you care about someone you don't wish loneliness on them." I stood and took a step closer to her. "I love him and I'll wait here for hours. I will sleep in this unbelievably uncomfortable chair just to see him because that's what love is. It's about them, not you."

Her narrowed eyes widened. She looked away. She sat down. After five minutes or so of silence, she said, "I'll leave you two alone."

I wished there would still be an us two after it all.

****

The female doctor led me into Brandon's room but did not follow me inside. "I'll leave you two to talk."

"Three actually," an old woman said from inside the room. She laid back on her bed on the opposite side of the room. "I'm Helen, his roommate."

"Um, nice to meet you." I stepped into the room

and stopped in front of his bed. "Brandon?"

"That's me."

"Ar-are you doing okay?"

"I still don't remember you."

I hid my flinch as well as I could. "I—"

"You're his girlfriend, right?" the old woman, Helen, asked me.

"Yes."

"You two are just like my soaps. Now that he has amnesia, y'all can fall back in love again."

"She's obsessed with soap operas," Brandon explained, not even commenting on the potential rekindling of love.

I took a step closer to him. "The doctor said it would help for you to go back to your routine so you can start remembering…maybe if we hung out—"

"As long as by 'hang out' you mean…" He wiggled his eyebrows and flexed his muscles under the thin hospital robe.

From her bed, Helen made a disapproving noise.

I glanced down at my shoes. Even his eyes were different, the way he looked at me, the tone he used with me was wrong. All wrong. "N-no. I was thinking we could eat together or study… We've been doing that for the past four or five weeks, so it might help you—"

"Sorry but I don't do study dates. I like to snore *after* meeting up with a girl, not during."

"We could—"

He raised his hand up to stop me. "Listen, no hard feelings. You seem like a nice girl and you're super hot, so I'm not going to say it'll never happen. I'm just going to say that I have a lot of time to make up for."

I hated the whimpering noise that escaped me.

"Don't you want to get your memory back?"

"Sure, I do. I'm just not in a rush, you know?"

Helen grumbled, "Ass."

****

After learning Brandon had amnesia, I spent the rest of the night in a haze. Somehow I managed to get back to my room from the infirmary. Ashley suffocated me with a hug. Apparently, Lucas told her about his condition before I could.

My heart broke in my chest. The first tears slid down my cheeks and clung to my chin before dropping onto her shoulder as she held me. It all sank in after my talk with him. "He doesn't remember me."

Her arms tightened around me as though the harder her grip, the less pain I would feel. For some reason, it had the opposite effect. "I'm so sorry."

"I just don't understand." Sobs racked my body; I was helpless to stop them. "Everything was perfect. He was so perfect, Ash... We were finally..." I could not even fathom that he didn't remember me. "He doesn't even look at me the same."

"He'll remember you, I know he will."

"But you don't know." I cried harder. "You don't know... I love him, and he doesn't even know my name."

"He barely even called you by your real name in the first place." She patted my back. "Maybe that's a good sign."

I pulled away from her embrace. "He said he was in no rush to remember anything... I finally told him how much I love him and now this..." My mind kept replaying his hurtful comments in my head. The way his gaze held lust and no other emotion. Nothing like what I was used to when he looked at me. "He-he's a jerk now. He's nothing like the guy I fell in love with."

"That's because your love changed him. He wasn't even close to a gentleman when you first met. Remember? He thought you were there to sleep with him even though he had no idea who you were. Sweetie, knowing you… You made him better. You owe it to him to try to change him back, to be patient."

I sank down onto my bed after my weak legs failed to hold me up anymore. "What am I going to do?"

"Maybe this is the universe testing you. Brandon was the one who had to work hard to keep your attention and make you love him the first time. Now, maybe it's your turn."

"I hate the universe."

"Considering it gave your boyfriend amnesia, I think the universe kind of hates you, too."

I put my head in my hands and groaned. "I have class with him tomorrow." How would I deal with looking into his eyes and not seeing…him?

"Then use the time you have together to show him why he fell in love with you in the first place." She nudged me and I curled up into a protective ball on my mattress. "Show him that old Mandy charm."

"The reason he was interested in me before was because I hated him."

"Then hate him like he never said 'I love you.'"

Chapter Twenty-Seven
Jake's Girlfriend

Brandon

It took them forever to release me. CAT scans and MRIs did not make my list of fun things to do on a Saturday night. Once I was set free, I headed to my dorm room. Everything around me felt different. Bushes were bigger; grass was longer. It was evident that time had moved on.

"Jake," I announced as I swept into the room. "How's it going, man?"

His computer laid in his lap while he reclined on the bed. "I heard about the concussion," he responded without answering my question. "Is that true?"

I fell back onto my bed and regretted it due to the slight pain that came from my head. "Yup."

"And the amnesia?"

"Last thing I remember is my mother feeding me tofu turkey on Thanksgiving." I grunted. "A terrible memory by the way."

"You don't remember anything after Thanksgiving break?"

A part of me felt suspicious at his tone but I had no idea why. Jake was my roommate and even though we were not best friends, I still trusted him.

"Nope. Apparently, I got pretty messed up."

"What do you mean?"

"Natalia and some blonde were fighting over me in the infirmary."

He dropped the pen he had been spinning with his fingers. "Blonde?"

"Yeah… I don't remember her name." I guess I could just call her Blon—

"Mandy," Jake offered quickly as if he saw the wheels in my mind turning and jumped in to help me. "Her name is Mandy."

"Do you know her?"

"Yeah… She's my girlfriend."

I stopped breathing for a moment after his confession. What? *His* girlfriend? The thought of the blonde with him made my chest hurt worse than my head. An iron fist wrapped around my lungs. Something about it felt…wrong. Utterly wrong.

"What? Two hours ago, she told me that she was *my* girlfriend."

Jake swallowed. "Huh, weird." His voice wavered. Was that a tinge of nervousness? "She's a jokester, that one. I bet she was just trying to make me jealous."

"I guess." Something was so familiar. The blonde, Jake, jealousy… God, it was like déjà vu. Maybe her hitting on me for his attention was a regular occurrence.

"What are your classes going to be like tomorrow? Will you remember what you've been learning?"

"I didn't remember things from classes before my amnesia. I feel pretty normal about it all." I closed my eyes to rest but something gnawed at me. "The blonde is your girlfriend?"

"Yup."

There was a sinking feeling in my mind that I assumed originated from my need for sleep. "Damn."

****

I chose a random seat in the lecture hall. As usual, all the girls in the room flocked to me like seagulls to bread crumbs. Hell yeah, I had been waiting for this. A redhead leaned in to whisper in my ear, "I bet your head isn't the only thing that's aching."

A loud sound of a binder hitting the desk next to mine stole my attention. It was the blonde girl I supposedly knew. The banging sound made the other girls frown and drift back to their original seats. Was she cursed? How had every female within ten feet of me disappeared once the blonde sat down?

"Damn, you're killing my game." Why couldn't she just leave me alone? I needed to get back to my normal, which she was not a piece of.

"You must not have much game if it only takes me sitting next to you for them to leave. Maybe your amnesia affected your flirting skills. I would give you a few pointers but I wouldn't want to waste my time."

Her statement stunned me. No girls talked to me like that... What the hell? And why was I so turned on by it?

"Who are you?" It slipped from my lips. I knew her name and that she was Jake's girlfriend but... God, something just felt off about it all.

"As I told you before, I'm Mandy."

"Why are you in my class?" I frowned at her. "Are you really stalking me?"

She huffed at my statement. "Of course not, we just happen to be in the same class. You're the one who sat in our seats."

"Our seats?"

"We always sit here."

Always? Since when did I attend class enough to have a permanent seat? "Together?"

"Why is us being together so hard to believe?"

Her eyes resembled a blue flame as they burned themselves into my brain. She looked angry and sad at the same time, and I had no idea why. I hated feeling so clueless.

I hung out with the guys on my team and a few down the hall in my dorm. That was it. No girlfriends and no girl friends. "I don't have friends who are girls."

"I guess I'm special."

"Hmm." I tilted my head so I could better see her expression. "I'm starting to see that... What flirting tips would you give me? I'm the champion at it after all, so I doubt your minor advice will help."

Her entire manner whispered 'challenge.' "Have dinner with me and I'll show you."

"For real?" I never 'had dinner' with girls. It sounded like Dating-101. But she was with Jake so she must not have meant anything by it. Maybe we were friends... She certainly interested me.

"No, I don't mean the things I say," she stated, sarcasm clear from her tone.

A light chuckle escaped my throat. "Okay."

She looked away but my eyes caught the way her lips pulled up into a small smile. "Cool." I wanted nothing more than to see her fully smile, fully laugh, fully moan— *Whoa, where did that thought come from*?

"Will Jake be there?" Her boyfriend being present while she gave me flirting advice would be extremely uncomfortable. Especially since I wanted her to teach me in every touchy-feely detail.

She appeared amused and confused by my bringing

up Jake. "Do you want him to be?"

I tried to appear nonchalant about it even though I wanted to scream at her 'no.'

"Yesterday you would have slapped me if I asked Jake to come along."

Why? Did I not like Jake anymore? Why would we hang out without him around? Why would—

Oh. Light bulb. "We're having an affair."

Mandy's right eyebrow shot up. "Excuse me?"

"It all makes sense now. You telling me we're dating and Jake saying you two are together. We're having an affair. Oh man, I never expected you to be so naughty."

"What the hell are you talking about?"

"You're dating Jake but you've been sleeping with me in secret. I understand now—"

"I am *not* dating Jake." The room got colder.

I was just as confused as her, if not more. I had amnesia after all. "Um, he told me you two were together."

Mandy began gathering her books as she stood up to leave. "Excuse me."

Class hadn't even started. "Where are you going?"

"I'm going to kill a man."

Words that ordinarily would have scared me had the opposite effect. Who was this girl and why did everything about her fill me with...warmth?

Chapter Twenty-Eight
Killing a Man

Mandy

I skipped the class with Brandon after he told me what Jake said. I knocked on Jake's door with a bit more power than necessary. The whole thing shook by the time I finished banging on it. Jake opened it with a frown that turned upside down at seeing me.

I cut right to the chase and grabbed him by the shirt collar. "Why in the world would you tell Brandon that you and I are together?"

"I don't know, I guess it just kind of slipped out."

The way he shrugged increased my rage. "Are you a pathological liar? Something like that doesn't just *slip out,* Jake."

He swatted my fist off his shirt collar and moved back. "Stop being so mad at me."

"What were you thinking?"

"I was thinking that I like you. I like you and this is our chance. Brandon doesn't even remember you—"

"Jake, I need to make something clear," I said. "I thought it was clear before, but I guess not. Even if Brandon *never* remembers me, you and I will never be together. Now, you either help me get the man I love to remember he loves me, too, or you can get the hell out of my way."

He took a minute to think it over before opening

his mouth again. "I'll help."

"Thank you. You can start by telling him you lied."

"No can do. I don't admit to lying. It's a fact that makes my lies more realistic."

"I will literally kill you," I said with a straight face so he would understand my seriousness.

Jake made a face and shrugged again like he thought my death threat was a joke.

"I've watched murder documentaries. They will never find your body."

"I guess I could tell Brandon that I was kidding about us being together." He sounded in pain after saying such a thing but it still made me sigh in relief.

"You do that," I growled and went straight for the door to leave.

"You were joking about the murder stuff, right?"

"I never joke about murder."

****

"This is perfect," Ashley said. "Now that Lucas and I are together, I can get you around Brandon all the time. Like, today there's a football practice, and Brandon is going to sit and watch because the coach said it might help trigger some memories. Lucas invited me to come watch, so you should come too and try to talk to him."

"I don't know, Ash. I don't want him to think I really am stalking him."

"You said he seemed interested during your conversation in class before you found out that my idiot, jack ass of a brother lied to him."

"He seemed interested because I was trying to challenge him. If I show up to his practice and talk to him, then he might take it as less of a challenge and more of me throwing myself at him while attempting to play hard to get."

"But you are playing hard to get."

I threw up both arms in exasperation. "Because that's all he responds to."

"What if you show up and don't pay any attention to him? That way you're at least putting yourself out there. The more he sees and is around you, the more of a chance that he'll start to remember."

"Fine, I'll go. But I swear to God, if Natalia is all over him on the sidelines..." Seeing him flirt with the girls in the class we shared together had already killed me enough for one day. She may have promised to stay away from him, but she lied better than a politician.

"Then you'll have to be all over someone else."

"Hmm, making the guy, whom I once used to make another guy jealous, jealous." I pretended to think it over. "No thanks."

"Fine, you don't have to flirt with someone else, but don't forget about how much attention he paid you when you started out-flipping Natalia."

"What then? If he's talking to a cheerleader, then I should just start doing cartwheels at random?"

"I would pay good money to watch you randomly fall into a split."

****

Lucas ran over to greet Ashley seconds after we walked onto the field. "You're here."

She poked his cheek. "How could I miss my little pudding cup throw balls around and sweat for an hour?"

He grabbed and kissed her. I felt sick. Half due to my loneliness of not having Brandon around to do the same thing, and also because their tongues made a play.

I cleared my throat and Ashley pushed him away from her with reluctance.

"Make sure to watch me run." Lucas grinned at her with pride. "Coach said I might be one of the fastest players."

"Oh, I know exactly how fast you are."

I had to clear my throat again in order to get them to stop.

His smile slipped down on one end. "I should go." He ran over to the other players. Michael waved at me and I waved back.

Once Lucas was out of earshot, I could not resist teasing Ashley. "Pudding cup?"

"He has a six pack. Pudding comes in packs. It made sense at the time."

I forced myself not to watch Brandon stretching. He needed to be the one to look at me first. That was the one way to keep his interest.

"I know it's hard right now but it'll get better," Ashley said.

"When?"

She touched my shoulder. "When you watch him fall in love with you all over again. And it'll definitely get better soon. He's walking over here right now."

His voice came from behind me. "Mandy?"

I had to remember to appear uninterested. I nodded at him. "Brandon."

"Can't stay away from me?" He got close enough to kiss me. I had forgotten how much of a fan he was of popping my personal bubble. "I understand. I have a rare type of animal magnetism—"

I crossed my arms over my chest to fight the

instinct to wrap them around him. "I'm here because my best friend is dating one of the players."

"A likely story."

"A true story," I defended myself. "This is Ashley and she's with Lucas."

Brandon turned to look at Ashley for the first time since he walked over to me. He then frowned. "You look familiar to me."

My breath caught from excitement at his words. *Please, Brandon. Remember. Remember.*

"You're Jake's sister," he said. "Right?"

My disappointed sigh was audible.

"I'm going to go sit down." Ashley looked at me before walking over to the bleachers to give us privacy.

"So…" I began but didn't have much else to go on.

"Have you been to practices before?"

"Once." I gave him a smile. "You invited me."

"Are you serious? We're only allowed to invite— huh," he paused and appeared to think something over. "Interesting."

"What?"

"Nothing, just… I've never invited anyone before." He continued to look at me with surprise and intrigue. "Were you bored?"

"No." I let out a small laugh. "It ended up being pretty interesting."

Brandon's eyebrows shot up. "How so?"

"Natalia challenged me to a cheer off."

Brandon chuckled. "No way. What happened?"

"Oh, you know." I used my over confident voice. "I wiped the field with her."

"You did not." His eyes filled with their usual joy and child-like wonder. "You're a cheerleader?"

"Used to be," I corrected.

"Wow, okay. I can see why I must have liked you so much."

I nodded. "I'm pretty amazing."

He grinned again. That grin always made the butterflies in my stomach come to life.

Our moment got cut short when a football fell at my feet. Before Brandon had time to say anything, I picked it up and threw a perfect spiral to another player on the field.

"Whoa." Brandon took in a deep, raspy breath as his eyes darkened. "That was fucking hot." The temperature outside felt ten degrees hotter, which was magical considering it was chilly and December. "How did you learn to throw like that?"

"My father taught me when I was younger." My hands fidgeted when I thought about how much I used to love my father. Before he left.

"He sounds cool."

"Not really, no."

"Oh…" He tilted his head and examined my awkward stance. "I'm sorry. My dad sucks, too."

Brandon had never spoken about his dad like that before. It was funny how even when he had amnesia, I was able to learn new things about him. "Yeah?"

"He's constantly telling me about how I can do better in football, in school, in life… It sucks because my best is never enough for him."

"Is it enough for you?" I had never thought about how insecure he must feel about the pressure his parents put on him. When he agreed to spend Christmas with me, I thought it was because he wanted to be with me. It could have been he just didn't want to go home.

"What do you mean?"

"I mean you don't need your dad to tell you when you've done a good job. As long as you're happy with yourself, that is all that should matter."

He stared at me for a minute. "You're not like other girls."

"I hope this isn't the part where you tell me I'm just like one of the guys and punch me in the shoulder."

"Nah, you're too hot to be one of the guys." This was the Brandon I was used to. The fast-paced conversation. The flirty, yet endearing comments. "Are you still up to the challenge of showing me some of your famous flirting techniques at dinner?"

I bit the inside of my cheek so my smile appeared less wide. "You want to go to dinner with me?"

"You're kind of growing on me, Mandy."

In that moment, all I wanted him to call me was 'Blondie.'

****

When I got home from a date full of laughter and heated glances, I was more inspired than ever before. I knew exactly what my art project would be about. The moment my paint covered brush hit the canvas, I thought about Brandon and the way he looked at me before the head injury. The love, the adoration, the wanting in his eyes...

I needed to capture every aspect of it because the successive paintings would be all I had for reminders—until I saw the real thing in his eyes again.

Chapter Twenty-Nine
Mistletoe Madness With A Jerk

Brandon

Mandy. Fascinating. Funny. Smart. Sexy.

Having dinner with her had been the most fun I'd had in a while. Whenever she leaned in, I'd catch her looking at my mouth more than my eyes. I couldn't tease her much though because I had the same problem focusing.

I had wanted nothing more than to wrap that golden hair around my fist and pull her into a wild, hungry kiss. The moment I realized how badly I wanted to kiss, hold, and touch her was also the moment I realized that it felt familiar. Something about her was just so normal, comfortable, and yet...perfectly new.

The next night, Lucas texted me and asked if I was interested in going on a double date with him, Ashley, and Mandy. I responded, a little too quickly, 'yes,' and wondered about what would happen when Christmas break came along. There were three days left. What would change when Mandy and I parted? Would she find someone else? Obviously not someone better looking or with a better sense of humor, but maybe... Someone else. Why would I care if she did? It wasn't like I...I mean I liked her, but I should not feel so possessive.

The double date was at an ice cream parlor, which

was the best location for such a thing. The sugar in the ice cream created more energetic conversation and the cooler temperature provided a good excuse to get closer to each other. Plus, I couldn't help fantasizing about Mandy licking an ice cream cone for half an hour. Sadly, she ended up getting a bowl instead of a cone.

"People who eat their ice cream in bowls are the same kind of people who don't know how to have fun," I said as she picked up her cup of mint ice cream.

Ashley and Lucas had already ordered and sat down with their frozen desserts. Mandy and I, however, shared the same idea and proceeded in trying out free samples of each flavor until the worker cut us off.

She raised her eyebrows at me and put a hand on her sassy hip. She was so cute when she did that. "It's fun to have it be messy and drip all over you?"

"Duh." The guy working behind the counter handed me my cone of cookies and cream, and I took my first bite. "Then you get to lick it off."

Her nose scrunched up in the most adorable way possible. "That doesn't seem very fun."

"Maybe I should demonstrate." I plopped my scoop of ice cream on her chin, and she gasped from the cold. Moving as quickly as I could, I leaned in to lick the remnants off her jaw. My tongue slid over her lips before retreating. "See? Yum. Fun."

She looked to be in some type of shock. "You just smeared ice cream on my face and licked it off."

"And you and it were delicious by the way." I devoured more of my ice cream as we walked over to the table that Ashley and Lucas had found. "Do you lick or bite?"

Her cheeks turned bright red and a choking noise

escaped her throat. "Excuse me?"

I chuckled. "Do you lick or bite your ice cream?"

"Um, neither? I eat it like a normal person." She looked at me like I was crazy, nothing new there. "Why do you bite it?"

"Don't get me wrong, I love licking." I winked. "But yeah, I bite it."

"Doesn't it hurt you?"

"I don't have sensitive teeth."

"Do you like to chew the ice crystals in it or something?"

"Yup."

Her eyes held a sparkle that I did not even know I had been waiting and wanting to see until I saw it. "You are the weirdest guy I have ever met."

"I think you meant to say 'the most interesting' or maybe 'the most attractive' guy you've ever met."

Her mouth turned into a smile. "I stick by my original wording."

We sat down at the circular table and I pulled my chair even closer to hers, hoping my action was not noticeable.

"Mandy." Ashley stole her attention from me and I frowned. "Your art show is soon, right?"

"Yup. A couple of days. I just finished my entire portfolio last night."

Ashley gawked at her. "That's like five paintings."

I was impressed as well. I did not know Mandy liked art. It seemed like the perfect fit for her though, so it wasn't surprising.

She blushed and glanced at me from under her long eyelashes before looking away. "I was inspired."

"Will I get to see your work?"

She blushed an even darker red and played with her thumbs. "I mean, if you want to."

"Of course, I do."

I suddenly could not wait for her art show. It would show me yet another interesting side to Mandy; so far I had found nothing not to like.

****

Over the next couple of days whenever both of us were free, we would eat together or do homework in the library while sitting across from one another. I became addicted to seeing her, talking to her…and all I ever wanted to do was kiss her.

Just as I was about to walk into Mandy's art show, my phone rang. My spirits dropped. 'Home' called me. Labeling my parents' number as 'Home' always felt a bit ironic.

"Hello?"

"Brandy!" My mother's voice sounded clear through the speaker. "I got your message about missing Christmas. I'm disappointed, but I understand that you want to spend it with your *girlfriend*," she squealed the word. "Tell me everything."

Her words shocked me into silence.

"Fine, not everything. But at least a little. It must be serious if you want to spend the holiday with her."

I had no idea what she was talking about. Then again, she had no idea about my injury. I had filed for emancipation at age seventeen—too impatient to wait another year for legal independence. Now at twenty-one, my parents had even less of a tie to me. On every medical paper, I made it a habit of changing the last digit of the phone number. It was a stupid idea. After such an injury, I wouldn't make that 'mistake' again.

From the conversation with my mother, I assumed Mandy had invited me to spend Christmas with her. I did not tell my mother that we were no longer dating. I did tell her that she was right and I would spend Christmas with Mandy. Avoiding a Gage family Christmas was an opportunity too amazing to miss.

Would Mandy still be okay with me spending the holiday with her? Would it be weird?

The moment I walked into the art show, I zoomed in on her. Finding her was a skill of mine, even in a place packed with people. It felt like following a pull. She talked to another artist and laughed. I had never seen her quite so happy; her face lit up like Christmas lights. Her happiness rubbed off on me. I had not even talked to her yet and from fifty feet away she already had me smiling.

Then I saw it. Her exhibit.

They were all of me.

All were blurred except the one hanging in the middle, tying all the pieces together. The main piece was so crystal clear that at first it appeared real. Like looking into a mirror or at a photograph taken in the future. My face was the same but my eyes...the emotion in them... I had never—

"Amazing, isn't she?" An older man said from behind me. Her art professor? "She has a lot of potential."

I tore my gaze away from her work long enough to make eye contact with the man. "She does."

"You must really love her."

The statement almost knocked my legs out from under me. "What?" How in the world could he know such a thing? Besides, it wasn't true. It couldn't be true.

"See the way she's captured every speck of emotion in your eyes? The different shades of brown coming together to show happiness, insecurity, amusement…love. Those kinds of emotions can only be captured with a real life subject. Artists can do many things, but we cannot create such a striking, realistic visual without a clear memory or model for us to draw upon."

His words churned the wheels in my head as thoughts raced through my mind. If what he said was true, Mandy must have seen this in a memory. Before my amnesia…had I loved her? Love. What does loving someone even mean? If it meant wanting to see her smile every hour of every day, then yeah, I loved her. If it meant also wanting to rip her clothes off, then yeah, I loved her a lot.

I loved her obnoxious laugh. I loved the way her glare turned me on more than hatred ever should. I loved how she thought of herself after everyone around her was taken care of. I loved the way she loved a challenge. I loved her. I loved Mandy…

No. I *had* loved her, before my accident.

"Hey," I said to her and she turned around to smile at me before enveloping me in a hug and thanking me for coming. "My mother called me today asking about Christmas. Apparently, I told her last week that I wouldn't be coming home because I was spending the holiday with my girlfriend. I suppose that wasn't just a lie to get out of it?"

Her smile slipped and I hated myself for making her sad on such an important day. "You were going to meet my mom."

"I was wondering if I still could." I shrugged in

order to make my suggestion seem more nonchalant than serious, but her eyes still widened like I had just laid down a bomb.

Surprise seemed to affect her ability to draw in enough air. "What?"

"I don't really like my parents, so if the invitation is still open… I would love to come to your house for Christmas."

"It'd be at Ashley's house."

"Ashley's house?" I blinked a couple times in confusion. Damn, I would have to be around Jake? He had annoyed me ever since I discovered his lie about dating Mandy. Who did that to a friend?

"We always spend the holidays there."

"Sounds fun." Anything with Mandy sounded fun. "Can I still come?"

Her voice cracked. "Yes." She then repeated her words in a less freaked out and excited tone. "I mean, sure, that would be fine."

"Great."

"Great."

And it was.

****

The rest of the week went by in a blur because of my impatience to spend Christmas with Mandy. Sleeping in the same house and opening presents with her, everything excited me. We drove to her house together, bickering most of the way about what music to play on the radio.

After parking in Mandy's driveway, I realized I was nervous. What if her mom didn't like me? What would that mean for us? Wait—*us*? There was no us. Girlfriends were…complicated. Being around Mandy was dangerous. I had to remind myself of that so I wouldn't continue to fall under her spell.

A woman in her fifties raced out of the raised rancher house like she had been a track star all her life. She tackled Mandy in a hug, and, for a moment, I worried that she would take her down to the ground and break something in the process. When Mandy's mother pulled back from the embrace, she marched right up to me and gave me a thorough visual exam.

"This is the guy that my daughter has told me so much of *nothing* about because she never answers my calls." Her blonde hair matched Mandy's even though there were streaks of gray worked into the mix. Her face also resembled her daughter's and a part of me instantly liked her due to their similarities.

Mandy wore the same painful expression that I did whenever I had to be near my parents. The difference was she actually did appear happy to see her. "Mom…"

Her mother's head tilted as she continued to survey me. "And what's your name, mystery man?"

"Brandon Gage."

"Mmhm, and Brandon Gage, what exactly are your intentions with my innocent, faultless, angel of a daughter?"

A million answers filled my mind, but more than half of them would get me skinned alive by her mother, if I said any of them out loud. "She's just a good friend," I responded and flinched when from behind me, Mandy released a hurt noise.

"Really?" Her mother's eyes narrowed like she did not believe me. "Mandy, you're not doing the whole 'friends with benefits' thing, are you? You know how I feel about that stuff."

Mandy looked more uncomfortable than I had ever seen her. She kept glancing to the house like she wanted to escape the driveway, run in, and hide. "Mom."

"Fine." Her mother read her mind. "We can go inside but just know that you two will be sleeping in different bedrooms, and because of my chronic insomnia, I'll wake up from any loud noises."

"Got it." I couldn't resist. "No loud sex."

Mandy's and her mother's jaws dropped at the same time. Appearing ready to faint, Mandy swayed.

Two seconds later, her mother grinned at me and slapped my arm. "Aren't you daring? I like you. Mandy, I like him," she said. "I'll wear my noise canceling headphones tonight."

Mandy looked absolutely mortified and I laughed.

"Come on in, you two. We've got decorations to put up and gifts to open."

****

Mandy's mother, Kristina, put me in charge of small decorations and knickknacks to place around the house. Mandy received the chore of hanging ornaments on the tree while her mother sat back in the living room and watched TV.

"I feel like I should be getting paid for my labor," I joked. She let out a small laugh—but a small one wasn't good enough.

I held a piece of mistletoe at the top of the doorway as Mandy walked under it. The amusement and heat in her eyes made my lips stretch into a grin. "Are you seriously going to be a cliché right now?"

I leaned in. "What do you think?"

She took a step back. "Strange. I didn't think 'good

friends' kissed."

"What are you talking about?"

"What you told my mo— you know what, never mind. It doesn't matter."

She went to walk away from me, but I pinned her to the wall. "I'm sorry, okay? I just don't understand this... I can't date you. I've told you that. I don't know what you want from me."

"I just..." Her nails dug into my sides as if to restrain herself. "I want you to remember."

She abruptly grabbed my head and pulled me to her until her lips met mine. No other word but 'fire' described the way my body reacted. My blood turned into hot liquid flames that flowed and fueled the steamy kiss. My hands gripped her waist and when her tongue flicked mine, I pretty much lost it.

I pushed her harder against the wall and proceeded to kiss the living day lights out of her. There was something so familiar about all of it that I felt a click in my brain. Like if I could kiss her for just a bit longer, then something inside of me might unlock—

Kristina clearing her throat was like a gallon of ice water being poured into my veins. "I didn't know good friends could kiss like that, Mr. Gage."

"You'd be surprised." I trailed a finger over my lips because I still felt the tingle. "Mistletoe." I lifted my stiff hand that held the fake plant. "It's the working of holiday magic."

"It sure looked like it," Ashley stated.

Jake trotted in behind his sister. They said their hellos to Mandy and we all stood in awkward silence.

"Didn't you say something about exchanging gifts early, Kristina? How about we do that now?"

Mandy's mother laughed at me. "Sure."

I moved like a zombie and barely registered what happened as I replayed the kiss again and again inside of my head. Kristina, Mandy, Jake, and Ashley all took a seat around the tree and I sat in a chair more toward the corner of the room. I needed some time to think. Never in my life had I experienced a kiss like that. Every part of me burned for her, yearned for her.

Mandy was more than dangerous. I shouldn't have come here. She wasn't one to sleep around and that was all I could offer her. I needed to leave. Every minute around her hurt me because I knew if I stayed with her, I would break her. Breaking Mandy was not an option.

"Brandon?" Her delicate voice pulled me out of my thoughts and I returned her stare. "I got you this." She handed me a package covered in Santa gift wrap and I was stunned. When had she gotten me a present?

I hated myself. "I don't have anything for you."

"Oh, it's fine. Trust me, no big deal." She smiled and my fingers itched to open the gift in front of me. "I can see you're dying to, go ahead."

At her approval, I ripped into the covering until I could see what was underneath... Needless to say, I was perplexed.

"You got me beef jerky?"

She nodded and bit back a grin. "Because you're such a jerk."

My laughter erupted from my throat, harder and louder than it ever had before. "Oh my God." I suffocated from trying to breathe. "I love you." It slipped out of my lips and I stopped. I hadn't meant it. I couldn't. "I mean, not really." She winced at my words. Underneath the packet of jerky was a piece of canvas. It was one of her miniature paintings from her art show depicting me holding a football. "This is a great gift, thank you."

"You're welcome."

The way she made me feel was too much to handle, and now that I had kissed her, tasted her... I couldn't stay here. I couldn't stay here and end up breaking her heart.

****

I went to my room immediately after dinner and re-packed the things I'd already taken out of my suitcase.

Mandy walked into my room, however, and interrupted my fast packing. "I—" She cut off as she stared at my full bag. "You're leaving?"

It tore my heart out to admit. "Yes."

She looked heartbroken. "Why?"

"I'm sorry, but I can't be who you want me to be. I know you want me to remember, but it's not that simple, okay? I *don't* remember and I might never remember. And having you look at me like that everyday...like you're waiting for someone else in my eyes... I can't do it."

"Brandon—"

"I'm sorry."

"I'll tell everyone you're leaving. Ashley was baking cookies," she said in a shaky voice and rushed out of the room.

I sat there on the bed and lost track of time as I put my head in my hands and groaned. Why couldn't I be who she wanted me to be? Why couldn't I just remember everything? As I wallowed in my self-pity, another person paid me a visit.

Ashley appeared at the door. "I made strawberry

cookies if you want to take some home."

My body stiffened at the heavenly aroma coming from the baggie she handed to me. Why did the smell feel so familiar? Strawberries were nothing new, but that smell…

Ashley looked at me with concern. "Brandon?"

I grabbed the baggie from her and lifted it to my nose. Why was the smell of strawberries affecting me so much? It felt like a balloon rose in my brain, a drifting memory lifting. Taking a bite from one of the cookies set me off.

"Fucking strawberries." My head hurt as everything rushed back in that moment. I fell back onto the bed when I finally remembered…everything. "Mandy tastes like strawberries."

"That's too much information—"

"Strawberries." I grinned and grabbed Ashley by the shoulders to shake her. "Ashley."

"Um, are you okay?"

"Strawberries." I laughed and hugged her with all of my strength. "Where's Mandy?" I pulled back but didn't stay in the room long enough to hear her answer.

"Mandy," I shouted in the upstairs hallway. She wasn't in her room, so I ran down the stairs as fast as I could. "Mandy!"

I raced through the house until I found her. "Mandy." God, she was beautiful; no one had ever been so beautiful. She sat on the living room couch, looking extremely too sad while reading a book titled, *Concussions and Amnesia*. Small amounts of sunlight streaming through the windows, highlighted the golden blonde of her hair. I ripped the book out of her hands and threw it to the side.

She gaped at me with a confused and distressed expression. "What's wrong? Is your leg hurting? Is it your head?"

Apparently, amnesiac Brandon made her think the only thing to stall his leaving would be pain. Not the fact that she was the most perfect girl in the world and there was no way to walk out on such a person.

"No." I dropped to my knees in front of her and she jumped in alarm. "Nothing hurts anymore."

"I don't understand." She shook her head in confusion and I wanted to soothe the worried lines in her face. I wanted to never make her worry again.

"I know you don't, Blondie." I cupped one of her soft cheeks in my hand and moved my face closer to hers so that I breathed in her sweet scent. "You still smell like strawberries." Her distressed expression took a minute to understand what I had just said to her, and faded into a look of hope.

"Brandon?" Her stunning blue eyes shined with unspent tears and I kissed the runaways as they fell onto her cheeks when she blinked. "You-You remember me?"

"Oh, Trench Coat." I kissed her nose, her eyelids, her head...everywhere. "I could never forget you."

I kissed her lips so that she would know that my words were real. I kissed her so that she would know that I would never want anyone else. I kissed her so that she would know that everything would be okay, because I loved her.

Epilogue

Mandy

I balanced my phone against my mug as I attempted to make coffee for two with one hand. "No, Mom, you can't wear white to my wedding."

After challenging Brandon and his NFL pals to a game of basketball, I tripped and sprained my right hand. I had won before it happened, but only because Brandon glared at anyone who got too close to me while I dribbled or took a shot. The injury came from falling during my victory dance. I have since retired my intense but amazing victory dance moves.

"But Ashley said she gets to wear white," my mother whined through the speaker.

"Ashley is wrong." I let out a sound that mixed a sigh and a laugh when Brandon walked into the kitchen of our apartment and wrapped his arms around my waist. His head buried into the nook he made out of my neck and shoulder. "I will be the only one wearing white at my wedding."

"And nothing underneath?" Brandon nibbled on my ear, and my jaw dropped as I suppressed a moan from what he did and a groan at the fact that my mother heard his comment.

"Good morning, Brandon," my mother rejoiced. She loved him and knew what he was like, so hearing something inappropriate come from my fiancé no longer fazed her.

"Good morning, Kristina." He grinned and responded in the same lighthearted tone that my mother always used around him. "How's the dress search coming along?"

"It would be a hell of a lot easier if Mandy would approve one of the twenty dresses I've asked about."

"Mom, I shall repeat my rules again since your tone has become persnickety." Brandon's arms tightened around me and he chuckled in my ear. "One, no white. Two, nothing shorter than to your knees. Three, no sequins because they will give Aunt Liza a seizure if they shine under the spotlights."

"Oh please, I heard she went to Tom's Halloween party and danced under the strobe lights and never had a problem," my mother grumbled. She really loved sequins.

I laughed and elbowed Brandon for tickling me while I was on the phone. "That still doesn't mean you should dress like a disco queen."

"You're my daughter so you know I love you, and you're entitled to your own opinion and I respect that... But it's wrong and I hate you."

"Love you too, Mom."

"Wait, before you hang up, what do you two want as a wedding gift?"

"Some peace and quiet," Brandon whispered into my ear and started kissing down my neck. Heat flooded me and I wasn't sure if it was from embarrassment or the fact that the man I loved was trying to seduce me so early in the morning.

"Surely you want something more expensive than that," my mother stated firmly.

I giggled as he continued kissing me, but Brandon tore his mouth off me long enough to respond to her. "Maybe you can call back later?"

"I'm a very busy woman."

He picked me up by the waist and lifted me onto the marble kitchen counter. Wrapping my legs around himself, he looked back at my phone. "I'm pretty busy too. Your daughter is extremely demanding."

"Oh honey, trust me, I know. If you ever need to talk about it—"

"Mom," I yelled as heat filled my cheeks.

Brandon grinned and laughed at my expression. "I know where to reach you."

"You two are horrible." I frowned at him. "I'm not that bad."

"Your daughter barely even lets me sleep at night."

My jaw dropped and my cheeks burst into flames as usual when Brandon was around. "Brandon!"

My mom took his comment a different way than I had which embarrassed me even more. "She always was a snorer."

"Mhm, she's really loud." The look on Brandon's face told me he was not talking about the snoring. Excitement flooded my body when his hands grabbed my hips and our bodies were pulled together. His breath on my lips made me forget that my mother was on speaker.

"How soon until you can give me grandchildren, Brandon?"

"Mom, I'm only twenty-six," I reminded her.

Brandon and I had dated for six years and now that our lives had settled, we were finally getting married. I had no plans to start a family right away, no matter how much he pushed. He said he wanted 'little Blondies' running around. I worried too much about having to deal with 'little Brandons.' Whenever I thought about it, I imagined smug smiles and lies about not eating the last cookie all the while chocolate smeared their lips.

"Exactly," my mother agreed. "Prime age for child bearing."

"That's not even…" I rolled my eyes. "No." We were in no rush.

"I want a grandson and a granddaughter." My mother ignored my rejections and spoke to Brandon. "Think you can do that?"

"If you would hang up, Kristina, then I would certainly start trying."

I closed my eyes and sighed, my legs still wrapped around Brandon's waist. "You guys are the worst."

"She's always so rude to the people she loves." My mother giggled and Brandon nodded in agreement. "She'll keep your life interesting."

"You're right about that." The love in his gaze when he looked at me made not kissing him impossible. His lips claimed mine, and my knees weakened from the power of him.

"Ugh, I hear lips smacking."

"Bye, Mom." I laughed and hit 'end call' before she made anything else awkward.

"I love your mother." Brandon kissed my cheek and poured coffee for both of us in our special mugs. His cup said 'My Heart Belongs to an Artist,' and mine was labeled 'Dating a Player…of Football.' They were both lame, but we couldn't *not* buy by them when we found them at a yard sale for a dollar.

"She loves you too." I took a sip out of my coffee

but it was too hot, so I put it back down on the counter. "A little too much. It's creepy. Sometimes I think you're her favorite."

"Oh please, your mother loves you more than she loves anyone else in the world. Including the top ten sexiest men alive that she tells me about every year at Christmas."

"Aren't mothers not supposed to like their sons-in-law? Isn't that a rule somewhere?"

"If it's not in the Declaration of Independence, then it's not relevant." Brandon pecked me on my lips and dumped three packets of sugar in his coffee. He had the biggest sweet tooth known to man.

My lips curled up into a smile. "You are so weird."

"Me? I'm not the one who picked orange flowers for a wedding."

"You said you liked the orange," I whined. Ever since I put down the deposit for them, he had not let me live them down.

"I said I liked you and even if you picked the orange, I'd still like you."

"I swear you said you liked the orange," I remarked as he sat down at the kitchen table and pulled me onto his lap.

He leaned over my shoulder and grabbed a grape from the fruit bowl I had put out for breakfast. His legs bounced up and down underneath of me as he popped the green grape into his mouth. "Is this the way it's going to be when we're married? You're going to only remember what you want to?"

"I had to deal with you when you couldn't remember me at all, the least you can do is deal with me when I choose to believe you say 'yes' to me even when you say 'no.'"

"When have I ever said no to you?" His laugh made me want to shut him up with a great example.

"I can think of a few times." I stalled while I racked my brain for a moment when he had denied me something I wanted.

"You cannot. You're just stalling, trying to think of something." He knew me so well. Damn, I couldn't wait to marry this man.

"You told me I couldn't go to Hillary's Bakery down the street to try flavors for our wedding cake." I pretended to pout but he kissed my scrunched expression away.

"We had already been to five other bakeries when we knew exactly who would make our cake in the first place and what flavor it would be." We had chosen strawberry shortcake because Brandon said it somehow represented our relationship. Sweet but tart seemed right to me.

"I like cake. Sue me."

"I could think of a better s-word to do with you."

I shook my head at his antics. He could do so much better. "Is this what your flirting has become? Cheap innuendos that pack no real punch?"

"You want me to try harder?" The excitement in his eyes told me he was more than happy to accept the challenge. "That shirt really brings out your mouth, I mean eyes."

"Lame."

"I'm going to call you butter because I can't wait to spread you and make you melt."

"Weird."

Brandon pulled my chest against his. The space

that divided us was enough for him to look deep into my eyes. "Fine, how about this?" His warm breath against my lips made it hard to focus on his words. "I can't wait to wrap those long, sexy legs of yours around my waist and show you exactly why we are, in every way, a perfect fit for each other. And when I kiss you and you moan like you feel my lips everywhere else on your body, then I'll know how much longer I can last before I take you right then and there."

The heat that flooded my body was evident under his intense gaze. My breathlessness was also a dead give away for how much he affected me.

He leaned in for the big finale. "I should call you apple because I want to bite into you and lick the juices away."

"And you ruined it. I think I'm going to buy you a muzzle for Christmas."

He tugged on my bottom lip with his teeth and then pulled back to kiss the tip of my nose. "Joke's on you, I'm into that."

"I love you." I smiled at him and he pressed his forehead against mine. "I'd do anything for you."

He wiggled his eyebrows up and down at me, and I didn't know if I should regret my statement. "Anything, you say?"

I ran my fingers through his silky hair and he grinned wider than ever before. "What did you have in mind?"

"Well." He pulled my body hard against his and leaned in to whisper in my ear, "If you still have that trench coat..."

M. K. Hale

A word about the author...

M. K. Hale published her first novel, *Shatter*, in high school and decided one was not enough. *Hating Him* is her second novel and her first debut romance. She currently attends University of Maryland and continues to pursue her love of writing. In her free time, she performs comedy and devours romance novels as quickly as boxes of chocolates.

You can find M. K. Hale on Instagram, Twitter, and Facebook: @mkhaleauthor.

She loves to hear from her readers so shoot her an email at: meredithkh22@gmail.com.

Thank you for purchasing
this publication of The Wild Rose Press, Inc.

For questions or more information
contact us at
info@thewildrosepress.com.

The Wild Rose Press, Inc.
www.thewildrosepress.com

To visit with authors of
The Wild Rose Press, Inc.
join our yahoo loop at
http://groups.yahoo.com/group/thewildrosepress/

CPSIA information can be obtained
at www.ICGtesting.com
Printed in the USA
LVHW011757230120
644586LV00014B/895